CHRISTMAS WITH THE COOKES

MATCHMAKERS IN TIME, BOOK 1

KIT MORGAN

WITH A LITTLE HELP FROM GERALYN BEAUCHAMP

Christmas with the Cookes
(Matchmakers in Time, Book 1)

by Kit Morgan

(With a little help from Geralyn Beauchamp)

Cover design by Angel Creek Press and EDH Designs

❀ Created with Vellum

LICENSE NOTE

A SPECIAL NOTE TO READERS

Okay, so Kit Morgan had a LOT of help from Geralyn Beauchamp in writing Christmas with the Cookes. This of course means that ...

For readers of Kit Morgan – the cat's out of the bag concerning a couple of characters you've probably been wondering about for a long time.

For readers of Geralyn Beauchamp – here's a little something to whet your appetite until TM4 comes out. (Geralyn's readers know what this means).

And for those of you who haven't read either author, this is a mash up story of two worlds by two different authors that write in two different genres. Kit Morgan – contemporary and historical western romance and Geralyn Beauchamp, who in reality is the alter ego of Kit Morgan, and who writes romantic science fiction time-travel with a lot of action adventure. Because of the bringing together of these two story worlds, some definitions are in order:

Time Travel: *The action of traveling through time, either into the past or the future, but you already knew that.*

Compatible: (Of two people) *Able to have a harmonious relationship; well suited.*

Time Master: *A Muiraran male (or Human in rare cases, such as the current Time Master) whose job is to bring balance and protect the Muiraran and Human races.*

Chaos: *What happens when a Time Master isn't around.*

The Time Master's current job: *Make sure there will be future Time Masters by matching compatible individuals (be they Muiraran or Human) to ensure a particular bloodline doesn't die out. If that happens, no more Time Masters, folks, and everything's toast!*

And because I know some of you are wondering …

Muirarans: *A race of elfin aliens who escaped some meaner, nastier aliens (who thought Muirarans made a tasty snack) by making a huge jump through time and space to Earth. They've been here ever since. You just don't know it because you don't know what to look for. Yet.*

That explains the time-travel component of our story, because hey, every time-travel story has to have one. As to the rest, well, let's get to our story and find out …

CHAPTER ONE

Clear Creek, Oregon, present day

HER HEART IN HER THROAT, Lorelei Ingrid Carson signed on the dotted line.

Mr. Plumb pointed at the lease agreement. “Initial here and here.”

She swallowed hard, her hand shaking, and initialed where he’d indicated.

“Nervous?”

Lorelei looked at him. “I’ve never rented an apartment before.”

“There’s a first time for everything, young lady. Pay the rent on time, take care of the place and you’ll have no problem with the Cookes.”

She swallowed again. The Cookes were the richest family in the area. Every girl from high school dreamed of dating one. For some, any Cooke would do as long as he came with a huge trust fund. But Lorelei was a realist – she knew she didn't have a shot at a Cooke. What would a rich rancher want with someone like her?

"One more signature, Miss Carson, and we're done."

She signed where he pointed. "Have you worked for the Cookes long?"

"About ten years. I handle their real estate and property management, including this old gal." He glanced around the living room of the apartment. "This is a grand building. I used to play out back when I was a boy."

"You did?" she said in surprise as she handed him his pen.

"Oh, yes. I love this part of town – Dunnigan's Mercantile, Mulligan's Bar & Grill, the old sheriff's office, the bank, livery stable, and especially the hotel. I know 'historic downtown districts' are for the tourists these days, but that everything is so well preserved, it makes me proud. I remember when it was pretty run down about twenty years ago."

"I never saw it. I didn't come to live with my current foster family until the sixth grade."

"It didn't look like it does now, that's for sure. Thanks to the town council and the Cookes, this whole area is on the nation's list of historic places now." He looked around. "Okay, some basics. Take care of the furniture." He patted the antique sofa they were sitting on. "Some of it's very old. If you don't want the responsibility, I'll have it moved into storage and you can move in your own furniture."

Lorelei smiled weakly. "I don't have any furniture. It'll be fine."

"Oh, well, then." He gathered up the papers from the little coffee table. "Do you have dishes?"

"I'm working on getting some." She stared at the antique furniture in the room. She loved it and didn't want to change a thing. To think the people that built this place used to live here. It made her feel like she'd be living in a museum of sorts, and she liked museums.

"There are a few dishes in the kitchen cupboards and the hutch. I'm not sure where they're from. Maybe Mr. Jensen took them from the store downstairs and put them here. Mind the porcelain wash basin and pitcher in the bedroom. The washstand is also antique."

"Why are they here?"

"The original plan was to rope off the rooms so folks could see how the original owners lived. But someone thought there'd be more money in renting out." He smiled. "I know I've asked this before, but it is affordable for you, isn't it?"

"Yes, sir. You don't have to worry – I have three jobs and I've had all of them for a few years now. Including working downstairs for Mr. Jensen."

He smiled again. "Mr. Jensen tells me you're his best worker. Since it looks like you aren't attending college for a time, he's mentioned hiring you on for more hours, especially with Christmas just around the corner. You know how busy it gets around Old Town. In fact, you can thank him for this place – it was on his recommendation that we chose you."

She blushed as tears stung her eyes. "Thank you."

He stood and offered his hand. "Congratulations, Miss Carson. Enjoy your new place."

She rose with a smile, took his hand and shook it. "Thank you again, Mr. Plumb. I'll take good care of everything, I promise."

"Don't make promises you can't keep," he told her with a wink. "Besides, I know you will. The store and gift shop downstairs look wonderful. Mr. Jensen tells me you keep things nice and tidy."

Her cheeks grew hotter. "I try."

He smiled, nodded and headed for the door.

She followed and stood on the landing as he headed

downstairs. "Goodbye, and thanks again!"

He turned when he reached the last step. "You're welcome." He stepped through the long gingham curtains that separated the front and back of the building instead of an actual door. She didn't know why there wasn't a door, but it did make the place look more authentic.

Lorelei went back inside, closed the door and studied her new home. A settee a little bigger than a love seat graced one wall, a mahogany coffee table in front of it. A large oval frame hung on the wall above them, with a picture of an old man and woman. She'd always liked it, probably because everyone assumed it was the original owners. There was a name and date on the back – *Dunnigan, 1889* – and nothing more. The old man looked kindly – he was even smiling, rare for photos of that era. The woman had a scrunched-up face and beady eyes.

On the opposite wall was a bookcase with another oval frame on the wall beside it. This couple looked about the same age, the man with a long droopy mustache and hair parted down the middle, the woman matronly with a half-smile on her face. On the back was written *Mulligan, 1889.* The couples were probably proprietors of the mercantile and restaurant in the old days.

Two antique chairs sat in front of the two windows facing the street and a lovely lamp (electric, definitely not original) on the table between them. There were lace curtains in the windows, and no television, which was fine. She never watched TV anyway. If not for the lamp, one could think one was transported to the Gay Nineties.

She left the living room and went into the kitchen. It was as large as the living room, with a table and four ladder-back chairs, not too old but with an antique flavor. The stove and refrigerator were modern, but the porcelain sink and countertops looked like they were from the 1940s. So did the cabinetry – she liked the glass cupboard doors and open shelving on one wall. There was a cute corner hutch, also from the '40s if her guess was right, holding a few pieces of pretty blue and white china.

Someone had put gingham curtains in the windows, the same as the curtains downstairs. She wondered if Mrs. Jensen made them. She was quite the seamstress and worked at the local fabric shop.

She looked at the bathroom next, even though she'd seen it a dozen times. Ever since Mr. Jensen told her the owners were thinking of renting the upstairs out, she'd dreamed of living here. Now it was a reality, and all her hard work and suffering was over. She hoped.

She went back to the living room, picked up her suitcase and carried it into the master bedroom. The apartment had two, but the other was too small – it had been divided in two to add the bathroom. She could use that one for a study – there was already a small desk and chair in there, so someone else had thought of that too.

Lorelei began to unpack. There were no closets in the apartment, just an armoire and a small dresser in the main bedroom, along with a very old bed and the antique wash-stand. She liked the bed's brass headboard, but hoped the mattress wasn't as ancient. She sat on it, bounced a few times, and it squeaked loudly. "What a racket." She stood and fingered the old but well-preserved quilt – had Mrs. Jensen made it too?

With a shrug she went back to unpacking, hanging up a few things in the armoire (happy day, it had drawers too!) and putting the rest in the dresser. She checked her watch and found it was almost time to go to work.

With a sigh she reached for her only towel (she'd have to get more) and went to wash her face. In the bathroom she stared at herself in the mirror. Her gray eyes looked tired, probably because she was. But that didn't matter as much as the knowledge that she was free.

Lorelei closed her eyes against tears. No more being yelled at for something she didn't do. No more staying up all hours of the night doing unending chores for her foster parents. No more babysitting the other kids, no more going hungry …

She opened her eyes and took a deep breath. She knew not all foster homes were like hers – she had friends who were in fairly good ones. When Julie's foster mom found out Lorelei had so few clothes, she bought her some … which she'd had to hide from the Browns. But that was behind her. She could now live her own life as she saw fit.

She went downstairs to a smiling Mr. Jensen. "Hello, Lorelei," he called happily. "Off to your other job?"

She smiled back. Mr. Jensen was middle-aged, short, pudgy and balding with a white Santa Claus beard and mustache. Little kids that came into the store often called him Santa, especially at this time of year. "Yes, though I'd rather be working here this afternoon and evening."

"I can fix that. Business is starting to pick up. With Christmas just a few weeks away I'll need the help."

"Mr. Plumb said the same thing when he brought me the lease agreement."

"So you're official?"

"I am." She glanced at the ceiling. "I love it."

"It's nice to know you'll always be around."

The bell over the door rang, drawing their attention. Lorelei's jaw dropped. The man coming in was huge, well over six feet, broad and handsome. He held the door open for a woman as pretty as he was handsome, though much shorter. She didn't look much older than Lorelei, with long auburn hair and bright green eyes. His eyes were the same color. They wore matching jeans, hiking boots and blue ski jackets.

"Welcome to Dunnigan's," Mr. Jensen said. "Looking for anything in particular?"

The man stepped inside and closed the door behind him. "Aye, my wife fancies a few ornaments for the tree," he replied in a thick Scottish burr.

Mr. Jensen's eyebrows rose. "Well, I have plenty of those around the shop." He waved them toward the Christmas displays on the left. "Right over here."

The woman smiled at him. "Do you have any lights?"

"I'm afraid not. You'll have to go to either the hardware store or Branson's Variety."

"Oh," she said, looking disappointed. They began to browse the ornaments.

"You folks visiting?" Mr. Jensen asked.

The couple exchanged a quick look. "Nay, not exactly," the man said.

"We bought a cabin off Powers Road," the woman offered. "We're fixing it up."

"Oh? The old Cotter place?"

"Aye," the man said.

Lorelei watched them, fascinated. They were both so striking, it was almost as if they weren't real.

"Scotland?" Mr. Jensen stated.

The big man smiled. "Aye."

Mr. Jensen beamed. "My wife's Scottish. What clan?"

The man's smile broadened. "MacDonald."

"Wonderful – so is my wife! Her maiden name's MacIain!"

The behemoth's green eyes twinkled. "Is it now?"

"Yes, yes. We go to all the Highland and Celtic games in the state," Mr. Jensen continued. "We hope to visit Scotland one day."

Lorelei glanced at her watch. "I'd better be going," she said to no one in particular.

Mr. Jensen turned to her, about to say something, when the bell over the door rang again. And in walked trouble. "Welcome, girls," Mr. Jensen said. "Shopping for Christmas?"

Cindy Crankshaw, Melanie Dickle and Heather Reeves each looked Lorelei up and down as they sauntered into the shop.

She swallowed and headed for the door. "I have to be going, Mr. Jensen."

"Heading to work?" Cindy teased as she spied the big Scotsman. She looked him up and down too.

"Yes." Though why she bothered to ask was beyond Lorelei.

"Laundromat or Daisy's Café?" Melanie scoffed.

Oh, that's why ...

"It's Thursday – it's the laundromat," Heather said. She grabbed Lorelei's hand. "Sheesh. See how old her hands look?"

Lorelei yanked it away.

"If you'd been able to go to college, you wouldn't have to work there," Melanie said.

Cindy wrinkled her nose. "She'll never go to college."

The woman with Mr. MacDonald turned to Mr. Jensen. "We're having a big Christmas party. Do you have any big, fresh Christmas wreaths?"

"Only what you see," he said. "If you want fresh ones you'll have to go to either Stone's Tree Farm or a tree lot. Most folks go to Stone's."

Lorelei took the opportunity to head for the door again.

"Oh, miss, where is the laundromat?" the woman called after her.

Lorelei turned around. "It's across town – 451 Smith Street. I'm sorry, but I have to go, or I'll be late."

"Maybe you should be," Cindy said. "That way you'll get fired and can go work someplace else." Melanie and Heather giggled at the taunt.

Lorelei rolled her eyes. She was tired of the mean girl's baiting. Unfortunately, Cindy and her cronies never tired of doing it.

"Dallan, we could wash the quilts this afternoon," she said. "I want to be home in time for Titus' visit."

Everyone stared at them. "You're having Titus Cooke over?" Mr. Jensen said.

"Aye, the Cookes are friends of ours," Dallan said. "We're having him over for dinner. 'Tis been a while since we've seen him."

Cindy looked him up and down again. "You're Scottish," she said, stating the obvious.

The Scotsman ignored her. "We havena a washing machine or dryer yet," he explained to Lorelei.

"Well then, why don't you have Lorelei show you the laundromat?" Heather prodded. "She's heading there."

The woman looked at her husband, her eyes bright. "A brilliant idea."

"But I'm walking to work," Lorelei said in a panic. Mrs. Deets, the owner of the laundromat, hated when she was late – especially since she was the only employee.

"We'd be happy to drive you," the woman offered, her voice like silk. "It's no trouble."

"Oh … no, I can meet you there." Lorelei didn't want to get into a car with strangers.

"I insist," the woman said. "I'd feel guilty if I made you late."

She stared at her. The woman's eyes were so beautiful and looked brighter than before. Before she could stop herself, she was nodding.

Cindy and her cronies' eyes were glued to her as well and

watched as she touched Lorelei's arm. An unexplainable warmth seeped into her bones, and Cindy and her taunts melted away.

"Come," the woman said. "Let's go."

"We'll come back and look 'round yer wee shop later," the Scot told Mr. Jensen.

Lorelei turned to the door and followed the woman out, the big Scot behind her. *I shouldn't be doing this, these are strangers.* But she couldn't stop her feet from moving forward.

Outside they approached a brand new white Ford F-150 extended cab. A girl was sitting behind the steering wheel. Lorelei looked at her as the Scotsman bounded into the back of the truck bed and sat. Wow – was he some sort of professional athlete? How else could he jump in like that? She pushed the thought aside as they approached the passenger side of the vehicle. "Really, I could walk," she mumbled.

"Nonsense." The woman offered her hand. "My name is Shona MacDonald."

Lorelei shook it then looked at the man in the truck bed. "Is Dallan your brother?"

He turned, smiled and waved. "Ye have a good ear for names, lass. And nae, I'm her husband."

"Why is he riding back there? Won't he get cold?"

"He likes the cold. Besides, we have some things back there I don't want flying out." Shona opened the door for her.

"What was in there? Did they have any wreaths?" the young woman in the truck asked. She had jet-black hair, hazel eyes and a bright smile. She also looked about Lorelei's age. "Hi!" she chirped, then glanced at Shona. "Who's this?"

"Oh, I'm sorry. Lorelei Carson, this is my best friend in the world, Kitty Morgan. She's helping us set up our house."

"I'm helping her *shop*," Kitty said with another bright smile. "One of my favorite things to do."

Lorelei couldn't help but smile as she climbed in. If they were a bunch of ax-murderers, then she'd just passed the point of no return. Yet somehow she was sure she could trust them. In fact, she'd never felt so comfortable around *anyone* before.

As soon as they were belted in, Kitty started the engine. "Is there a mall in this town?"

"No," Lorelei said. "Just little shops and boutiques."

"Pity. It's still a cute place. Shona, did you see the old drive-in?"

"Yes, I noticed it when we drove into town."

"I think you're going to like the cabin," Kitty said. "Especially after we fix it up."

"What cabin is it again?" Lorelei asked. She was familiar with some of the old farmhouses outside of town, but not all of them.

"The Cotter house – it's a little past the tree line," Shona said. "You can see Ruby's Peak from there."

"Down Powers Road, you said? I didn't know there was a cabin back there."

Shona smiled. "It's old, hasn't been lived in for decades. But the foundation and frame are still good. We're fixing it up as a vacation house." She glanced around. "Are we going in the right direction?"

Lorelei blinked a few times. She felt so relaxed she'd forgotten she was going to work. "Turn right at the light, then the first left is Smith Street."

"At least this place is small enough to get around quick," Kitty said. "In Portland it can take forever."

Lorelei nodded. Thank Heaven they were taking her in the right direction and weren't heading out of town to murder her. "We only have about eight thousand people."

"Big enough to have everything you need," Shona commented.

"Except a mall," Kitty added in disappointment.

Lorelei smiled. She liked these people. And they were friends with the Cookes – that said a lot, since the Cookes were the most prominent family in the area. She supposed she shouldn't have jumped to conclusions, but she couldn't help it. After all she'd been through in her life, she rarely trusted anyone.

CHAPTER TWO

"I can take those for you if you want," Lorelei offered.

Shona peeked over the armful of old-fashioned quilts. "Thanks." She set them on the long table near the washing machines the laundromat used for drop-off and pick-up. "I didn't think a town this small would have a service like this."

Lorelei began to unfold the quilts. They smelled musty and old. Had they purchased them from an antique shop? "We're the only laundromat in town." She examined the quilts. "These have beautiful patterns."

"Yes, they do."

Kitty brought in another armload and set them on the table. "Wow, how many of these are you going to need?"

"The cabin sleeps eight," Shona told her. "So at least that many."

"Eight?" Kitty said in surprise. "Oh, yeah, I forgot about that loft in the attic."

"Plus the bedrooms downstairs," Shona added, then smiled at Lorelei. "So where can a person buy sheets around here?"

"There's a boutique in Old Town that sells fancy ones. It's right next to Mulligan's."

Shona nodded. "So how long have you lived here?"

"About six years."

Shona glanced at Kitty and back. "I couldn't help but overhear what your friends said in Dunnigan's about college?"

"They're not my friends," Lorelei replied, perhaps a little too quickly.

"Do you attend the community college?" Kitty asked.

A chill went up Lorelei's spine. She didn't like talking about college and why she couldn't go. But they asked, so ... "No. I can't afford it. Besides, I don't have time right now."

Kitty sat on the table as Lorelei put several quilts into a machine. "I was pre-med at Portland State, but I quit."

Lorelei took a breath. She dreamed of just being able to attend community college. "Why?"

Kitty shrugged. "It was what my parents wanted me to do, not what I wanted."

"So ... what do you do now?"

Her face lit up. "I'm a novelist."

"You're a writer?"

"Yes, I can give you a bookmark!" She hopped off the table and headed for the door and her truck. Or was it the couple's truck? Not that it mattered.

"You'll have to excuse Kitty," Shona said. "She gets very excited talking about her books."

"Books? She's written more than one?"

"Dozens."

"What has she written?"

Before Shona could answer, Kitty trotted back in. "Here, I got you two!"

Lorelei looked at them. They both showed book covers of

women and men in old-fashioned Western dress. She read the title on one. "His Prairie Princess?"

"Yes, that was my first book ..."

"Kitty, we need to get going." Shona turned her toward the door.

"Okay, okay, you don't have to shove." Kitty turned and waved one last time, followed by Shona.

Lorelei waved back, then waited until they left the laundromat before she sighed. "Strange folks. But nice." She looked at the bags of laundry customers had already dropped off and got to work.

Mrs. Deets shuffled out of her office. "Who was that?"

"Customers."

"Hm." Mrs. Deets looked at the piles on the table. "Get as much of this done as you can before the evening rush."

"Yes, ma'am." Thursday nights were always busy. People liked to have their laundry done before the weekend. If she thought there were piles now, in a few hours there would be a mountain. Lorelei looked out the big front windows and thought of the handsome couple and the novelist she'd just met. Maybe one day she could write a book. But would anyone buy it? Probably not. Nothing exciting ever happened to her – what on Earth would she write about?

With a weary sigh, she got back to work.

IT WAS near midnight when Lorelei trudged home through the snow. When the MacDonalds returned for their quilts, Kitty the author wasn't with them. Did she live nearby? She'd mentioned Portland ...

Lorelei meant to ask, but they started talking about their upcoming dinner with Titus Cooke and the huge Christmas costume party they were planning. It all sounded so wonderful and glamorous. Guests would be flying in from New York, Los Angeles and other places she would never see in her lifetime. She should've asked what they did for a living. They must make a lot of money to host parties like that.

By the time she reached Old Town she was chilled through. The mile walk would only get worse as the weather grew colder. But it was shorter than when she lived with the Browns, two miles *outside* of town, and Patsy her foster mom rarely gave her a ride. It meant loading everyone into the car and that wasn't about to happen.

She stopped in front of a shop with pretty lights in the window, showcasing beautiful clothes and a wedding dress. Lorelei had never been into Bella's Boutique and Bridal. The owner made all sorts of costumes and custom wedding dresses, but Lorelei would never be able to afford anything inside. She wondered if Shona MacDonald had seen the shop yet. Would she buy a costume for her party there, or did she already have one?

She was about to continue home when she heard a woman's laughter followed by a moan. Lorelei's eyes widened. It sounded like it was coming from the alley – the same alley she'd have to cut through to get to the back of Dunnigan's Mercantile and her new apartment. She went to the edge of the building and peeked into the alley. "Ew." Cindy Crankshaw was making out with Erwin Brown, Lorelei's foster parents' son. He was two years younger than her and had just gotten his first car - really, his dad's beat-up old Toyota Tacoma. Still, did Patsy and Bob know he was out this late?

Erwin stopped sucking face with Cindy when he spotted Lorelei. "Well, well, if it isn't Lowlife. Getting an eyeful?" He turned to Cindy, who was licking her lower lip. "She just moved out. She's eighteen, you know – a *legal adult*."

"Which means you need to be getting home," Lorelei replied. "What are you doing out so late, anyway?"

"I just got off work."

"You have a job?" But that explained a lot. Besides, how would she know – no one told her anything in that house. One more reason to be glad she was out of it.

"Yeah, it was my first day at Pizza Pub."

"We might ask you the same thing," Cindy slurred. "But we know where you've been. The question is, what are you doing *here*?" She looked her up and down. "Looking for a little action? Have another late-night job you haven't told us about?" Erwin laughed and pointed at her.

Lorelei rolled her eyes and ignored the jab. At least Erwin was working, but he hadn't put any effort into looking for a job until he knew he could drive to town. He didn't want to walk like she did.

"Well, loser?" Cindy teased. "Looking for a customer?"

"Shut it, Cindy," Lorelei said.

"She got an apartment, did you know?" Erwin told her. "She's all moved out of our house – and good riddance."

"Right back at you, Vermin." Lorelei turned to leave. She didn't want the Browns to know where she lived. Not that they'd come knocking on her door, but she'd rather keep the knowledge to herself for a few days. She'd just moved out that day.

"Run along, loser," Cindy called after her.

Lorelei refused to stoop to Cindy's level – which from the looks of it, was about to be prone with her legs in the air. She hurried around the block the opposite way. When she reached the back door of Dunnigan's she heard Cindy moaning again and made a face before unlocking the back door and entering the building.

She shivered and decided to make herself some tea, then remembered she didn't have any. She had no food in the place, come to think of it. She'd been so preoccupied with the MacDonalds and their friend, she forgot to at least grab something from the store for breakfast. Good thing her first job tomorrow was at Daisy's Café. Beatrice, who was the cook tomorrow morning, would fix her something before she started. If Carl was cooking, he'd complain and tell her she should have thought of it earlier, but Beatrice was more laid-back.

She went into her bedroom and flopped onto the bed. "My life sucks." Then she reminded herself that it sucked worse before today. She was out on her own. Maybe next year she'd have enough money put away she could work a little less and have more time for college. She could get financial aid; she was poor enough. Time was the problem. Between her three jobs she was already working over fifty hours a week, and now she had rent to pay. If they weren't minimum-wage jobs, then maybe she could make more time, but as it was, she was stuck.

She sat up and rubbed her face. She should brush her teeth and go to bed. But after her short time spent with such fascinating people, she wanted to daydream about traveling, having a little extra money … dare she think, dating someone and getting married one day? "Yeah, right. Like that'll happen."

She went to the bathroom, brushed her teeth and stared at her reflection. She was attractive enough, but no one had ever asked her out in high school. She was "weird," everyone said, including the Browns. None of her other foster parents thought so, until the "incident." The day she started staring off into space and gave no emotional reaction to anything for days. Then it was gone, and life was normal again. But she'd carried the stigma of being different ever since. At least she was smart, and given her experiences, could she be blamed if she'd rather spend her time reading than socializing?

Or maybe she wasn't attractive enough. Her eyes were too far apart and almond-shaped, slanting upwards slightly like she had some Asian blood in her. And she was stoic, standoffish. She didn't used to be, but since she'd moved in with the Browns, she'd lost interest in people. Books were her comfort and she could live vicariously through the characters in them. They had adventures. They went places. The only time Lorelei ever got to venture beyond the town limits was on field trips, and with school over, those were a thing of the past.

She went back to her bed and pulled the quilt back. No sheets. "Figures," she said with a sigh. At least there were cases on the pillows. She'd have to budget the sheets in for next month. In the meantime, she'd have to wrap herself in the quilt and hope it was enough.

She looked at the used cell phone she'd bought just days before and was still learning to use. The device had taken a lot of her savings, as had giving Mr. Plumb first and last month's rent, so her funds were now sadly depleted. She'd have to figure out how to get blankets too. She couldn't afford a huge electric bill, but didn't want to freeze either.

She curled up in the quilt, the bed squeaking with every movement. Okay, the place had its quirks, but she was going to love living there. She knew she was.

Lorelei smiled at the thought and tried to get some sleep.

"WEEL, 'tis nice to see ye again, lass," Mr. MacDonald said as Lorelei approached their table.

She poured them each a cup of coffee. "Nice to see you too."

"So this is your second job?" Shona asked. Her long, wavy auburn hair was pulled back today. Lorelei noticed her eyes were shaped a little like her own. It made her feel better knowing someone else had similar eyes. She wondered if Shona ever got teased about them.

"Third, actually. I also work at Dunnigan's Mercantile part-time."

"Three jobs?" Shona said. "I thought perhaps your ... *acquaintances* were teasing you yesterday. But I'm glad you're working hard. It will all pay off one day."

"I hope so." She nodded at the menus already on the table. "The specials on are the back."

"Are they big portions?" Dallan asked.

"Pretty big, yes."

He beamed. "Pancakes – a big stack, if ye dinna mind. Four eggs, over easy. Six of those wee sausages if ye have them. Rye toast, and, hm ... grapefruit juice."

"Dallan," Shona scolded. "You'll spoil your lunch."

"Nae, I won't."

Shona pondered this. "Sadly enough, you're probably right. A cheddar cheese omelet, fried potatoes and fruit." She handed the menus to Lorelei.

Dallan reached for his coffee cup. "Oh, and bring two more of these. We're expecting company."

He'd no sooner said it than in walked Titus and Lincoln Cooke. Lorelei took a quick breath. They rarely came into the café, preferring the more high-end eateries in town. The father and son headed straight for the MacDonalds' table.

Lorelei backed up a few steps as Dallan stood and shook their hands. "Morning, gentlemen. Have a seat and we'll get down to business." He turned to Lorelei. "Coffee, lass."

She nodded, turned and went to fetch two more cups.

"Is that Titus Cooke and his son out there?" Beatrice asked quietly. "My gracious!" She patted her hair. "How do I look?"

Lorelei tried not to roll her eyes. Beatrice was around

sixty but spry, with blue streaks in her salt-and-pepper hair. "Why do you bother?" She looked at the elder Cooke and reached for more cups. He had to be seventy at least. "I know he's single, but every woman in town has tried to nab him …"

"They have not," Beatrice cut in. "Did Patsy tell you that?"

Lorelei filled the cups. "Yes."

"Not true. Though quite a few have thought about it." She sighed dreamily. "Just look at him. He could be Sam Elliott!"

Lorelei shook her head and returned to the table. But Beatrice was right – Titus Cooke did look a lot like the veteran actor. Lincoln Cooke could pass for Viggo Mortensen, come to think. She set the coffees in front of them. "Would you like more menus?"

"No need – we already ate," Titus said in a gravelly voice. He even *sounded* like Sam Elliot! No wonder Beatrice was smitten. "The MacDonalds tell me you work at Dunnigan's Mercantile."

She swallowed. "Er … yes, sir."

"I also hear you rented the apartment upstairs."

She swallowed again. Why was she so nervous? "That's right."

"Good, that place needs some love. Take good care of it."

"I will, sir." She hurried back to the kitchen where Beatrice stood, tapping her foot with impatience. "What?"

"Well, what did they say?"

"Not much. They know about my new apartment …" Which was a little creepy – it made her feel exposed. Would they check to make sure she was keeping the place up? Evict her on a whim if they didn't think she was? Tell the Browns? All of that was ridiculous, but her fear of things not going her way (which they usually didn't) was clouding her thinking. "They didn't ask after you, if that's what you want to know."

"Awww …" Beatrice walked back to the grill.

Lorelei served coffee to a few more customers that came in, then checked on the MacDonalds and Cookes' orders. She hoped Beatrice was on her game this morning. She was fast when she wanted to be. She noticed other customers stealing glances at the Cookes, which made sense – they were the town's most prominent family. And one of the oldest – they'd helped found the place back in 1849. For Daisy's Café it was the equivalent of some famous actor or athlete coming back to town and sitting down for coffee.

The Cookes were such a big deal that the burg's unofficial nickname was "Cooketown." They owned at least half the buildings downtown. There were statues in the city park of three of their ancestors and one of the Turners'. The Turners weren't as wealthy as the Cookes, but they were pretty substantial themselves. Lorelei had had a crush on Wyatt Turner when she was a sophomore and he a senior. But it was thoroughly unrequited, and she rarely saw him after he graduated, just from a distance at the annual town picnic in Canyon Park.

"Orders up, sweetie." Beatrice placed the plates under the warming lights. "Best get these out there. Unless you'd like me to take them …"

She gave her a look that said *nice try,* picked up the two plates and carefully carried them to the table.

"… That's going to be some party," Lincoln was saying when she arrived.

She stepped away from the table. "Will there be anything else?"

"Yes." Shona smiled at the men, then at Lorelei. "We were just discussing our party this weekend, the one we told you about yesterday?"

"I remember. It sounds like it'll be wonderful."

"Yes, it will. And I wanted to know if you could come?"

Lorelei's eyes went wide. "Me? But … why would you …?"

Dallan waved off her concerns. "Ye did a fine job with those antique quilts yesterday. They handled the washings. Ye didna toss them into the machines and wash them any old way – ye made sure they were taken care of properly. So think of this as a wee thank you."

She had to remember to breathe. "Wow, I … I mean … thank *you!*"

Lincoln Cooke exchanged a look with his father. "The party starts at 7 p.m. Saturday. Do you need a ride? We could pick you up along the way."

She stared at him. Ride with the Cookes?! "Well, I …"

"That's very kind of you." Shona smiled at Lorelei again. "And very convenient for you. Unless you'd rather drive yourself?"

She looked away a moment. Was this really happening? "I don't have a car." She didn't even have a driver's license – the Browns had refused to put up the money for lessons.

"Well, that settles it, then," Lincoln said. "We'll pick you up at 6:30."

Lorelei nodded as she backed away from the table, almost tripping over her own feet. It would just be her luck to fall on her rear and embarrass herself. Thank Heaven she was able to retreat to the kitchen.

"Well? What were they talking to you about?" Beatrice took a closer look at her. "Why are you so pale?"

Lorelei blinked and managed to say, "I'm going to a party."

CHAPTER THREE

Lorelei tried not to think of the MacDonalds' Christmas party the rest of the morning. Shona said she'd call or stop by the shop after they had exchanged phone numbers. Thank Heaven she had a phone now! But her shift that afternoon at Dunnigan's was slow, which meant she had some time on her hands – and mind.

"Why?" she asked herself. "Why invite me?" She was nobody, nothing. Heck, she was hardly noticed at school – and given what happened when she was noticed, she liked it that way. She could act out on occasion, pushing back when someone like Cindy made snide remarks or Erwin got ratty about something. But she didn't have to deal with them anymore other than the occasional chance encounter like last night.

She sat on a stool behind the front counter and took out some crochet she'd been working on. Patsy and Bob Brown might not have been the best foster parents, but that didn't mean she hated them. She wanted to make them each a scarf for Christmas and had almost finished Patsy's.

Christmas. Neither Bob nor Patsy had made any mention

of Christmas to her. She'd spent the last six Christmases with them. Would they invite her to spend it with them now that she was out on her own? She didn't see why not ... but she didn't assume it would happen either. Still, time was growing short. Christmas would be here before any of them knew it.

She stared at the scarf, a tear in her eye. She'd never spent Christmas alone before. They weren't great up to now, and some Christmases she *wished* she'd been alone, but now that she was staring the possibility in the face, she didn't like the empty feeling it gave her.

It was that same horrible, hollow feeling she got whenever she thought of her deceased parents. She was only six and sound asleep when they died in that fire. She wasn't sure how it started, only that a fireman found her and carried her from the building. Now she could barely remember them. All she had to remind her was an old picture someone had given her. They had no relatives, no friends willing to take her in. So into the system she'd gone.

Sometimes she didn't think it fair that they died, and she lived. But life wasn't fair, was it? She wiped away the tear and started crocheting again. She had to get this finished, then work on Bob's when her shift was done.

"Is it true?" a familiar voice said as the door burst open. "You got invited to the costume party?"

She looked up to see Cindy and Erwin blocking the doorway. "What?"

Cindy marched across the store to the counter. "You? I don't believe it."

Lorelei's face twisted with confusion. "What are you talking about?"

"The Cookes' Christmas party, stupid," Erwin said. "Their costume party?"

"Cookes?" They weren't talking about the MacDonalds' party, were they?

Erwin rolled his eyes. "It's being held someplace else this year, but yeah, that one."

Her jaw dropped. How would *they* know about it? "The old Cotter cabin?"

"That place is more like a lodge, not a cabin, but yeah," Cindy spat. "What I want to know is, how did you get an invite to one of the most coveted parties of the year?"

Lorelei stared at her a moment and giggled. Was she serious? "What do you care?"

She leaned across the counter. "Because you're no one! I've been trying to get an invite to that party since I was a freshman!"

Lorelei laughed in her face. She couldn't help it.

"Shut up and tell us," Erwin sneered. "Or shall I guess? You slept with one of them, didn't you?"

"I bet she did," Cindy snapped. "Maybe more than one."

"I didn't sleep with anyone," Lorelei stated as calm as she could. But her insides were starting to shake, and she felt something welling up inside of her. It wasn't anger so much as ... well, something.

Thankfully, before any of them could say anything further, the bell over the door rang again and in walked Shona and Kitty. It was all she could do not to sigh in relief.

"We thought we might find you here," Shona said.

Kitty went to a display of colorful socks with funny patterns. "Oh, look how cute these are!"

Shona joined Cindy and Erwin at the counter. "Are you busy? I can come another time."

"No," Lorelei said with a glance their way. "Not busy at all at the moment."

"Good. I was wondering if you had a costume for the party?"

Cindy's mouth had fallen open and her face was turning an interesting shade of red. Erwin didn't look much better.

Lorelei thought she shouldn't enjoy the sight, but boy, did she. "No, I hadn't thought about it."

"That's okay. Kitty and I have a few extra outfits and thought you might be interested in one."

Her temporary gloating was tempered by wondering why she'd received an invitation in the first place. It seemed too good to be true and, with her luck, probably was. "I don't know what to say."

"You can try them on, decide which one you want to wear, then one of us will pick up the others tomorrow. Does that work?"

She nodded, speechless. The woman's generosity was almost more than she could bear. She felt like Cinderella going to the ball. Too bad there wouldn't be a handsome prince there.

"So you're new in town?" Cindy ventured.

Shona looked at her. "Yes and no."

Kitty, meanwhile, set three pairs of socks on the counter. "I'll take these. They're just so cute!"

Shona sighed. "Kitty, we don't have time."

"Think of them as souvenirs," she said. "Do you have any CDs?"

"Kitty …" Shona warned.

"Oh, okay, never mind."

"Who buys CDs anymore?" Erwin scoffed. "Don't you listen to music on your phone?"

Kitty stared at him. "You can do that?"

"Kitty!" Shona grabbed her arm. "Let's get the costumes out of the truck." She began to pull her toward the door.

As soon as they were gone Erwin shook his head. "She's weird."

"Which one?" Cindy asked with a laugh.

Lorelei stared after them. She could see the same big white truck parked outside. Maybe Kitty had an old flip phone or something. Still, her statement was odd – who didn't know you could download music?

"Costumes?" Cindy said like it was a dirty word and turned back to Lorelei. "She's loaning you a costume?"

She shrugged. "So?"

Cindy tossed a hand in the air. "Unbelievable!" She grabbed Erwin by the jacket. "Let's go. I can't be around this loser another minute."

Lorelei rolled her eyes. "Get over yourself, Cindy."

Cindy stopped and turned to her. "You did *something* to get that invitation. I know you did! How else would you get invited? I bet when everyone finds out what a loser you really are, they'll think twice about letting you come." She grabbed Erwin's jacket again and dragged him out the door.

Lorelei shook her head. Cindy was vindictive and could be a real witch (though most pronounced it differently) when she was mad.

But she didn't have time to think about it. Shona and her friend came back in, carrying several huge garment boxes tied with string. Shona set the two she carried on the counter. "Here they are."

Kitty did the same and smiled, her eyes bright. "I think you should wear the red one, but that's just my opinion."

Lorelei stared at the boxes, still recovering from Cindy's jabs. She hoped she didn't start spreading rumors all over town. But then, Lorelei could fire back with facts – she was an eyewitness to Cindy having a sexual encounter with an underage male.

Kitty pulled the string off a box, opened it and pulled out a green velvet gown with black buttons down the front.

"That's pretty." Lorelei reached a tentative hand toward it.

"It's okay," Kitty said. "I still think you should go with the red."

Shona opened up the next and pulled out an ivory dress

with buttons that looked like diamonds. "What about this one?"

"What kind of costumes are they?" Lorelei asked. They looked very old-fashioned, like the dresses the women on covers of Western novels wore.

"Period dresses from the 1870s," Shona explained. "They're very elegant, I think. Our party has an Old West theme."

Lorelei glanced out the store windows. There was no sign of Cindy or Erwin. "Is it your party, or … the Cookes'?"

Shona's eyebrows shot up. "Where did you hear that?"

She shrugged. "Cindy and Erwin found out I got invited to a party and insisted it was the Cookes' annual Christmas party."

"I see," Shona said. "Well, actually, we combined parties."

"So all the Cookes will be there?" The thought made her nervous. It was bad enough when she thought she wasn't going to know anyone there, but to have the whole Cooke family present was even more overwhelming.

"Yes, the whole family. You know them, don't you? Aren't some of them your age?"

"Well, maybe Avery. But she's younger than me and still in high school. So are Nathaniel and Winston. The others are all older than I am and have been out of school for years."

"I see," Shona said with a smile. She was staring at her, her eyes bright. "Well, how about this one?" She took the lid off the last box.

Lorelei gasped as Shona pulled out the red dress and shook it so it unfolded to its full length. The skirt was covered in red ruffles, the sleeves trimmed in red velvet. There was some sort of wrap or cloak in the box that matched. She thought the neckline was a little low, but perhaps you wore the cloak with it. She touched the cloak still in the box. Kitty lifted it out to show an ivory-colored lace scarf underneath, and Lorelei lifted the delicate lace out of the box. "It's beautiful …"

"Three pieces!" Kitty gushed. "One more reason it's my pick."

Lorelei studied the dress. The neckline was trimmed in the same dark red velvet as the sleeves. Tiny red bows ran from the scooped neck to the bodice. It looked like something out of a fairy tale.

"I think she likes it," Shona told Kitty.

"Ya think?" Kitty giggled.

Lorelei stared at them open-mouthed. "I … I don't know what to say."

"Say you'll wear it," Kitty chirped. "Or I will."

"No, you won't," Shona said. "And from the look on her face, I'd say we have a winner." She nodded at Kitty to fold the cloak and put it back in the box. She did, then helped Shona do the same with the dress. "It should fit fine – but if not, call me and I'll have it altered."

"That fast?" Lorelei said in surprise. "But Mrs. Clifford at the alterations shop is gone. She always visits her son in California this time of year."

"Don't worry, I know someone who's pretty handy with a needle and thread."

Kitty sighed. "Yeah."

Lorelei stared at her a moment.

"Oh, it's not me. Just someone we know."

"Well, if you don't mind waiting a few minutes, I'll run it upstairs," Lorelei volunteered. "I wouldn't want anything to happen to it."

"That's right, you live in the apartment over the shop," Shona said.

She nodded, gathered up the box and taking the stairs two at a time, hurried to put it away. She left the apartment unlocked. There was no sense locking it when she was right there in the shop. Besides, almost no one knew anyone lived up there yet.

"Remember, call me if it doesn't fit," Shona reminded her when she returned. "But I think we'll be fine."

Lorelei smiled and, before she could stop herself, gave Shona a hug. "Thank you so much!"

Shona hugged her back. "Think nothing of it."

Lorelei felt so good in that moment, she couldn't begin to describe it. Nothing like this had ever happened to her before. Was she dreaming?

Shona stepped away. "We have to be going. The party is Saturday, remember."

"How can I forget?" she teased.

"Oh! Shoes!" Kitty blurted, then ran out the door.

Lorelei laughed. "Is she always that excitable?"

"You haven't seen anything yet," Shona commented. "As you can see, I'm the calm one."

She laughed again as Kitty came back with another box. "Shoes!" she exclaimed and set them on the counter. "I hope they fit. If not, we have access to other sizes."

"Do you outfit everyone for your parties?" she asked as she opened the box.

"Not everyone," Shona said as Lorelei pulled out a pair of off-white ankle boots. "But a few people usually have trouble finding outfits, so we try to have it covered."

"They're pretty." Lorelei held them up to examine them. "Are they comfortable?"

"You won't find out until you try them on," Shona said. "I have a pair, though, and I'm fine in them."

"They're lovely, they really are." Lorelei brushed a tear away. She didn't know why she was suddenly so emotional. No one had ever been this generous to her before. And why would they? She was a nobody. Sometimes she felt as if she didn't exist.

"We should go." Shona nodded at Kitty's socks on the counter.

"Oh, yes. I'm sorry," Lorelei said. "I forgot all about these."

"Understandable," Kitty said. "New clothes make me forget everything."

Lorelei's jaw dropped. "I'm just borrowing the dress and the other things, aren't I?"

Shona shot Kitty a funny look, then nodded. "Of course. You can return them the day after the party."

She nodded in relief. What would she do with a fancy ball gown anyway? But to wear it for one night would be awesome! "I'll take good care of it, I promise."

Shona smiled and looked at Kitty. "Pay for your socks, then we must go."

Kitty sighed. "I wish we could shop more. There's so much cool stuff in here."

"Not now, Kitty ..."

Lorelei quickly rang up the socks, put them in a bag and ran Kitty's card. "Thank you."

"You're welcome!" Kitty headed for the door, bag in hand. Shona smiled and followed.

As soon as they were gone Lorelei had to fight the urge to run upstairs, take the gown out of the box and admire it. If the dresses being worn at the party all looked as pretty at that one, she could only imagine what sort of people would be attending. How would she talk to anyone? She had visions of sitting in a dark corner all night. Would there be a dinner? Dancing? She never thought to ask! All she knew was that it was a Christmas costume party with a Western theme. Did that mean the men would be dressed as cowboys?

She glanced at the clock on the wall. Four hours before closing, then she could try the dress on. She hoped it fit. She also hoped she could be cured of her shyness around strangers in the next few days, but that wasn't likely.

Once again the shop was quiet. This time of day there was always a lull as folks got off work and headed home. The evening would be busy, though, and that would keep her occupied until she could see how the dress fit. She still couldn't get over her luck at being invited to one of the biggest parties of the year.

The problem was no one would know her, or she them. The thought made her shiver. Books were better friends than people in her world, but she'd kept it that way for far too long. Now she was on her own and about to make a life for herself – she should put herself out in the real world more often.

She grabbed the feather duster and tidied some shelves and displays. She was most comfortable in this old place, which dated back to the town's early days. She couldn't explain it, she just was. She could almost see the wagons, horses and cowboys in the street outside. There were some other shops across the street the same age, and the old doctor's house a half a block down that was now the city museum.

Without thinking she set the feather duster down, went to the mercantile doors and stepped outside. Cars were parked along the sidewalks, the historic street beginning to fill with folks shopping after work. Some would go to Mulligan's or the Van Cleet Hotel for dinner. She could only imagine what the hotel looked like in its heyday – it was still being restored. Only a few rooms were available to rent, but it was a popular wedding reception venue, so the first floor was always in operation.

Chilled, she went back inside and closed the door. Another wave of emotions hit as she stared around the store. To Lorelei, Dunnigan's had always been a magical place, a safe place. But a part of her knew she couldn't hide behind its walls forever. Especially not after Mr. Jensen hired her on for more hours. If there were enough, she could give up one of her other jobs.

But first she'd wait and see what her favorite employer had in mind. Right now the only thing she had to worry about was surviving the upcoming Christmas party.

CHAPTER FOUR

By the time Saturday rolled around Lorelei was exhausted. Setting up house wasn't as easy as she'd first thought – she hadn't planned for all the little incidentals, and because she didn't have a car, she couldn't travel to a larger town with better shopping. Besides, she'd been so busy this last week she wouldn't have had time anyway.

She'd bought cans of soup on sale earlier in the week, then brought them home only to realize she didn't have a can opener. She'd bought bread, figuring she could have a piece of toast in the morning for breakfast. No toaster. Heck, she didn't even have a pot to heat up her soup in. She'd at least been able to get the can opener and a saucepan, but she'd have to save up for the toaster. And this went on all week. It was amazing how much she took for granted the little conveniences stowed in drawers and cupboards in Bob and Patsy's kitchen.

Finally, she made a list of everything she needed. It was large enough to be daunting. She added everything up and sighed. "I can't afford all of this. Not all at once." She let go a frustrated sigh, went into the bedroom and took the dress

Shona loaned her out of the armoire. That would get her mind off her troubles. It was so beautiful she could stare at it for hours. When she first tried it on, she was speechless. There was an oval mirror on one door of the armoire, and she had to back up almost to the other side of the room to see her entire reflection, but she didn't care. It was the most beautiful clothing she'd ever laid eyes on. When she put on the cloak and lace scarf, she felt like a princess. She'd even walked around the apartment a few moments and pretended she was in another time.

That is, until she caught herself and felt silly. What if Mr. or Mrs. Jensen came knocking on her door for something? So she'd taken it off, hung it up and called Shona to tell her it fit perfectly. So did the shoes, which was a surprise. Did Shona and Kitty take a lucky guess?

She yawned. She'd taken on more hours at the laundromat and Daisy's this week, not to mention Dunnigan's, to help pay for the household items she'd need. But tonight was the party – she hoped she had the energy to get through the evening. She'd look ridiculous if she fell asleep in a corner at such a coveted event. If Cindy heard, she'd come into Dunnigan's every day for months to rag her about it.

She shrugged the thought off. She had more important things to think about – like what she'd do with her hair. She went into the bathroom and tried putting it in French braids, then wrapping the long braids around her head like a crown. But naturally, she couldn't. "Pins! I don't have any bobby pins!"

She sighed and stared at herself in the mirror. Her golden blonde hair looked pretty with the red of the gown, but how would she get it to stay? She let the braids fall and wrapped small rubber bands around the ends to hold them in place for now. Maybe she could think up a hairstyle while she put on some makeup? But she didn't wear a lot, so that didn't give her much time.

She blew a stray hair out of her face and had a sudden cold feeling in the pit of her stomach, the kind that told you something wasn't right somewhere. She turned from the mirror, stepped into the hall and glanced around. Nothing. Maybe she'd feel better if she took a quick shower?

Lorelei got her one towel and returned to the bathroom. She wanted to enjoy herself tonight. She didn't want to worry about her hair or makeup or any of that. But that wasn't her biggest worry and she knew it.

NO SOONER THAN she got out of the shower she heard a noise. "Mr. Jensen?" But why would he be in her apartment? She thought a moment. She didn't remember locking her door. She was so used to not being able to …

Thud.

Lorelei froze for a moment, her heart in her throat, then realized she was wrapped in nothing but a towel.

"Ha ha ha …"

Her eyes widened. "Who's there?!" She reached for her jeans and pulled them on as the sound of feet hurried down the hall. Why would whoever it was be running? Were they trying to surprise her with something?

She pulled on a T-shirt and put her ear to the bathroom door just in time to hear the door to the apartment close. Without thinking she ran out and down the hall. By the time she opened her door and stepped onto the landing, the curtains leading to the store front were just settling back into place. "What the heck?" She hurried down the staircase, her footfalls soft. She'd always been light on her feet. Sometimes she seemed to float on air when she moved and right now her blood was racing so fast she wanted to keep running.

When she reached the bottom, she ran into the storefront and looked around. "Something wrong?" Mr. Jensen asked. "And why aren't you dressed? Didn't you say your ride would be here at 6:30?"

"Someone was just in my apartment."

"What?"

"Who was in here?"

"Well ..." He glanced around. "I was helping a couple pick out some ornaments for their grandchildren, and I thought I heard the bell over the door ring."

There were a half a dozen people browsing the store. "Did you see anyone run out?"

"No, though it looks like a few customers are gone now."

"Did you recognize any of them?"

"Yes, one was that Cindy Crankshaw. She was with your brother Erwin."

"He's not my brother, he's ... never mind." She went to the door and looked out. It was snowing. Great.

"Don't you think you'd better get ready?" Mr. Jensen pointed at the old cuckoo clock on the wall. The hands pointed to 6:19.

"Argh!" Lorelei ran back through the curtain and up the stairs. As she ran back to her apartment, she had a sinking feeling. Why on earth would Cindy and Erwin be in there? Not to see the place, that was sure. To badger her about the party again? Beatrice told her that now that Patsy and Bob knew where she lived (she couldn't keep it away from them forever), Erwin and the others would have heard. She'd been waiting for the inevitable knock, but not this.

She went into her room and realized the dress wasn't hanging in the same spot as before. "Oh, no, she wouldn't ..." But she knew Cindy would. She checked it, and sure enough, several ruffles on the skirt had been rent, as if Cindy had tried to tear them off. "No. No, no …"

Lorelei shut her eyes and counted to ten. She couldn't afford to be mad right now. She had to get ready. She also had to figure out what to tell Shona. The dress probably cost a fortune, and now it was ruined. And she didn't even own safety pins …

A knock sounded on her door. "Oh no!" She ran down the hall to open it. "Mr. Jensen! They're here, aren't they?"

"Yes, Titus Cooke is downstairs. You'd better hurry – you don't want to keep him waiting."

She shut her eyes, nodded, shut the door and ran back into her room. She changed as fast as she could then went to put on the shoes Shona had loaned her … and they were gone. "What!" she screeched, turning a full circle. "She took my shoes?!"

She caught the panicked look on her face in the armoire's mirror. "What am I going to do?" But that wasn't the part that made her blood boil. It was that Erwin helped. The stab of betrayal was overwhelming. Sure, they'd never had much to do with one another unless they had to, but they'd lived in the same house for six years! That had to count for something. They'd done chores together, made meals together, exchanged Christmas gifts … and he'd never done anything like this to her.

Tears stung her eyes as she realized her foster brother couldn't care less about her, not if he'd helped Cindy do something like this. Cindy was a bully and a snob, but now she'd sunk to a whole new low. She'd jealously ruined what had promised to be a magical evening, all because Lorelei got an invitation and she didn't. Never mind that her family attended parties at the Cookes' Triple-C Ranch all the time.

Another knock on her door told her she needed to hurry. She grabbed the only other acceptable shoes she had, a pair of white Converse Chuck Taylor high-tops. She only had two pairs, and the worn black Mary Janes weren't going to cut it – they were almost falling apart. Beatrice had warned her she'd have to get a new pair soon, because she couldn't waitress wearing shabby shoes. But she wasn't the one who had to pay for them. Mr. Jensen and Mrs. Deets didn't care what her shoes looked like.

She put them on, took one look in the mirror and sighed in relief. The dress covered them. She'd have to tell Shona what happened and promise to pay for the shoes and the damage to the dress. She wasn't sure how she would, but she'd have to worry about that later. For tonight, so long as she didn't let anyone see her feet, she'd be fine.

Lorelei looked at her hair. It would have to do. She put on the cloak and scarf and prayed that nothing else happened tonight. She'd have a hard enough time as it was.

THERE WAS little conversation between Lorelei and the Cookes. As soon as she climbed into the big black Cadillac Escalade, she felt like she was on another planet. Mrs. Cooke insisted she call her Mavis. She was a pretty woman in her late forties with dark hair just graying at the temples. Her blue eyes were inquisitive, and she spoke softly. They sat in the back while the men took the front.

Lincoln drove, and Lorelei took a few moments to study him when the streetlights illuminated the cab. He was a few years older than Mavis with light brown hair and dark eyes, and the more she studied him the more she noticed the kindness in his face, much like his wife's. She couldn't see Titus well from right behind him, but she'd get to see him and his costume at the party.

All were dressed like they'd stepped out of the Old West.

Titus looked like a gambler. Mavis was wearing a long cloak similar to her own over an ornate blue gown. Lincoln, though dressed like a gunslinger, was the most authentic – Mavis told her the handkerchief around his neck came from one of his settler ancestors and had been passed down for generations.

Lorelei listened, speaking only when spoken to. She felt so small and insignificant compared to these people. They lived a life she could only dream of. Maybe one day she'd have nice things, but she'd have to work for them and that would take time.

They left Clear Creek and drove several miles out of town before turning onto the road leading to the MacDonalds' cabin and the party. "Have you been out here before?" Mavis asked.

"No, never." Lorelei looked out the front window at the snow. If it kept coming down, they might have a time of it getting back to town. "Is this four-wheel drive?"

"Yes. Are you worried about the weather?" Mavis asked.

Lorelei half-smiled. "A little."

"Don't be," Lincoln said. "This rig can handle it."

"Do you have your driver's license yet?" Mavis asked this time.

"No," she told her. It was embarrassing – most of the kids from her class had one already. Thank Patsy Brown for not being willing to pony up the fees for the foster kid.

They pulled into the drive and headed toward a grove of firs and pines. Lights shone through the branches until they rounded a corner that opened up into a large yard. The cabin came into view and Lorelei's jaw dropped. Cindy was right – it looked more like a small lodge, two stories with several dormers on the second floor. The house and front walk were trimmed in white Christmas lights, and gold Christmas ornaments hung on some small evergreen trees in the yard.

She continued to take it in as Lincoln looked for a place to park. Several men milled around the front door in Western garb, like they were waiting to do a scene in an old movie. A couple had drinks in their hands. A woman dressed in a beautiful pink gown with a white fur wrap came out of the house to join them. Lorelei wondered if the wrap was real.

"Isn't it lovely?" Mavis whispered. "This is going to be fun." She reached over and patted Lorelei's hand. "You're going to have a wonderful time."

Lorelei smiled and tried to swallow the lump in her throat. She wasn't sure how much fun she'd have after she told Shona MacDonald about the dress and shoes. No one had noticed when she climbed into the SUV, but would they when she climbed out? She didn't want anyone saying anything to the MacDonalds before she could.

Lincoln parked, got out, and went to open Mavis' door. Titus did the same for Lorelei. "Shall we, m'lady?" He offered her a hand.

Lorelei took a breath. It was stupid, but she felt a little like Cinderella. In her world, Titus Cooke was the equivalent of a prince, and she was very much a peasant. She forced a smile, took his hand and, being careful not to let her Chuck Taylors show, carefully slid out of the vehicle.

As soon as her feet touched the ground, Titus offered her his arm. "Let us away to the ball," he said with a smile, then leaned toward her. "Always wanted to say that."

She couldn't suppress a snort. He had no idea how many times she'd dreamed of a handsome young man telling her that. She'd settle for the patriarch of the Cooke family. She lifted her skirt just enough to not trip over it and took quick steps to keep her shoes hidden. They followed Lincoln and Mavis up the front walk to ooohs and ahhhs from people around the door.

"Look at you!" a man said. Lorelei turned to find John Turner of Turner Ranch & Winery. He smiled and looked at Titus with Lorelei. "Titus – who do we have here?"

"This is Miss Lorelei Carson," Titus said. "A guest of the MacDonalds – we're acting as her private coach for the evening."

"Nice to meet you, Lorelei," the woman in the pink gown and white fur wrap said. "I'm Angie Turner and this is my husband John."

Lorelei smiled and nodded. Good grief, she couldn't talk! She'd better get a grip or people would think she was weird. "N-nice to meet you," she managed. A shiver ran up her spine. She was way out of her element. She hated being so shy, but what could she do about it?

The front door opened and out stepped Dallan MacDonald. "Well, look at you!" Titus looked him up and down. "Hey, I thought this was supposed to be a Western themed Christmas party. That's not a Western outfit!"

Dallan smiled. He was dressed in a long-sleeved white shirt, a black dinner jacket and a kilt, with a holster on each hip. "Western Scotland, mayhaps."

"Oh, come on," Lincoln scoffed. Titus just laughed.

Dallan smiled at them. "Host's privilege, then."

"Oh, stop, you two," Mavis said. "It's cold out here."

"Aye, but it's hot in there. Why d'ye think I came outside?" Dallan looked at Lorelei and smiled. "Ye look bonny, lass. Shona will be pleased with herself."

Lorelei blushed to her toes as her stomach knotted. She hated to have to tell Shona about the dress and shoes, but what else could she do? She took a deep breath to brace herself and hoped the woman wasn't too mad. But then, she was used to being yelled at. She'd been listening to people yell at her for as long as she could remember.

CHAPTER FIVE

When they followed their host inside, Lorelei found that what she thought was a second story, was instead an open-beamed ceiling over twenty feet high. The dormers she'd noticed earlier were high on the front wall, accessible by a wraparound mezzanine with doors leading off it on the other three sides. There was a staircase at one end of the huge room – a room over fifty feet long and at least twenty-five wide – that led up to the mezzanine.

The stair rail and balustrade of the mezzanine were wrapped in fir boughs, red velvet bows and white Christmas lights. A floor-to-ceiling Christmas tree filled the center of the room. There was a kitchen at the other end of the house with a large pass-through in the wall, in front of which was a dining room table that seated at least twelve. Lorelei glimpsed an old-fashioned cast-iron cookstove in the kitchen and wondered if it worked.

"There you are!" came a familiar voice. "I'm so glad you came."

Lorelei slipped her arm from Mr. Cooke's and cringed,

hoping the tears in the skirt weren't noticeable. Shona was wearing the green dress she'd brought into Dunnigan's. It was beautiful on her, with her auburn hair piled on her head and a few ringlets framing her face. She looked just like she'd stepped out of the 1800s. Which was the point, Lorelei reminded herself.

Shona took her hand. "You're going to have a wonderful time!"

Lorelei let out the breath she'd been holding. "Shona, I … I need to talk to you. In private."

"Oh, about what?" Shona said, concerned.

Lorelei's heart sank to her toes. She hated disappointing the woman. Would she be angry? Only one way to find out. "It's about my dress," she whispered.

Shona's eyes flicked over her. "What about it? It looks fine to me." Of course, she couldn't see it. Lorelei was still wearing the cloak. "I'll explain, but can we go somewhere else?"

"Certainly." Shona motioned toward the kitchen, then glanced at Dallan, whose back was to them.

Lorelei saw him stiffen just before he turned. They exchanged a look, and she swore something passed between them. Did Shona suspect the dress was damaged? Had they talked of the possibility when they loaned it to her? Great – then they already thought she wasn't capable of handling things. It wasn't her fault, but she was responsible for the dress no matter what happened.

With an overwhelming sense of dread, she followed Shona to the kitchen. She shouldn't feel this bad, but she did. Cindy, Melanie or Heather wouldn't care less if it happened to them. But that was the difference between Lorelei and those three – she cared.

"What is it?" Shona asked when they were alone.

Lorelei took off the cloak and pointed at her dress. "See it?"

Shona bent down and looked. "Oh, dear ..."

"I'm so sorry!" Lorelei hoped she didn't sound too pathetic. "I was taking a shower when someone came into my apartment and ... and they stole the shoes too!"

Shona glanced at her sneakers, straightened and arched an eyebrow. "Who?" She sounded like a policeman interrogating a witness.

She sighed. "Some ... old classmates from high school ..."

Shona nodded as if she'd confirmed something. "Anyone I've met?"

"I think so. I'm pretty sure it was Cindy and Erwin. Look, I'm so sorry, and I promise I'll pay for it. The shoes, too."

Shona held up her hand. Those green eyes boring into Lorelei like twin lasers, but they held no anger – not for her, anyway. Somehow she could tell. "I see. Cindy from Dunnigan's? The one that made those snide remarks the day we met? And I gather Erwin was the boy toy she was dragging around."

Lorelei hesitated. What would Shona do? If she spoke with Cindy, her old classmate would make her life miserable for as long as she could. "Um, yeah."

Shona nodded to herself. "Don't worry about it. She seemed the type."

"You believe me?"

"Of course I believe you." She thought a moment. "And I know just the person to fix the dress. I'm not a good seamstress."

"If you have some safety pins, I can do it."

"I'm not sure ..."

"Please, let me pin it," Lorelei said. "I don't want it to tear further."

Shona sighed. "All right." She went to a drawer and dug

through it, emerging finally with a packet of small safety pins. "Let me. I can see what I'm doing."

"Thanks." Lorelei watched Shona deftly pin the ruffles into place. "I can't tell you how sorry I am."

Shona looked up from her work. "Like I said, don't worry about it. You can't be responsible for every jerk who wants to give you grief. I'll give this to my friend Melvale when I see him – he can sew circles around most women."

Lorelei was almost faint from relief. The woman took it well and didn't come unglued on her like she thought she might. Patsy would have, but this woman was nothing like Patsy. There was an elegance and sophistication about Shona MacDonald that Lorelei had never seen before. It was as if the woman was royalty.

Shona's husband entered the kitchen. "What's amiss, then? And what're ye doing on the floor, Flower?"

Shona looked at him. "Pinning Lorelei's dress."

"What happened?"

"It will only upset you."

Lorelei's stomach churned anew. But she also noticed the tender look the man gave his wife, and the nickname he'd called her. How pretty.

"Och, aye? Weel, ye ken me best. Dinna say a word if ye think 'twill bring me to blows with someone."

"It will." Shona stood and poked him in the chest. "But what worries me is that you'd enjoy it."

To Lorelei's surprise, the man blushed. He looked into Shona's eyes and smiled. "Aye, no doubt I would if justice is to be served."

"And you know that in this time and place, that won't go over well." Shona returned her attention to Lorelei. "Have a good time tonight. And don't worry about the dress. Or the shoes."

Lorelei opened her mouth to reply but Shona held her hand up again.

"Best do as she says, lass," Dallan cut in. "She kens what she's about."

Lorelei stared at him a moment. She didn't understand some of the Scottish words he used but got the gist. "I will, sir."

He smiled. "The dress looks fine." He looked her up and down. "Aye, mighty fine indeed."

Her cheeks grew hot and she gave the man a shy smile. These had to be two of the nicest people she'd ever met. "Thank you for inviting me."

The couple's eyes grew warm. "Thank you for coming," Shona said. "I'm sure this will be a night you'll remember for the rest of your life."

Lorelei stared at her a moment. That the couple's eyes were so similar in color was one thing, but they seemed to brighten at the same time as well. How could that be?

"Dallan," Shona cooed. "Don't you need to go change?"

He rolled his eyes. "Fine, I'll put my costume on."

Lorelei giggled, quickly covering her mouth.

"Oh, go ahead and laugh," he said. "I was so busy decorating, I didna have time to change." He glanced at his tuxedo jacket. "Though I did think the jacket made me look dashing." He turned to Shona who cast him a look that clearly said, *get going.* "Fine, I'll do it now." He made to leave then turned around. "Everything ready, Flower?"

She glanced at Lorelei and back. "It is now."

"Good." He turned again and left the kitchen.

"Come along," Shona motioned to the party. "Let's see if Kitty has come downstairs yet. Last I checked she was trying to put her hair up." She glanced at Lorelei's braids. "Hmm, we'll have to do something about those."

"What?" She tried to keep the worry out of her voice.

"Follow me." Shona led her back into the massive main room and went to a huge Christmas wreath hanging on one wall, covered with tiny red velvet bows. She untied two and turned to Lorelei. "Here, this will make your outfit perfect." She tied a ribbon around the end of one braid, covering the rubber band, then did the same with the other.

"Thank you," Lorelei said. "You've been so nice about this whole thing."

Shona smiled. "Well, I'm glad you think so." She turned away and waved at the party going on around them. "Enjoy yourself." She left Lorelei to fend for herself. But then, the woman had a lot of guests to see to.

Lorelei swallowed hard as she glanced around the room. There had to be more than sixty people talking, laughing and eating. She saw the Cookes near a couple of long food tables against one wall. More trays of food were set on the counter of the pass-through, more still on the dining table. She recognized folks from town besides the Cookes and Turners, but most were strangers. She suddenly felt very alone, too self-conscious to hang around the well-to-do guests. Maybe when Kitty came downstairs ...

Before she knew it, she'd backed herself into a chair in the corner. Her comfort zone, found.

"Enjoying yourself?"

She looked up and saw a man dressed more like an English lord than a cowboy, with a plate in his hand. "Have you tried these?" He held up a Ritz cracker covered in spray cheese. "They're jolly good."

She tried not to make a face. "Er, no."

"You really ought to. I've never had it before." He took a step toward her and offered her his plate.

She didn't want to be impolite, so she took one. He was

handsome, with dark hair and eyes, and spoke with a British accent. Had he come all the way from England to attend the party? Shona did mention they had friends coming from all over, but that far? "Thank you," she finally said, and took a bite. Actually, it wasn't bad – certainly better than the Cheese Whiz that was a staple in Bob and Patsy's house. Bob loved the stuff. Lorelei thought it smelled like Vaseline.

He winked. "No one else has any," he whispered conspiratorially. "I made my own in the kitchen."

She stopped chewing as her eyes fixed on the dining table covered with all sorts of tasty treats. Everything looked better than Patsy's cooking – or her own.

"Would you like another?" the man offered.

"No, thank you," she said as she finished the cracker. "I'll just see what they have over there. Nice talking to you."

He smiled. "You too. Have a good time."

She hurried off, still nervous from the encounter with the English stranger and his fascination with aerosol cheese – didn't they have that in Europe? Mm, probably not. She spotted a large punch bowl and headed straight for it, suddenly desperate for a drink.

"Kitty, you can't keep putting us into your books!"

Lorelei froze at the end of the dining table by the punch bowl, recognizing Shona's voice from the kitchen. What was going on?

"But what else would I write about?" Kitty replied. "Besides, everyone thinks it's fiction. And the books are being published now, not back then."

"I understand, but our assignments are our private business. If my father found out, he'd be very upset."

Lorelei heard Kitty sigh, then say, "Well I can't very well go back and change everything. My readers would kill me."

"I'm not asking you to, just … be more careful in the future. We can't risk exposure."

Lorelei's eyes grew wide. What were they talking about? What was Kitty Morgan writing? Maybe she ought to get one of her books and find out. For now, she got a glass of punch and wandered to the opposite corner. She'd never been good at mingling. She'd never been much good at anything, when one got down to it.

She spied an empty chair and sat, tucking her feet beneath the ruffled skirt of her dress and doing her best to be invisible. She felt like a stranger in a strange land. Some of the guests looked so glamorous in their period dress. She knew she should talk to people but couldn't bring herself to leave the safety of the corner.

She blinked a few times as a chill went up her spine, then blinked some more. What was wrong with her eyes? She rubbed them with her free hand, took a sip of punch and hoped the sudden bout of dizziness she was feeling wasn't from the squeeze cheese. Worse, she hoped she wasn't coming down with the flu. That was the last thing she needed – how would she work?

She rubbed her eyes again and leaned back. When she did she felt as if she kept going, like there was no chair back or wall behind her. What was happening?

"Lorelei," Shona asked, or was it Kitty? "Are you all right?"

She blinked again but couldn't bring whoever it was into focus. "Noooo …"

"Are you sick?" came another voice. Kitty's? Or Mavis'?

"Yeeeess …"

One of them sighed as two more people hovered over her. "Aerosol cheese?" Shona scolded someone. "Really?"

"You said …"

"Oh, I know what I said …"

Lorelei hoped she didn't throw up on them. Stupid spray cheese. Should've known better.

"Time to take her upstairs," Shona said. "Best go through the kitchen."

Before she knew it, she was lifted into a man's arms and being carried. She really *was* sick! She had no idea that cheese in a can could go bad. Was the Englishman sick too?

"You said, find something no one else is eating. That's what I found." Was that him? Or another Englishman?

Lorelei's mind became so fuzzy she wasn't sure who was talking anymore. The last clear things she heard were, "Doesna matter," as she was set on a bed, followed by, "Shona, take us to Clear Creek."

Great, they were going to the hospital to have her stomach pumped! It was only one cracker – and the cheese-like product didn't even taste bad!

She could barely keep her eyes open as a brilliant white light appeared and shot toward one wall. The light narrowed to a beam, moving up and down in an odd pattern. With effort, she forced one eye to open and for a second saw the nearest wall outlined, as if someone was using a light pen to trace everything on the wall. And what was that singing? She swore she heard someone singing. Her only conclusion was that she was having a spray-cheese-induced drug trip. Is this why Bob devoured Cheese Whiz? Oh yuck!

And then it was gone, all of it – the voices, the light and hopefully the squeeze cheese. The room fell dark and quiet. She could no longer hear the party downstairs. But she was in the hospital now, wasn't she? Naturally it would be quiet. Had they already pumped her stomach? How would she feel in the morning? Was it morning? She couldn't tell, couldn't open her eyes.

There was a floating sensation, and she thought she heard music again. Peaceful, serene, soothing, like an Enya record playing in another room. The sound made her feel wonderful, much better than she'd felt moments ago. But … how much time had passed? She had no idea at this point and didn't care. She just knew she didn't want the feeling of peace to end, nor the sensation that she was tucked into a comfy, warm bed in a dark, cool room.

Nothing else mattered as Lorelei slipped into a deep and dreamless sleep.

CHAPTER SIX

"Lorelei? Are you awake?"

Lorelei's eyes fluttered open. Daylight shone through the windows, the sharp kind that came after a night of snowfall. She let her eyes focus, then looked at the woman standing over her. "Who are you?" Her voice was raspy, her throat dry. She tried to clear it and coughed instead.

"Oh, dear, let me get you some water." The woman crossed the room, poured some water from a pitcher into a glass and brought it to the bed. "Here, this will help."

Lorelei tried to sit up but couldn't. Her head swam and she felt disoriented.

"Don't rush. Take your time."

Lorelei decided to focus on the woman. She had blue eyes, and golden blonde hair much like her own, put up in an old fashioned hair-style. Had she spent the night here after the party? She still had on her costume, but it wasn't a fancy dress like so many others, just an olive-green calico with simple ivory buttons down the front and a knitted black shawl around her shoulders.

The room felt cold, like someone had left the windows open. Lorelei shivered, pushed herself onto her elbows, then slowly sat up. "Oh, my head …"

"It's all right." The woman sat on the edge of the bed. "Mrs. MacDonald said you'd feel dizzy when you woke up. Drink this." She handed her the glass.

Lorelei took a long swallow. It was wonderful and cold. "Shona … where is she?"

"I'm afraid they're gone. They had urgent business to take care of. They left you in our care."

Lorelei could only stare. "What?"

"I'm Belle," the woman said with a warm smile. "Belle Cooke."

Lorelei blinked again. One of the Cookes? But not a name she'd ever heard – was she visiting from out of town? She didn't remember seeing her last night. "Lorelei Carson."

"How do you do?" Belle offered her hand.

Lorelei reached out and shook it. The woman's hand was calloused. She must garden a lot. But this was winter – did she have a hot house? "I need to get back to Clear Creek."

"Back? I was under the impression … well, never mind. Do you think you're up to it?"

"Impression of what?"

Belle sighed. "The MacDonalds told my husband and I to take you home with us. They'll come fetch you when they're done with … well, whatever it is they're doing. They didn't tell us specifics, but then, they never do." She chuckled.

"That's odd." She noticed she was not only still wearing her party dress, but that she wasn't in a hospital. "They didn't take me to the hospital?"

"I beg your pardon?"

"I was sick last night. I … ate something bad." She wasn't about to go into details. It was embarrassing enough to be done in by a single cracker covered with spray cheese.

"Oh, you poor dear. But don't worry, we'll get you home and fix you right up."

Lorelei smiled weakly. Couldn't Shona and Dallan or the other Cookes have just taken her home? But as sick as she obviously was, they must've decided against it. Maybe they could still drop her off. She wasn't still that sick. She'd had food poisoning before and been able to handle it. She licked her dry lips. "Where do you live?"

"A few miles on the other side of Clear Creek, but with the added distance, we're looking at about six."

"THEN IT WOULD BE easy for you to drop me off. I live above Dunnigan's Mercantile."

"You ... do?"

"I just moved in. I appreciate you giving me a ride – I really need to get out of this dress."

Belle gave her a funny look, then glanced at the dress. "It's beautiful. Did you make it?"

"Me?" Lorelei laughed. "If only. I can hardly thread a needle. Shona lent it to me for the party."

Belle smiled. "I see. Where are you from originally?"

"Portland. But I've lived in Clear Creek for years."

Belle gave her a look as if what she was saying didn't add up. Then she studied Lorelei's dress while running a hand over her own. "I used to have beautiful clothes when I lived in Boston. Seems like a lifetime ago."

Lorelei studied Belle's worn clothes. "Did you make that dress?"

"Yes – do you like it? It's not my best work, I had to rush to finish it because I was also sewing new dresses for my daughters at the time. They're going to be Christmas gifts."

"You sew a lot?"

"With as many children as I have, yes," she said with a laugh. "Can you stand?"

"I can try. Besides, I need to use the restroom."

Belle stared at her. "The what?"

"The bathroom?"

"Bathroom," she drawled. "You mean … a water closet?"

Lorelei stared at her. "Water closet, yeah." It was the 1800s word for "bathroom," but why was Belle using it?

Belle sighed, reached under the bed and pulled out an old-fashioned porcelain chamber pot. It looked brand new. Lorelei wondered where Shona and Dallan found it. More important, why was the woman offering it to her? Was this some kind of joke?

"I'll leave you to it," Belle said as she handed it to her and stood. "I'll let my husband know we can leave soon." She gave Lorelei a nervous smile and left the room.

Lorelei shoved the heavy quilts off of her – the same ones she'd washed for the MacDonalds over a week ago. Only now, they looked almost new. "What the …?" She fingered the fabric, then the stitching. There were no old stains, no musty smell … what was going on? She got out of bed, shivered and went to the dormered window. She must be in the back of the house. Had the electricity gone out? It was freezing.

She rubbed her arms and looked outside at the snow-covered trees, more trees than she remembered. "Wow." It was a beautiful sight. The trees were very tall, the woods thick. She noted the frost on the windows, went to the bed, noticed her cloak and scarf at the end of the bed and put them on. After another shiver she grabbed the top quilt and wrapped it around her. She had to find a toilet and fast.

She went to the door, opened it and stepped into a long hallway illuminated by a window at either end. There were several other doors and she was confused as to what part of the house she was in. Where was the mezzanine? The place must be bigger than she thought. And when was there a power outage? Brrr! She hoped the electricity was on at home.

She opened the first door she came to – another bedroom. She went to the next – another one. She opened every door on the second floor but still found no bathroom. Lorelei remembered Shona said the cabin had eight beds upstairs – that's what she needed the quilts for. But the quilts on the beds – and the one she'd was wrapped in – though they appeared the same, looked much newer.

She found the staircase at the end of the hall, went down it and found herself in a large living room, with a wide door leading to a dining room. Where was she? Was she even in the same house? She crossed the room to a door and opened it. Another bedroom.

"All done?" Belle said as she came into the house through what had to be the front door. "I'll empty the pot."

Lorelei gaped at her. "Um … I didn't use …"

"Oh, would you rather use the privy? It's out back in the trees. The trail's covered in snow, but you can follow the footprints."

"Out back?!" Had she heard her right?

"Yes, follow me." Belle went into the dining room.

Lorelei could only follow. Maybe this was some sort of hunter's cabin behind the main house. Were the MacDonalds shooting for a rustic vibe? She reached the kitchen and stopped. "Oh, wow. Definitely rustic."

"I beg your pardon?" Belle said.

"Nothing." Lorelei stared at the wood-fired cookstove, the dry sink, the hutch against one wall. Nothing looked less than a hundred years old, but it had all been made, or restored, to appear brand-new.

"Yes, I know, it's not everything one needs. Amon built this to replace the original men's camp but never finished it. He left for England and none of us have had time to work on the place."

Lorelei nodded, not knowing what to say. Did this Amon still own part of the property? "How far is this from the main house?"

"Main house?" Belle said, confused.

Lorelei's bladder reminded her where they were going and indicated this wasn't the time to argue. "Never mind. Where's the trail?"

Belle led her through a back door and into a small yard. There was a clothesline strung between two small pines and a trail of footprints that disappeared into the thick trees.

Lorelei nodded at Belle and, doing her best not to fidget, took to the trail. It led about sixty feet away to an honest to goodness outhouse. "Great." But beggars couldn't be choosers. She took a deep breath, prayed it wasn't full of spiders, and went inside.

"AND THIS IS MY HUSBAND COLIN." Belle waved at a man readying an old-fashioned buckboard. It had a two-horse team and Lorelei wondered if they trailered the horses in from the Cooke ranch or some other ranch or stable. If this was part of the MacDonalds' idea, it was certainly working on her. She *felt* like she was in the Old West. People that stayed would love it.

"Hello," Lorelei said, too softly. Then, a little stronger: "Nice to meet you."

He turned. "My pleasure. My wife tells me you're feeling much better."

Her brows shot up at his British accent. "Oh, yes. Last night was, um ... a little rough."

"We understand," Belle said.

Lorelei smiled and studied Mr. Cooke. She hadn't seen either of them around town and an Englishman would have stood out as soon as he opened his mouth. She wondered if they were there to help the MacDonalds out. "Do you live around here?"

The couple exchanged a concerned look. "Yes, I thought I explained," Belle said. "We live on the Triple-C."

Lorelei's brow furrowed. "I haven't seen you around town."

"We don't get to town as much as we used to," Mr. Cooke said. "It's easier to send our foreman or one of his sons."

She smiled. "That makes sense." She didn't know what half the Cooke family looked like anyway. She was only familiar with the three youngest – Nathaniel, Winston and Avery – because Clear Creek had just one high school.

"Let's go." He offered his wife a hand.

Lorelei glanced around. She didn't see a car or truck anywhere.

"Coming?"

She looked at them and her breath caught. "We're riding in the wagon?"

They exchanged another look. "You don't want to walk, do you?" Mr. Cooke asked.

"No ... it's just that I thought you'd drive me home."

"We are, but to our ranch," Belle said again. "It's what the MacDonalds said. They were quite ..." She glanced at her husband. "... insistent."

She stared at them. What *did* happen last night? "Was I that sick?"

"We wouldn't know," Belle said. "We weren't there. But according to them, you definitely need looking after."

She thought about that and hoped the panic rising in her chest didn't show on her face. Was something wrong with her, something she didn't know about? Had they taken her to the hospital and brought her back?

"Come along, Miss Carson," Mr. Cooke said. "We really must be going."

"You're not feeling ill again, are you?" Belle asked from the wagon seat.

Lorelei looked up at her. How was she going to climb up there in her dress? But more importantly … "Did they take me to a doctor?"

"Not that we know of," Belle said. "But if you're feeling sick, we could always drop by Doc Drake's on the way home."

"Doc Drake?" Who the heck was that? "Is he at Clear Creek General?"

Belle blinked a few times. "I'm sorry, at what?"

"We'll talk about it on the way," Colin insisted. "We must get going before the snow starts up again." He held a hand out to Lorelei. "Come, dear."

Lorelei looked at the two big bay horses, then at him. She'd never been this close to horses except at a Fourth of July parade. But she wasn't being offered an alternative. She took his hand and gathered a handful of voluminous skirt with the other, not wanting to tear the dress any more than it already was. The quilt didn't make it easier.

"Right then, here you go." To her surprise, he led her to the back of the wagon. "You'll ride here."

"Oh, okay." At least she wouldn't have to climb onto the seat.

He lifted her into the buckboard like she was nothing. "There – you can sit on those bags of oats behind us."

She turned, saw the grain sacks and some crates of what

looked like groceries, then sat and pulled the quilt tighter. A biting cold wind was kicking up.

"You don't have a heavier coat?" Belle asked.

"No." She rearranged the quilt and put part of it over her head. Belle, she noticed, had her heavy shawl, a scarf around her head and neck, and a blanket across her lap.

Colin climbed up, put part of the blanket over his legs and picked up the reins. He got the team moving and the wagon lurched forward.

Lorelei was afraid to question the Cookes about much yet. For now, she was hungry, cold and disoriented, but all in all still felt better than last night. She'd been so sick and ... something else. Didn't she feel unexplainably good at one point? She thought she had, right before she went to sleep. Maybe they gave her some sort of medicine. She hoped it wasn't addicting – she'd read about the opioid epidemic.

The wagon bumped through the snow-covered woods. She liked the sound of the horse's hooves on the snow and the jangle of harness, but boy, could this thing use some shock absorbers! She was facing backwards and could see other wagon tracks, some of which were already covered with new snow. Did they all belong to this wagon, or did the MacDonalds have two or three? She'd have to ask them when she saw them again. The sky looked like it was going to snow again. She saw the landscape, sighed at the beauty of it all and ... "Oh no!"

"What is it," Belle asked as she turned on the wagon seat to see her.

"I have to go to work!"

"Work?" Mr. Cooke said. "But it's Sunday. And where the devil do you work?"

She tapped her forehead. Think, think, think, Sunday ... "Okay, I think I have time. I just have the four-to-eight shift at Dunnigan's."

"Dunnigan's?" Belle said.

"Shift?" Colin added.

"Yes," Lorelei said, as if it should be obvious. Why wasn't it obvious? "I work part-time at Dunnigan's Mercantile. And at the laundromat, and at Daisy's Café."

Belle stared at her in confusion. "And before, you said you live above Dunnigan's?"

"Yeah. What about it?"

"My aunt and uncle *own* Dunnigan's."

"Oh, you're related to the Jensens?"

The Cookes gave each other another look. Mr. Cooke eyed her this time. "Oh, yes. The MacDonalds told us you wouldn't be yourself and that you also wouldn't be … working for a time. Though I thought they meant something else."

"What? No, I can't afford to lose hours! I have to work this afternoon!"

Colin smiled, but his gaze was firm. "My dear child, you're not yourself and you'll not be going to work. If you're worried about your wages, I've been told that they're taken care of. In the meantime, you're to stay with us, on the MacDonalds' orders, and we'll look after you until they come fetch you. Is that understood?"

She stared at him, mouth open. He'd been nice enough when he said it, but she could tell he meant business. "You kidnapped me?!" she finally shrieked.

"No," Belle quickly replied. "It's all right. You're free to go wherever you like – we won't hold you against your will. But you're here as our and the MacDonalds' guests. Free of charge, if that helps."

Lorelei was a little less alarmed – but only a little. "Is this some kind of a cult?"

Now Belle looked confused again. "I don't know what that means … but no, I don't think it's that. Please, I think it will all make sense soon enough." Belle sighed. "And I should probably talk to the MacDonalds when they return about …" She trailed off with a shake of her head.

Whatever happened last night, they obviously weren't going to tell her yet. Lorelei knew she'd just have to play it cool, see what happened and be prepared to escape whatever weirdness these so-called Cookes and the MacDonalds had planned. "All right. Sorry for freaking out on you." She turned and faced the road behind them.

After what seemed like forever but was probably no more than an hour, she saw another wagon. Then a horse and rider, and another, and still another. She turned, knelt on the sacks of grain and faced front. "What's going on?"

"What do you mean?" Mr. Cooke asked.

Lorelei didn't clarify, just kept looking around. They'd left the woods for the open prairie, and now … this. A well-traveled dirt road was fronted on either side by wooden houses and storefronts and boardwalks. Everyone on the street was in costume. There wasn't a car in sight or power lines to pull her from this dream land. But how in the *heck* was there an entire Old West town in the middle of nowhere?! She didn't know of any Western-themed parks in the area. "This is like *Westworld* IRL. Do you have robots?"

"Lorelei, are you all right?" Belle asked. "Because I'm afraid you're speaking gibberish."

She gaped at the town as her lower lip trembled. Where was she? Where were they taking her?

"Lorelei?" Belle repeated.

She tried to speak but nothing came out. This didn't make any sense. Considering the direction they were traveling, she thought they'd come out on the other side of Canyon Park, but she must have been wrong. "Where … where are we?"

"You mean you don't know?" Belle asked.

Mr. Cooke turned to Lorelei as she shook her head, eyes wide. "My dear child, this is Clear Creek."

Her eyes widened further, her chest grew tight and her head began to spin. Or did everything else? She had no idea, for it all went suddenly black.

CHAPTER SEVEN

"Lorelei?"

The voice was gentle, caring, but she didn't recognize it.

"Let me try," a man said, and an unexplainable peace seeped into her bones. "Lorelei, can you hear me?"

She opened her eyes slowly, not wanting the peaceful sensation to stop. It reminded her of…

Her eyes popped open and darted around the room. There wasn't much furniture, just a hutch with a few small baskets of bandages and some brown bottles full of who-knew-what, a bedside table between two beds – one of which she was in. Finally, she looked at the man hovering over her and holding her hand. He was in his late forties, brown hair graying at the temples with a day's growth of beard and blue eyes. "Who are you?"

"I'm Doc Drake. And you are?"

Didn't he already say her name? "Lorelei Carson."

"Good." He held up a finger. "Can you follow this?" He moved it right, then left.

Her eyes followed it as it all came back: the party, the

Cookes and MacDonalds, the handsome Englishman and his fascination with spray cheese, the ride with Belle and Colin into … "Ohhh," she groaned.

"Does your head hurt?" the doctor asked.

"A little. It's just …" She looked to her right. Belle sat in a chair watching them, Colin standing behind her. Cookes, or so they said. But not any Cookes she'd known or heard about before today. "Belle?"

The woman came and sat on the bed. "I'm right here. How are you feeling?"

"I dare say, you took a nasty tumble," Colin added. "You're lucky you didn't land on a crate of supplies."

She swallowed, her throat dry. There was something wrong, something terribly wrong, and she couldn't figure out what. A 19th-century town in the middle of eastern Oregon …

"Father?"

All heads turned as a young man entered the room. He took one look at Lorelei and froze, his hat in his hands. He looked like a young cowboy, straight out of an old movie.

"Jeff, stop staring – it's not polite," Belle said.

"Your mother's right," said Colin. "What is it?"

"Parthena and Sam are done helping Mr. Mulligan," Jeff said, his eyes darting between his parents and Lorelei.

Her cheeks grew hot under his perusal. She'd always liked cowboys – they were sturdy, tough and romantic. It was one of the reasons she loved watching Westerns. It was also why she'd wanted her time at the MacDonalds' party to be special, but this was getting a little *too* special.

"Jefferson," Belle said, voice laced with warning.

Jefferson – what a nice name. Lorelei watched him twist his hat in his hands a few more times. His eyes met hers, flicked to the other end of the bed and widened. He tilted his head from one side to the other, then stared at her. Her forehead crinkled with confusion. "What?"

"Begging your pardon, ma'am, but those are the strangest shoes I've ever seen."

"What?" She looked at her feet. "They're just Chuck Taylors."

"Who's Chuck Taylor?" Colin asked. "A friend of yours?"

"Um, no. I don't know why they're called that. I used to wear them to school."

"They make shoes just for schooling?" the young cowboy asked.

Lorelei stared at Jefferson. He looked like his father Colin, tall and with the same hazel eyes, though his hair was a little darker and he wasn't as broad. He still had a teenager's gangliness.

Then something he said before hit. *Mulligan's* ... the bar & grill? Her stomach did a funny flip – did he live in Clear Creek? She'd never seen him before. His clothes were well used, not new-looking like those at the party last night. They looked like he wore them every day. Did he get them at Dunnigan's? They sold a little Western wear, mainly for the tourists.

The doctor, Drake, was still holding her hand. His clothes looked worn too, as did Mr. Cooke's. The only outfit that looked newer was Belle's dress. But she had said she'd just made it.

"Are you all right?" the doctor asked.

She opened her eyes, not realizing she'd closed them. "Um, not really." Something wasn't right. Had Jeff the cowboy just come from Mulligan's? They must be in town, then, not that ... other place. But why had the MacDonalds left her with strangers? What was going on? "I ... I just want to go home," she whined, tearing up.

"Oh, you poor dear," Belle said. "We'll take you home with

us. You really shouldn't be alone." She looked at the doctor, worried.

Drake smiled at Lorelei and squeezed her hand. "I believe you've had a shock." He looked at the others. "I wish the MacDonalds had left us more information. Did they give *any* specifics?"

"No, other than to look after her for them," Mr. Cooke said. "I must say, it all happened rather fast. They met us here in town, led us to Amon Cotter's place, the one he built just past the tree line, and ... that was that. Gone."

Doc Drake sighed. "They must have had some sort of emergency. Still, it's odd."

"*They're* odd, if you ask me," Jefferson said.

"Jeff, mind your manners," Mr. Cooke scolded.

He sighed and looked at Lorelei. "Hello, ma'am."

She smiled cautiously. "Hiya."

"Bowen, is there anything we can do for our young guest that you haven't ... already done?" Mr. Cooke inquired.

The doctor shook his head. "Let her rest, keep her warm, feed her. And be patient. It's best after someone's had a shock."

"Wait a minute," Lorelei struggled to sit up through a wave of dizziness. "I haven't had a shock – I had some bad cheese, that's all. It must have given me food poisoning. I'm fine, really. But will someone tell me where I am?"

Each of them gave her a funny look. "You fainted," Belle said in protest. "Colin and Jeff had to carry you in here."

She stared at the Cooke men and swallowed hard. She hated being a bother to anyone, so the thought they'd had to hoist her up and haul her in here was embarrassing. "I'm sorry I fainted. I don't usually do that. But you brought me to some Wild West park, then claimed it was Clear Creek ... are you sure you're not a cult?"

"You must be disoriented." Belle took her other hand.

"Let's get you home now." She turned to her son. "Fetch your brother and sister."

Jefferson nodded, but his eyes didn't leave Lorelei's.

"Jeff, do as your mother says," Mr. Cooke ordered.

His son nodded, spun on his heel and left, his boots clomping into the distance.

"Now I want you to go home with Colin, Belle and their children," the doctor told her. "Rest up, eat right and you'll be back to normal in no time. Don't be afraid. You're in good hands."

His voice was gentle, soothing. She couldn't help but nod in return. But things still weren't adding up. She needed to find out where she really was, and how to get from here to home, no matter how nice everyone was acting.

Belle stood and offered her a hand. "Come along. I'm sure Parthena has a few peppermint sticks by now. I'll have her share one with you."

Her stomach growled. "Candy? Well, all right."

"Oh dear, perhaps some jerky instead?" her husband suggested.

Lorelei made a face. Was he kidding? "Can't we just stop by a Wendy's?"

Belle ignored that and gave Lorelei's hand a gentle tug. She took the hint and swung her legs off the side of the bed. No fast food in Wildwestville, apparently.

"Steady now," the doctor warned. "Wait for any dizziness to pass."

She nodded. Her stomach just felt empty, not the nausea she expected. She stood slowly, carefully, clutching Belle's hand the entire time.

"There now." Mr. Cooke took her elbow. "Let's get you settled. The children should've loaded themselves up by now."

They steered her out of the room, through an ancient

kitchen complete with cookstove, and into the hall. There was a staircase there, a living room on the left and a dining room on the right, both furnished with antiques.

A blond woman sitting on a Victorian-looking couch – a settee? – set some sewing aside. “Is she all right?”

“She’ll be fine, Elsie,” Mr. Cooke said.

“She don’t look fine, Colin.” An old lady pushed herself out of a rocking chair, came over and looked her up and down. “That’s some dress, young lady.” She smiled. “Call me Grandma.”

Lorelei’s eyebrows rose. She glanced at the Cookes.

“We all do,” Mr. Cooke said. “Everyone in town.”

She smiled at the old woman. “Grandma.”

Grandma shook her head in annoyance. “She ain’t right. Something’s wrong.”

You can say that again, Lorelei thought.

“Grandma, you needn’t worry,” Doc Drake said as he joined them. “Physically she’s fine, just a little woozy.”

“Case of the vapors?”

“Not exactly,” Drake said as he rubbed his chin with a hand. “But I trust Dallan and Shona.”

“Hmm,” Grandma mused. “Well, if’n they say she’s fine, she must be.” She smiled at Lorelei again. “Welcome to Clear Creek, child.”

Lorelei shuddered as she looked at the front door, then the windows in the parlor. But she couldn’t see what was outside through the lace curtains.

Before she knew it, she was at the front door. Mr. Cooke opened it, his hand still on her elbow, and ushered her outside. She looked around and, yeah, she was still in Wild-westville, just as she’d seen before she fainted. Was it a movie set? A place for Western re-enactments? Or some Amish-type cult that rejected modern technology? She remembered reading in one of Mr. Jensen’s travel magazines about a place in the Carolinas that didn't allow cars, only horses.

But how did she not know about a place like this in Oregon? And why did they keep insisting it was Clear Creek?

She let them lead her off the porch and across the street toward their buckboard. Jefferson was leaning against it, and a girl and boy who both looked about twelve sat in the back. All three looked like Colin and Belle. Okay, so that must be Parthena and ... Sam or Stan or something.

She took inventory as she settled in the wagon bed. She could see fine, hear fine. Her mind wasn't as foggy as before. But what *was* this place? "Is this town for actors?"

Belle smiled. "You'll find no actors here. Not until Christmas Eve, that is."

"What's Christmas Eve?"

"A most auspicious event," Mr. Cooke said as he snapped the reins and the horses began moving. "The town Christmas play. I'm Joseph this year."

"We don't know that," Belle said. "Annie isn't done giving out parts."

"Harrison got to be Joseph last year, Paddy the year before, Bran the year before that. It *has* to be my turn by now. It's a very coveted role," he added with a wink to Lorelei.

Lorelei, though, was too busy looking around at the buildings the buckboard was passing to notice. "Mr. Cooke? When was this place built? And why is it here?" She smiled at him. "It's remarkable. What is it used for?"

His face froze, as if he wasn't sure what to say. Belle looked much the same.

"I mean I know the MacDonalds were working on their cabin and stuff. Judging from some of the people at the party last night, they must have serious investors. Did they build this place?"

They continued to stare at her, their faces a blank. "Build it?" Belle said.

"Yes. And how did they build it? Did they use refurbished wood on everything?" She glanced around. "The buildings look like they've been here a while."

"They have," Mr. Cooke said. "Some of them almost thirty years."

Lorelei returned the same blank stare. "I was thinking they looked older than that."

Belle shook her head. "We can talk about that later. We'll turn around and get you something to eat from the mercantile. Maybe Paddy has some dried apples. He's helping to mind the store while the Dunnigans are away."

Lorelei's face fell. "The who?"

"The Dunnigans, they own it," Belle said. "Don't you remember me telling you I'm their niece?"

She glanced between them, then looked at the building they'd pulled away from. The sign was different than the one over the store she knew – newer looking, as if it had been painted recently. But the building front was the same as the Dunnigan's Mercantile she knew. And the house behind it similar to the one behind Dunnigan's in Old Town, but it was bare wood instead of painted lilac with white trim. Mrs. Randall owned that shop, selling various gift items, incense, crystals and the like. Mr. Jensen called it "the hippie store."

She took another look down the street. There were no power lines, no satellite dishes, but if you added them and replaced the horses and wagons with cars, it would look a lot like Old Town Clear Creek. She reached into the pocket of her cloak for her cell phone.

It was gone. "Hey!"

"Are you all right?" Belle asked with concern as the wagon stopped. "Should I fetch Doc Drake?"

"I … I don't need a doctor." Without thinking she climbed

down from the buckboard and walked toward the mercantile. Jeff and the kids were watching her, but she ignored them as she headed up the porch steps and inside.

A tiny bell over the door rang, announcing her arrival.

Lorelei glanced around the store as her chest grew tight. It wasn't as cluttered with gift items and knickknacks as the Dunnigan's she knew, but the built-in shelves and some of the bins were the same. She turned and looked at the windows. Those were similar too. But the ones in her store were double-paned; these were single.

"Well, good morning. How can I help ye, young lady?"

She turned around and looked into a familiar pair of eyes. She knew this man, but from where? He looked like he was in his late sixties. "Sir, can you tell me where I am?" She had no idea why she asked that – it was a stupid question. She *should* know where she was, but she didn't.

"Colin?" he said in an Irish brogue. "Mind introducing me?"

He reminded her of ... no. She took a breath and backed up a step.

"Paddy, this is Lorelei Carson," Mr. Cooke said. He must have come in while she was looking around. "She's going to be staying with us for ... well, a while. Probably not long. She's a friend of the MacDonalds."

"Ah, aye." The Irishman smiled at her. "Welcome to Clear Creek."

She stared at him as her mind raced. She knew him, *knew* him. But she didn't. "Okay, nice try. But I've lived in Clear Creek for six years, and ... this isn't it." She waved around herself nervously.

The old man looked confused. "Ah, lass, I think ye're mistaken. This is Clear Creek – I should know, I helped found it."

"Wha?"

Colin cleared his throat. "Lorelei Carson, this is Patrick Mulligan. I mentioned he played Joseph in the town play two years ago."

The picture over the bookcase in her apartment! Mulligan?! Lorelei could barely breathe.

"Oh, ye poor sweet lass. Ye've gone white as a sheet."

"Oh, dear," Mr. Cooke said. "I knew we shouldn't have moved her yet."

"Colin, you're not helping," said Belle. "Lorelei, are you ill again?"

She couldn't speak as her eyes fixed on the Irishman. He was younger than the man in the picture, a little thinner too, but it was him. She knew it. But how ...?

The bell over the door rang and she heard Jeff behind her. "What's taking so long? Parthena's liable to chew Sam's leg off, and she's not the only one. I'm famished."

Lorelei's voice was a numb mumble. "This is Clear Creek?"

"Of course," Colin replied.

"When ... is this?"

Lorelei didn't get an immediate answer. Instead she heard Belle yell, "Oh, she's going down again!"

CHAPTER EIGHT

"Father, she's awake!"

Lorelei blinked a few times, then blinked some more. Something kept getting in her eyes, but she didn't know what.

"Here." A male voice.

She tried opening her eyes again and blinked the wetness away. Was she crying? She saw a hat over her face and squeezed her eyes shut. When she opened them, it was still there. "Wha?" came out weakly, but at least she could talk.

"Sorry," said the same voice, and the hat disappeared.

It was snowing. She pulled her arm from beneath the quilt thrown over her and wiped her face. It was hard to see with big fluffy flakes coming down in her eyes. She tried to sit up, felt her head swim, and stopped.

"Jefferson, give her some water." She knew it was Colin Cooke without checking. She'd grown accustomed to his English accent. Did Jeff have an accent? She couldn't remember.

"Here, drink this." Jeff unscrewed the top of the canteen.

No, he didn't have much of one. She took it, not caring

how odd it looked, and took a long cool drink. "Where are we?"

"Heading home." He stared at her.

She stared back. He was a handsome boy – correction, young man – with nice eyes, light hazel. Not quite the same color as his father's, but close. "Thank you. Now for the next question: *when* are we?"

"Um," he said softly, then cleared his throat. "Mother? Should I answer that?"

A giggle sounded to her right. She forgot they had company. His younger sister watched them with mischievous eyes. She had golden blonde hair like her mother, blue eyes and a funny name – Pantheon or something. Too many unfamiliar people and sensations were boggling her mind – and underneath them all, the big unfamiliar: where she was. Or, if the sinking feeling she had was correct, when.

Lorelei handed the canteen back to Jeff. He took it, replaced the cap then set it to the side. "Do you feel all right?"

"No. No, I do not feel all right. I feel woozy. I feel disoriented. Someone slipped me a mickey yesterday, and now I'm in a place that's Clear Creek but not Clear Creek and no one will tell me what's going on and if I see the MacDonalds again I am going to rip them both a new one for doing this to me!" She took a second to catch her breath. "No offense to any of you, but this is very annoying, and I want to go home – my real home, not anyone else's – and to *my* Dunnigan's Mercantile, not the one with people from hundred-year-old pictures behind the counter."

There was a long pause as she fumed, everyone staring at her. She hated that she'd just thrown such a tantrum in front of these people, but by golly, she thought she'd earned a good blow-up.

Then Jeff spoke up. "Rip them both a new what?"

Lorelei looked at him in shock. Then she started

laughing and couldn't stop. She felt like she was going crazy, but the laughter felt good – especially when everyone else joined in. She remembered something a private eye said in a book she'd once read: "If logic takes me to a place in the Twilight Zone, I go there anyway." That got her laughing even harder, because she doubted Rod Serling could have topped *this* one. Finally, she was forced to stop due to lack of oxygen, and she wheezed a bit before sitting up against a crate in the wagon bed. But strange as it seemed, she felt a lot better now. Her mind wasn't playing tricks on her. No one was lying to her. Her situation was literally impossible – or, rather, she would have thought it was a day ago – but at least now she had a good guess as to what her situation was. She extended a hand to Jeff. "Lorelei Carson."

Jeff bowed his head to her. "Jefferson Wilfred Cooke, at your service."

"Don't you have a middle name?" the girl asked Lorelei.

"Yes. Ingrid." She locked eyes with Jeff. "I don't like it very much so please, don't use it."

"Ingrid?" he repeated, as if trying it out. "I like it."

"My name's Parthena," the girl said. "My middle name is Opal." She tossed her head at her brother at the back of the buckboard. "His middle name is Harrison."

"And his first name is … Sam?" She was still considering that this might be some elaborate joke by the MacDonalds, but no. Too expensive a joke to waste on a nobody girl from the back end of Oregon. She needed to ask the one question that would – hopefully – confirm what she was thinking.

But then she was distracted by the landscape. "Oh my …"

"What is it?" Jeff asked.

They were crossing rolling prairie like the ones Clear Creek Road ran through on the way to Canyon Park. It was some of the last untouched prairie in the state – one more reason Clear Creek attracted tourists. "How close are we to Canyon Park?"

"I'm sorry – Canyon Park?" Colin asked.

Crud – how was she going to explain this? If she was right – a big if – it probably wasn't a park yet. "Um … big stretch of Clear Creek Gorge where it spreads out. The annual town picnic is held there, and there's this ginormous oak tree they call 'His Majesty,' and –"

"Oh – I know where you're talking about!" Colin said in happy recognition. "We'll pass it on the way home. Our home, I mean."

"Canyon Park," Belle mused. "Most people just call it 'Cooke's Canyon.'"

"Can I ask a favor?" Lorelei continued. "When we get close enough to His Majesty, close enough to see it, could … could you pull over? I'd like to see it."

"You've never seen it before?" Jeff wondered.

"Well, I have, but … well, I'll explain when we get there."

"It's so cold out," Belle mentioned.

"Please. It'll all make sense if I can see it."

"If you're sure." From the sound of Colin's voice, he wasn't.

"You're trembling," Jeff said softly. He took off his coat and placed it around Lorelei's shoulders.

Lorelei's heart skipped a beat. No one had ever done anything like that before. "I, I really can't …" She tried to remove it.

He stopped her. "We're almost home. And I insist."

They locked gazes and something cut through the fear in her gut. Something nice … "Thank you," she whispered.

"It's the least I can do. You've been through a horrible ordeal, haven't you?" He spoke softly, as if he didn't want his parents to hear.

She almost started laughing again. "Oh, you have no idea."

They sat in silence for a few minutes before she recognized more of the landscape. Her eyes grew round as she looked to the left and noticed the canyon. She tried to stand.

"What are you doing?" Jeff asked in alarm.

She ignored him and got to her feet. Though the canyon was off Clear Creek Road about a quarter mile, you could see it. "Oh my Lord."

He stood too. "What is it? What's wrong?"

Tears streamed down her face, but she said nothing. The only possible truth was staring her in the face. You could spend millions on a practical joke, but a landscape was a landscape – it couldn't be faked. "Yep. That cinches it." She sat back down.

"Cinches what?" Jeff said in confusion as he plunked back down beside her.

"Here we are," Colin said, pulling the horses to a stop. "There's the canyon, and if you were to walk to the beginning of the road leading down into it, you can see the topmost branches of His Majesty. Does that help, Miss Carson?"

Surprisingly, it did. "Tells me what I need to know. Jeff … may I ask you a personal question?"

"Um, I, uh, guess so."

"How old are you?"

"Just turned eighteen, ma'am."

She knew she had to do this before she lost her nerve. Either she was right, or she was nuts. "And when were you born?"

Jeff looked confused, as if she should be able to calculate it herself. "First of November 1861."

Lorelei shivered, not from the cold, and nodded. Bullseye. "Well, I'm eighteen too. And I was born on the seventh of July. In 2001."

"Young lady, that's not amusing," Colin scolded.

"You're right about that. Any of you have an idea why the MacDonalds would drug me, kidnap me and send me back in time a hundred and forty years? Because I don't." She was verging on hysteria. But at least she wasn't fainting.

"Are you jesting with us?" Belle asked.

"I promise I'm not. For the last few hours, I thought you might be jesting with *me*. But you can't fake an oak that size. This is ... well, in my time it's Canyon Park. It's right outside Clear Creek. And that Dunnigan's Mercantile is the same building I work in ... and live above. And there's a painting in my apartment, dated 1889, of Patrick Mulligan and his wife – the same Patrick Mulligan I just ... okay, I'm getting woozy again."

Instantly she felt Jeff steady her and looked into his eyes. He had beautiful eyes, high cheekbones, a square jaw, thick brown hair and lashes any girl would die for. She could guarantee Cindy Crankshaw and her friends would go bonkers over him. Unfortunately for them, he was dead, at least in their time. But she was here with him in ... 1879?

Oh, yeah, she was going to rip the MacDonalds new ones. They couldn't have told her, or the people taking care of her, any of this?!

"We ... really should get going," Colin mumbled. "It's still another mile home."

Lorelei nodded. A mile or so past Canyon Park was the Triple-C Ranch. In the years she'd lived in Clear Creek, she'd never seen it. Well, she would now – like no one had seen it in over a century. "Sorry to hold us up. I just needed to check."

"But ... how can this be?" Belle said, her voice strained.

"I suppose we'll have to ask the MacDonalds that when they return," Colin replied.

Parthena and Sam didn't say anything, just stared at Lorelei in confusion. She couldn't blame them. How would she react if she met someone from the 2150s talking nonsense? She'd probably call 911 and have them locked up in the nearest psych ward. But there was no 911 here. Heck, telephones had just been invented. And psychiatry was still in the Stone Age. She sat and stared at the passing landscape for now, wondering why she was here (or rather, now) and what she was supposed to do about it besides lose her mind.

"Here we are!" Colin announced as they crested a rise.

Jeff leaned toward her, still with his arm around her. "Look, Miss Carson. We're home."

She turned in the direction he pointed and felt him pull her to her feet. She stood and leaned against the back of the wagon seat.

"It's not much," Colin said. "But we've had a grand time building it up over the years."

She gaped at the sight. They were looking down onto mile after mile of rolling prairie. There was a pair of two-story farmhouses side by side, a large barnyard with a matching large barn to the right of the homes, a small house beyond that and a cabin halfway up another rise. Oaks and a few junipers dotted the open spaces. Smoke rose from the chimneys and from an unseen source beyond the barn. There must be another building back there. "It's ... much," she whispered, then chuckled.

"Father, I think she's going to be sick again."

"No, no, I'm fine. Just a long way from ... a long time from home. Whatever." She sat back down, pulling Jeff with her.

"Quite right. Off we go!"

Jeff righted himself and stared into Lorelei's eyes. "It'll be okay." He swallowed, making his Adam's apple bob. She'd never noticed such a thing before.

"You sure about that, cowboy?"

"Well … I mean, I can't guarantee nothing. But … we'll take care of you, don't worry about that."

"Okay." She was starting to feel numb, like shock was setting in at the enormity of her circumstances. How could this be? Why had they done this to her? Could she ever get back home?

They descended into the ranch, the horses slipping now and then in the snow. She was aware of how Colin spoke to the team, coaxing them down slowly. Jeff alternated between watching his father and her. When they pulled up in front of the smaller two-story house, he breathed a sigh of relief and said, "Father, we need to get her inside. Something's wrong."

"Based on what she's saying, I'd agree," Belle added.

Colin jumped off the wagon seat and came around the side of the buckboard. "Hand her down to me."

Lorelei wanted to protest, but her mouth wouldn't work. She let Jeff scoop her into his arms and hand her down to his father, who carried her to the house, up the steps and inside. Warmth surrounded her, making her cold cheeks sting. She started to feel nauseous and wondered if it was a bad thing. But this whole situation was bad. Unbelievable. Either she was completely certifiable or … she was 140 years in the past. Which was the better option?

"Father, who is that?"

Lorelei noticed a staircase next to them as Colin looked around. "Adele, fetch Major over here, would you?"

"Yes, Father." A brown-haired teenage girl ran down the remaining stairs and out the front door.

"Right then – into the parlor," Colin said brightly. "Belle will fix you a nice cup of tea and make you something hot to eat." He laid her on an old couch much like the one she'd seen at the doctor's house but gave her a look that was anything but jolly. She recognized the panic in his eyes. She had enough of her own to know. She was too exhausted to reassure him – abject fear could do that do a person. Didn't she learn that in health class?

She decided to not worry about moving for now or talking. For now, she could lie there, stare at the ceiling and try to remember everything she could about 1879. Who was the president – Ulysses S. Grant? No, he was earlier. Was Oregon a state? She was pretty sure it was. The Civil War was over, Reconstruction … probably over too. Edison invented his light bulb around this time, like Bell and the telephone, but neither would've reached Clear Creek yet.

She could also hear what was going on around her, like the door opening. "Colin, what is it?" The voice was male and Southern.

"I need you to ride to town and fetch Doc Drake."

She heard them enter the room. "Who *is* she?"

"Someone the MacDonalds wanted us to look after. They brought her into our care, then left without much explanation. She's had a bad shock."

Lorelei hoped he'd leave the explanation at that.

"I'll go right away," the other man said. The door opened and closed again and there was some other commotion as Colin left the room. She heard voices, footfalls, another woman's voice.

"Lorelei? Can you hear me?"

Her eyes moved in the direction of Jeff's voice.

"Please stay with us. I don't know what's ailing you, but please hang on. The doc's coming."

She managed to nod, then tried smiling. Okay, good, she could do both.

"Are you thirsty? I can get you some water." His voice was soft, gentle, concerned and comforting.

She slowly turned her head in his direction. "Jeff …"

He smiled. "Yes?"

Her eyes met his as her first tear fell. She shivered all over. "Don't leave me."

He took her hand and held it between his. "I won't."

"WHO IS SHE, AUNT BELLE?"

Belle and her niece Honoria watched Jefferson kneel on the floor next to Lorelei and speak to her. The girl was deathly white, as if her life was suddenly slipping away. "We don't exactly know." She frowned a moment. "See if the tea is ready. We'll try that."

Honoria left the hall and went to the kitchen, her hand to her back. She was growing heavier with child – the baby was due around the first of March, according to Doc Drake.

Belle continued to watch Jefferson speak to her charge softly, the same way he did when handling a skittish filly. Animals loved him, felt comfortable around him, and would do anything for the young man. *Her* young man. But the way he was looking at Lorelei … well, she'd seen that look before. When she first met Colin in Aunt Irene's store and again here at the ranch.

She and Aunt Irene had come to the main ranch house for tea. She was new in town, a fact that brought the female population of Clear Creek high enough to start a sewing circle. Colin had a horrible black eye, a cut lip and scraped and bloodied knuckles; she later found out his brothers had purposely beat him black and blue so he'd have an excuse to be in the house and see her. She'd nursed those wounds under Grandma's careful watch, and thankfully Grandma was a terrible chaperone …

She smiled and closed her eyes. *Please don't let anything happen to this poor child,* she prayed. She didn't know her, and until the ride home hadn't a clue where she'd come from, only that Dallan and Shona couldn't take her with them and needed her cared for while they were away.

But was this girl really from the future? How could that happen? How could Dallan and Shona *make* that happen? Granted, they were known to do some strange things, but they'd helped the townspeople of Clear Creek numerous times since first showing up in town back in '59. So no one asked too many questions when odd events occurred while they were around, or why the couple never seemed to age.

Honoria waddled back with a tea tray, and Belle led her into the parlor. Honoria set it on a table by the settee and poured a cup. "Can you sit up?" she asked Lorelei. "I have some nice tea made. Do you … take sugar?"

Lorelei stared at her a moment and licked her lips. "I … yes, please."

Belle sighed in relief. "Jefferson, help her sit up." It wasn't proper for him to be so close to her, but he seemed to have a calming effect and Belle wasn't going to take that from her. Not when the poor dear had … well, whatever had happened to her.

The people of Clear Creek didn't question Bowen Drake's divine gift of healing. And they didn't question the MacDonalds about their appearance, despite twenty years having passed since she first met them. But there was something about this situation that was stranger than usual, even stranger than the MacDonalds' usual. Maybe, in light of this girl's statements about being from the future … maybe they should ask more questions. Either Lorelei had gone far around the bend, or – unlikely as it seemed – she was telling the truth.

But for now, Belle took a deep breath, pulled up a chair, and proceeded to take care of Lorelei until the doctor arrived.

CHAPTER NINE

"Physically, she's fine. But she's frightened to death."

Jefferson listened from the hall as Doc Drake spoke to his parents in the kitchen. He glanced toward the parlor, where Honoria was sitting and talking with Lorelei. It seemed to help to take the poor girl's mind off whatever was giving her such a tortured look. He hated that look. He'd seen it before on horses and other animals that had suffered abuse or been lost. She reminded him of a lost kitten he'd once seen hiding under the mercantile steps. The poor thing was so scared it was frozen with fright.

But what was Lorelei afraid of? What she'd said about being born in 2001 couldn't possibly be true … could it? Where did she *really* come from?

Jefferson returned to the parlor and watched Honoria's continued attempts at giving Lorelei some comfort. "Major and I got into a horse race and I lost. Really lost – my seat, that is. I fell off my horse and that ended the race. When he says I lost the *race*, he's just being kind." Honoria laughed.

Lorelei didn't laugh, just shivered.

Jefferson came closer. "Does she need another blanket?"

Honoria turned to look at him. "It wouldn't hurt."

He left the parlor, ran upstairs to his room and pulled the quilt off his bed. By the time he returned, Doc Drake was seated in a chair next to his patient and was taking her pulse. He let go of her wrist, put his pocket watch away, then took her hand and smiled at her. "Your heart is racing, my dear."

She looked at the doctor, her jaw trembling. "I think I've got a good excuse."

Doc Drake glanced at Jefferson's parents and nodded slowly. "Did you bump your head? That would explain the nausea and the ..."

"I told you. I was at a party the MacDonalds were throwing and I felt ill – I still think there was something in the cheese – and when I woke up, I was here. In the past. My past, your present ... gah, I know it's hard to believe, but there's no other explanation ..."

"Shhh, it's all right," Doc Drake soothed. "But you might have sustained an injury beforehand. Do you remember anything like that?"

She shook her head, tears in her eyes. "I told you no."

Jefferson bit his lower lip and clutched the quilt to his chest. Maybe she'd lost her memory or gotten it scrambled. If so, how long before she got it back? She'd started talking that nonsense on the way home – a bump to the head would explain it.

"Jefferson, spread that over her," Doc Drake instructed.

He moved to comply and lay the quilt over Lorelei. She smiled at him, and he smiled back, his heart racing. She was the most beautiful girl he'd ever seen. Where were her parents? Why hadn't anyone asked yet? He cleared his throat. "Do ... your folks live in these parts?"

She stared at him. "I'm on my own."

His mother and cousin gasped. "No family?" Honoria said.

"None?" Doc Drake asked to confirm.

Lorelei shook her head. "No. My parents died in a fire when I was six."

"I see." The doctor motioned to Jefferson. "Why don't you keep Lorelei company while I speak with the others?"

"Sure, Doc." He took the chair Doc Drake had vacated and watched everyone leave the room.

"They think I'm crazy, don't they?"

"Um ..." He couldn't bring himself to lie to those beautiful eyes. "Well, it does sound pretty loco. I mean, I don't know how it could be ..."

"Yeah, I get that," she whispered. "I don't mean to be such a bother."

He leaned toward her. It was improper, wrong, but he couldn't help himself. "You're not. Around here if a person needs help, we help. No matter what they need."

Her eyes misted with tears. "I'm afraid you and your family aren't going to be able to help me. The only people who can are the ones that left me here."

"The MacDonalds?"

"Yes, and I'd sure like to know what they were thinking. I don't understand why they'd do this to me."

"They always seem to have a good reason," he insisted.

She blinked back tears. "I should hope so, but it makes no sense."

He studied her face, her hair, and fought the urge to hold her hand. "You must have bumped your head like Doc said. It makes perfect sense."

She half-laughed, half-cried. It was an odd sound, as if someone was pulling it out of her. "But bumping my head doesn't give you eighteen years of memories – memories about the 21st century! And it doesn't make you think you're in the 19th century either." She rubbed her hand over her scalp. "Oh, and there's no bump. So there goes that theory." She scowled at the ceiling. "So either I'm 140 years in the past, or I'm completely cuckoo for Cocoa Puffs."

Jefferson couldn't understand a lot of what she was saying, but what he could grasp had his sympathies. He didn't want her to be halfway around the bend, or further. He sat on his hands to stop himself from taking hers.

"Are your hands cold?"

His heart skipped a beat and he had to swallow. "A little."

"Winters are cold here, even in my time. If there isn't a way to heat your house, it can be miserable."

"Well, who wouldn't have fires going? That's just plumb loco."

She looked at him. "Maybe they don't have anything to make a fire with."

His brow creased. "What? Only a fool doesn't stock up wood for the winter. How would you cook, let alone keep your fires going?"

She looked toward the fireplace but from her vantage point, couldn't see it. "Yeah, good point. I think I'm warmed up now."

"Are you sure?" She'd been shivering earlier. "Maybe we should leave the blankets for a spell."

She smiled. "I like the way you talk. Is it okay to say that?"

He pulled his hands out from under his legs. "There's nothing special about how I talk. Other than the accent, but none of us have as much of one as our parents and aunts."

"Do you have a big family?"

He grinned. "Yes, ma'am."

She shook her head. "Call me Lorelei."

"But ... that wouldn't be proper."

She sighed. "I suppose not. But it's not proper for me to

be here anyway, so let's lose the formality … Jeff." She grinned.

"Well, okay." He stared at his boots as he felt his cheeks redden.

"Can I ask you some questions?"

"Sure – whatever you like." He hoped the questions wouldn't be too embarrassing.

"Are you a cowboy?"

He shrugged. "I like to think of myself as a cattle rancher. The ranch hands are cowboys."

"Ranch hands? So your family has hired people on?"

"Sure – there's no way we could run the whole ranch without them. We have five right now, plus our foreman Logan Kincaid and his sons."

"So the Triple-C is a cattle ranch right now too. In my time it still is – a big one."

"Oh. Well, that's nice." She was talking nonsense again. He wanted her whole, undamaged in mind, spirit, body … whoa, where had that thought come from? It had popped into his head and heart as if it had always been there, just waiting to come out. As if he'd been waiting for her … but that was ridiculous. He'd just met her.

"It's really successful even now, I guess?"

"Well, yes. My parents, uncles and aunts built the place, with a lot of help from my Aunt Sadie's father. He's a big cattle baron in west Texas, and he gave Uncle Harrison a dowry of cattle when he married Aunt Sadie. Plus he's brought more cattle to join with ours over the last few years. We don't see him much anymore, as he and Great-Aunt Teresa are starting to get old."

She stared at him, wide-eyed. If he wasn't careful, he could get lost in those grey eyes of hers. "Must be nice to have so much family. Like I said, I've just got me."

"Well, are you feeling better?" Doc Drake asked as he re-entered the room followed by Mother and Father.

"I'm tired. And disoriented, for obvious but seemingly impossible reasons. But otherwise I'm fine. No bump on my head – I checked."

Doc Drake studied her a moment. "Well, all right. But something must have happened."

"And I told you what. But I don't blame you for not believing it. Ask the MacDonalds when they get back, is all I can suggest."

Father looked frustrated. "Is there anything else we should do for her?"

Doc Drake shook his head. "Just take care of her like the MacDonalds said, I suppose." He went to Lorelei, knelt beside her and took her hand again. Jefferson recognized the look on his face – he was *doing it.* No one knew exactly how, but Bowen Drake could heal folks with a touch. Everyone in town was aware of it and did what they could to protect the man and his family from any not-so-nice folks trying to take advantage of him.

"Lorelei," Doc said softly, "don't be afraid."

Tears filled her eyes and she nodded. Jefferson sensed some unspoken understanding had just passed between them.

Doc rose, put on his hat and gave everyone a parting nod. "You know where to find me if you need me."

"Thank you so much for coming, Bowen," Mother said. "We'll do everything you asked."

He smiled, whispered something in her ear, then left the house.

Father sighed. "Well, young lady, you heard the doctor. How about something to eat?"

"I'm not saying no." Lorelei slowly sat up and pushed the quilts off, then pulled one back over her. "Yikes, it's chilly in here," she said with a giggle. "Comes with not having central air, I guess."

Jefferson set the other blankets aside. "Central …"

"Never mind. Unless you *really* want an explanation."

Jefferson decided he could wait on that.

"I'll get you a change of clothes," Mother said numbly. "You look about the same size as Honoria. She'll have a dress you can borrow."

Lorelei looked at her clothing. "I'm sorry I don't have anything else. They didn't exactly give me a chance to pack."

"Don't worry," Father said. "Dallan left us some funds to see to your needs."

"He did?" Jefferson and Lorelei said at the same time. They looked at each other and exchanged the same smile.

"Yes, in case you needed things like … clothes."

Lorelei frowned. "So they really did plan this out." She shook her head. "Why couldn't they just ask me? Consent is important."

"They did come and go in a hurry," Father said.

"Where did they go, exactly?"

Mother headed for the hall. "As we said, we're not sure other than it was California."

"California?" she blurted. "Driving or flying?"

Jefferson made a face. "Flying?"

"Oh, boy," Lorelei groaned, but didn't elaborate.

"Oh." He eyed the tea tray. "You hardly touched that. I can fetch more."

"Good idea, son." Father looked at Lorelei. "If you're feeling better, then I've some chores to attend to. I suggest you get changed, have something to eat and make yourself at home." He smiled and left the room.

Mother picked up the tray. "I'll make a fresh pot. Jefferson, come with me? We'll be right back." She hurried him out of the parlor and to the kitchen.

To their surprise, Father was waiting there for them. "This is all so strange," he muttered.

"Stranger than I could have guessed," Mother replied. "You know what Bowen said to me before he left?"

"I was rather wondering about that."

Jefferson watched his mother shake her head in disbelief. "He said she's not loco, she's telling the truth."

"That she's from the ... the future?!" Jefferson blurted.

But Mother just nodded solemnly. "Don't ask me how or why – maybe only the MacDonalds know. But yes. From the future."

LORELEI SAT on the Victorian sofa and studied the room she was in. It was pretty, feminine, cozy – the kind of room she'd always wanted to have. Too bad it was before her great-grandparents were gone.

As impossible as it sounded, she had traveled through time to the Clear Creek of the past. It's the only thing that made sense. And the MacDonalds had brought her here. Which meant they had a plan – a plan that involved ... "Drugging me with spray cheese." Saying it out loud didn't make it any less bizarre.

She massaged her temples and tried to figure out why they'd done this to her. She went over everything that had happened since she met the MacDonalds and their author friend Kitty Morgan. They came to Dunnigan's, to the laundromat, and most recently to her home. They invited her to that party. They loaned her a dress and shoes. They had her wash some antique quilts ...

She got to her feet and picked up the one she'd been covered with. Yes – she'd washed this same quilt at Deets' Laundromat not ten days ago, she was sure of it. But now it was brand new, not frayed and yellowed. She looked at the dress she was still wearing. Had it come from the past too?

Lorelei looked around the room, examining some of the framed photographs on the wall. One was of the Cooke family – Colin, Belle and five children, looking as dead serious as people always looked in old photos. There was also one of the same couple as the other photograph in her apartment, the Dunnigans. "Belle's aunt and uncle," she said to herself.

Another photo was of a large group of people, dressed for summertime. She looked a little closer. One of the men looked familiar – *very* familiar. "You've got to be kidding me."

"Something wrong?" Jeff asked as he came into the room.

She spun around and caught herself before she stumbled and fell on her face.

Jefferson was at her side in a flash. "Come sit down. You shouldn't make sudden movements like that."

"You're right." She let him guide her back to the sofa and looked at the tea tray. He hadn't spilled a drop when he set it down and leaped to her aid. The man was graceful as a cat.

"Sugar?"

She blinked at him. He was pouring her a cup of tea as if it was the most natural thing to do, even if his hands were shaking a little. The sight of a handsome cowboy performing such an act was comical. If she had her cell phone, she'd take a picture. But the MacDonalds must have it.

That brought her back to the big question: why? Why did they leave her with these people? She tried to recall snippets of conversation from the times she spent with them. Didn't she overhear Shona and Kitty arguing, something about Kitty writing about Shona and Dallan's assignments? What did that mean?

"Do you take cream?" he asked as he poured himself a cup.

"I've never tried cream in tea," she confessed.

"I love it." He picked up the pink-and-white sugar bowl. "You never told me how much sugar you take."

"Oh, just a teaspoon, thanks." Some small part of her felt giddy at having afternoon tea with this man, like something out of a fractured fairy tale. But she liked it.

He stirred the sugar into her cup, then handed her the cup and saucer. She took it, watched him pour cream into his cup, add sugar and stir. When he was done, he raised his cup as if to toast. She automatically raised hers too. "Thank you."

"You already thanked me."

She blushed. "Well, now I've thanked you twice." She didn't want him to think she was some blithering idiot, but she was actually starting to have fun with all the weirdness.

They sipped their tea in silence a few moments before Belle came in, a dress in her hands. The woman stared at her a moment, as if she couldn't believe her eyes, then said, "This should fit fine. If you're up to it, we'll go into town in a day or two and get you something else."

She smiled. These people were so kind. "I don't know how to thank you."

"Don't worry about such things now. We're happy to help." She set the folded dress on the sofa next to her. "I have a petticoat that should fit – it's old but that shouldn't matter. We can always get you a new one."

Jeff took a quick sip of tea, catching her attention. Had he been staring at her funny too? And … was he blushing? But of course, he would be. This wasn't the 21st century – these people would have very different kinds of manners, the kinds she'd only read about in library books. She'd have to try to remember some history and fast. This might not be some city, but it was the same era – and these people were British besides.

She sipped her tea and did her best to stay calm. She

could be logical when she wanted – it was part of how she'd survived all these years. She might not be socially adept, and she had some hang-ups, but who didn't? Her shyness at meeting new people wasn't an option now – everyone would be new.

In short, Lorelei was stuck here until either the MacDonalds returned for her or she found her own way back, as impossible as that was. But if she got here, then there had to be a way to get back. Doors swung both ways. Now all she had to do was find one – and do her best to fit in until she did.

CHAPTER TEN

Lorelei watched Belle knead bread with fascination. She'd slept well after eating a delicious stew and biscuits for dinner, slept in Parthena's bed last night – Parthena shared Adele's – and was now wearing the blue calico dress Honoria loaned her. She'd met the rest of the family, and they were all really nice. If only the circumstances were different. After all, she didn't belong in this place – or more to the point, this century.

Jeff, at eighteen, was the oldest of Colin and Belle's children. Next came Adele, sixteen, who talked nonstop unless one of her parents told her to be quiet and eat. She was pretty, with light brown hair and the same hazel eyes as the rest of the family. In Lorelei's experience, sixteen year-old girls either talked a lot or very little. She'd been the latter in high school. Not this girl.

Thackary, fifteen, was the quiet one, with all the awkwardness you'd expect from his age. But he was so well-mannered, he'd be considered from another planet in her time. She'd already met Sam, fourteen, and Parthena, twelve. Five kids in eight years – it was amazing Belle wasn't worn to pieces. And a good thing they weren't worrying about sending them all to college.

Honoria, Colin and Belle's niece, was only twenty, but much more mature than women the same age in her time. She was better looking than Cindy Crankshaw too, even though she was six months pregnant. Her husband the major – no, wait, his *name* was Major – was handsome with a Southern accent straight out of *Gone with the Wind*. They'd come by earlier to see how she was doing, and Major fascinated her. To think he'd fought in the Civil War! Where was he when she had to do a special report on Sherman's March to the Sea as part of her senior project?

Of course, Major had fought for the Confederacy, so his views on the subject might be different from what she was used to, even in a town as redneck as Clear Creek in her time. She wasn't sure whether to ask him about it or not.

Belle wiped her hands on her apron. "Now we let the dough rest a couple of hours."

Lorelei looked at the bowl she'd covered with a dishtowel, then at everything cooking on the stove. Patsy had a hard time just heating up microwave dinners. How did Belle do it all? "Everything smells wonderful, Mrs. Cooke."

"Mrs. Cooke – where did that come from? Especially after yesterday. Call me Belle."

She smiled shyly. "What should I call Mr. Cooke?"

"He'll insist you call him Colin. I gather you're used to less formality."

True enough. "And your children?" She wanted to make sure what the proper etiquette was for the time period before she said something she shouldn't.

"Just use their Christian names," Belle advised as she turned the fried potatoes. "Would you like more coffee?"

"Please."

She watched the woman grab the handle of a large metal

coffee pot with her apron and pour her a second cup. The dishes were the same ones in the little hutch in her kitchen back home. "This is a lovely set." She held up her cup and saucer. "Where did you get them?"

"These old things? They belonged to my Aunt Irene. She had quite a few and gave some to us after we built this place."

"Where did you live before?"

"Next door in the main ranch house with Harrison, Sadie, Duncan and Cozette."

"Your husband's brothers and their wives, right?"

"You remember – good." She looked her over. "You're sure you're feeling all right this morning?"

She nodded. "It's still a little strange. I have so many questions, and I don't know which ones to ask – or who I should ask."

"Well, given your secret ..." Belle winked. "... you might want to stick to asking me or Colin or Jefferson. Or Doc Drake, since he knows. Dallan and Shona tend to keep their activities rather hush-hush, so I don't know who else in town is aware. But if we can answer your questions, we will."

That made sense. "And if it's something personal?"

"Don't worry – if we think you're overstepping your bounds, we'll say so."

Another nod. She didn't want to ask the woman her age – that was rude no matter what century you were in. She must be at least forty, since she had an eighteen-year-old son, but she looked good for having five children – not an ounce of fat on her. Must be all the ranch work. Hmmm ... she gulped.

"Are you all right?"

"Yes, fine. But ... I don't know how long I'll be here. And I want to earn my keep."

Belle smiled. "Of course you do. Just consider yourself part of the family until it's time to leave." She turned back to the stove.

Adele and Parthena entered the kitchen, went to the hutch against a wall and began to take out plates and utensils. "Good morning, Lorelei," Adele said happily. "You must be feeling better – you got up before we did!"

"I am, thank you."

Parthena took a stack of plates to the table and began to set it. Adele went to the back door, walked out, then stepped back inside, looking confused. "Where's the milk?"

Belle looked at her. "Jefferson didn't leave the bucket?"

"No. I don't see it anywhere."

Lorelei smiled. "Fresh milk?"

The three looked at her like she'd just grown a horn in her head. "Yes, don't you have it where you come from?" Parthena asked.

"Um … not exactly." How much should she say? Adele hadn't been privy to the conversation in the wagon, and Parthena probably hadn't understood it …

"She grew up in a city," Belle explained. "I'm sure her family didn't own a cow."

"Oh." Parthena got back to setting the table. Lorelei smiled gratefully at Belle, who winked back.

Adele reached for a shawl hanging next to others on pegs near the door. "I'll go see what's keeping him." She wrapped herself up and headed outside.

Belle spooned the potatoes onto a serving plate, then began cracking eggs into the same pan.

"You have chickens, cows and …?"

Belle smiled. "Steers, lots of steers. Thousands, in fact."

Lorelei tried to calculate in her head. The Cookes were well off – maybe not rich like future generations, but this is where it all began. She shouldn't be so freaked out but concentrate on learning as much as she could in the time she was here. The MacDonalds did say they'd return for her. But what then? What would they do with her? She trusted them, and they'd drugged her, dumped her almost a century and a half into the past and poof – gone!

The back door opened, and Jeff lugged in two buckets of milk. "Sorry it's late, Mother." His eyes met hers and she blushed. It didn't matter if she was in the present or the past – having a handsome young man look at her the way he was would make anyone blush.

He set the buckets down, Adele and Parthena took them to a sink and began to pour the milk into two porcelain pitchers. "How are you feeling?" he asked Lorelei.

She'd been so caught up in what the girls were doing, she hadn't noticed him come so close. "Much better, thank you. Still adjusting, of course."

He glanced at his mother and back. "Maybe later, after my chores are done, I could show you around the ranch."

"Me too!" Adele chimed in.

"And me!" added Parthena.

"You can all give Lorelei a tour of the ranch after all the chores are done." Belle put fried eggs on a plate and set it on a nearby worktable. "Adele, put these on the table."

Adele left the milk operation and did as her mother asked. "I can show you Uncle Harrison and Aunt Sadie's house. It's bigger than ours. We eat over there a few times a week."

Jefferson shrugged. "It's tradition."

Lorelei smiled. "It sounds like a nice one."

He smiled back.

Parthena, finished setting the table, was at their side in a flash. "Of course, Uncle Harrison and our aunt and cousins aren't here. They're visiting the Weavers in Nowhere."

Lorelei smiled. "Where?"

"Nowhere," Parthena said, then realized the problem. "The *town* of Nowhere, in Washington Territory."

"We mentioned it to you yesterday," Jefferson said. "We understand if you don't remember."

"I'm afraid I don't." She unconsciously put her hand to her head. Whatever it was they'd slipped her at the party had packed a wallop. "That's a funny name for a town."

"Yes, it is," Parthena agreed. "Mr. and Mrs. Dunnigan went with them."

Her heart leaped. "The Dunnigans?"

"Yes, my aunt and uncle," Belle brought more eggs to the table along with a plate of fried ham slices. "Do you remember much of yesterday?"

"Bits and pieces. I remember you mentioning your aunt and uncle. I …" *… have a picture of them in my apartment* almost slipped out. It was safe to tell Belle that, and Jeff, but not the girls. She was having to do a lot of self-editing. Even that photograph was a decade in these people's future.

"Sit down, children," Belle instructed.

Just then, Colin came through the back door. "Jefferson, I'll need you to do a few extra chores today."

"But Father …"

"No buts, I have to take care of things at the mercantile, so we need the help." He took off his coat and hat, hung them up by the door then went straight to the table and sat.

The entire morning so far had been run with an efficiency Lorelei had never seen. At Bob and Patsy's, once the morning alarms went off, the morning fights began – primarily over the bathroom but with plenty of variety in the subject matter. The worst were the actual fistfights between Erwin and Francis, a fifteen-year-old foster kid who'd joined the household last year.

The other two foster kids, Missy and Pete, were younger – Pete eleven. Missy eight – and were brother and sister. Though she eventually got sick of babysitting them all the time, Lorelei considered them lucky to not have been split up. Maybe not so lucky to be under Bob and Patsy's roof, but at least they were together.

Which made her think: had she been missed yet? She was supposed to work at Dunnigan's yesterday afternoon. How long before a missing persons report was filed?

"Lorelei?"

She stared at Colin at the head of the table. Everyone was seated but her. "Oh, I'm sorry." She went to the nearest empty chair – next to Jeff – and sat.

Colin glanced around the table, clasped his hands in front of him and bowed his head. Everyone else, including Lorelei, did the same. "Lord, thank you for bringing Lorelei to us safe and relatively unharmed. We'll do our best to take good care of her in the interim. I pray the MacDonalds have safe travels until they return. Bless my brother Harrison and his family on their trip to the Weaver farm, and keep Irene from causing too much trouble ..."

A few of the kids snorted. Lorelei, not in on the joke, stayed quiet.

"Take this bounty and bless it to our bodies. Amen." Colin looked around the table, his eyes fixing on her. "Feeling better, I take it?"

"Yes, sir," Lorelei said, her hands in her lap. "Sir" seemed appropriate with all the children present.

Jefferson picked up the plate of ham. "Would you like some?"

"Yes, please."

He stabbed a piece with his fork and shook it onto her plate, then took two for himself.

"Thank you."

He smiled. "You're welcome."

The food was passed around the table and each time something came to Jefferson, he asked if she wanted a portion and served her before taking any for himself. She'd never seen such manners. Last night she sat between Thackary and Adele and served herself. She couldn't envision Erwin doing anything near as polite. Was it because Jefferson was the oldest? Or maybe the Cookes raised their children better than the Browns did. She suspected the latter.

Conversation was light. This was a routine day for the Cooke family – chores had to be done, food had to be cooked. Lorelei watched them eat, listened, and learned in a very short time that a cattle ranch in the 1870s was a lot of work. It was nothing to sneeze at in the 21st century either, even with all the modern conveniences. They were polite and considerate to each other. They weren't perfect, because who was, but there was something at their center, something almost tangible.

Tears stung her eyes when she realized what it was. Love. She'd never experienced this, not even when her parents were alive. They both worked and she …

"Would you like to see the barn?" Parthena asked, pulling her from her thoughts.

Lorelei swallowed hard, then took a sip of coffee to push back the lump in her throat. "Sure."

"After you gather the eggs and feed the chickens," Belle said.

Parthena frowned. "Yes, Mother."

"I'm afraid our children's chores are taking longer than usual," Colin explained. "They're also covering for Harrison's brood while they're away."

Lorelei got an idea. "Can I help you with the chickens?" she asked Parthena.

"Sure!" Then Parthena turned to Colin. "Would it be all right?"

"Are you up to it?" he asked Lorelei

"I think some fresh air will do her good, dear," Belle said.

"But we don't expect you to work today. Doc Drake did say you should rest."

"I think I can handle gathering eggs," Lorelei volunteered. "If someone shows me how." She winked at Parthena.

"I can. And we have a rope swing in the barn ..."

"I would argue against using it today," Colin warned. "One dizzy spell and that would be it."

"Yes, Father," Parthena said, then grinned at her.

Lorelei could tell she was a mischief-maker. "I probably wouldn't try the rope swing anyway. I get vertigo."

Jefferson turned to her. "You get what-a-go?"

"I, uh, get off-balance at heights," she explained, hoping they wouldn't press it. Some of the girls in gym class never let her forget about it. She stopped taking gym as soon as she'd met the requirement for graduation. She didn't play sports in school. She didn't do drama class or band or choir. She wouldn't even join the chess club, even though she was a good player. She was too shy, too self-conscious all the time. Books were her thing, and all the wonders they held between their pages. She'd wanted to major in Library Science if she ever got to college.

But going to college was contingent on a lot of things. Now including getting back home to the 21st century.

"Hey," Jefferson said to get her attention.

She turned to him. "Yes?"

"Can you ride?"

Her eyes widened. "A horse? No, not at all."

He stared at the table a moment. "Would you like to learn?"

"Chores, children," Belle called from the stove. "Now."

Colin put on his hat and coat. "Go see Logan and find out what he wants you to do, Jeff. I need to get into town."

Lorelei blushed as Jefferson glanced between them. "Perhaps later?"

"Perhaps. Not today, though." It was fine to stand next to a horse, but to actually sit high upon one might be too much. She'd had a hard enough time with the buckboard yesterday.

"Jefferson ...," his father warned.

Jeff left the table, shrugged on his coat, put on his hat and taking one last look at her, went out the door.

She swallowed hard. He was attentive, polite, handsome, and unlike any boy she'd ever known. But Jefferson Cooke, she reminded herself, was no boy. He might be considered young where she came from, but around here he was a man full-grown and acted like one.

She finished her coffee and almost offered to do the dishes before noticing the lack of plumbing. Adele and Parthena hauling in buckets of water didn't go unnoticed either. They took them straight to the stove and set them on it one at a time. "Okay," Parthena said. "Let's go feed the chickens."

Lorelei smiled. She could handle chickens. How hard could it be?

Adele disappeared from the kitchen and reappeared with a coat. "Here, you can wear this. It used to be Honoria's but she grew out of it. It might be a little tight."

"Thank you." She took the coat and put it on. She noticed the lace-up boots the girls wore and glanced at the tips of her easily laced high-tops. She had a pang of guilt at having such comfortable shoes and was glad she'd had them on when she was ... what, taken? Kidnapped?

She pushed the thought aside. She was here now and would have to fit in if she was to survive. The problem was, she'd never fit in anywhere before. How would this be any better, when she was a hundred and forty years away from fitting in?

"Are you ready?" Parthena asked with a big smile.

Lorelei forced a smile back. "Sure. Let's go."

CHAPTER ELEVEN

Lorelei decided that she preferred chickens in a cardboard bucket with a side of potato wedges. Live chickens, on the other hand …

"Not like that," Parthena scolded. "You're giving them too much!"

Corn fell out of her hands as she tried to dodge twenty chickens chasing her through the snow to get their breakfast. "Get away from me!" She turned, slipped on some ice and down she went. The chickens were ecstatic.

Parthena rushed over to help. "Shoo, shoo!" She waved them away, grabbed Lorelei's hand and pulled her to her feet.

"Thank you." She brushed snow off the borrowed coat. "Aggressive, aren't they?"

"Not really. You just have to toss their feed *away* from you. Otherwise they'll be on top of you trying to get it."

"Now you tell me."

Parthena's hands went to her hips. "I thought you at least knew how to feed chickens."

"I *told* you I needed someone to show me how."

"No milk cow, no chickens. You really are a city girl."

Lorelei smiled weakly and shrugged. "Guilty as charged." She brushed her hands together and stuck them in her coat pockets. Her feet were cold, but otherwise she felt ... excited. She was on an adventure, with the chance of a lifetime to learn about the past. All she had to do was get past her screaming ignorance and paralyzing fear and she'd be fine.

Parthena headed back to the chicken coop. "Come along – we'll gather the eggs next."

"Great." Lorelei took a deep breath as they entered the chicken coop. Thankfully most of them were in the barnyard at the moment scurrying for all that spilled corn.

Parthena handed her a basket. "Here. All you have to do is take the eggs from the nest and put them in this."

"I can do that." She looked at the first nest – uh-oh. It had a hen in it. The bird looked at her with its beady eyes and clucked menacingly.

"Don't worry, just put your hand under her like this." Parthena demonstrated, pulling out two eggs and putting them in the basket. "Now you try."

"Are there any left?"

"One."

Lorelei took another deep breath as she slowly stuck her hand beneath the bird. "It's warm."

"Yes. I don't mind this chore when it's cold out."

Lorelei smiled and pulled the egg out. The hen continued to look at her but did nothing. "Wow, she didn't mind at all."

"Most of them don't. Some put up a fuss."

They gathered the eggs and took them into the house. She'd done her first farm chore. Talk about living history! "What next?"

"Well, let's see. We have to bring in wood for the stove."

"All right." They went back outside and chopped some kindling in a woodshed near the barn (Parthena had a mean swing with a hatchet), loaded it into a wheelbarrow, took it to the house, stored it in some baskets and bins and went back to bring in more. Lorelei was more familiar with this kind of work – Bob used to take Erwin and her up past the tree line to cut a couple cords of wood for the old stove in the family room and the fireplace in the living room. It was just for ambiance - their house had central heat. But here, wood was a necessity.

"What's next?" Lorelei asked when they were done.

Parthena made a face. "The mending."

"I take it you're not fond of that?"

"It's because she's not very good at it," Adele said as she entered the parlor. "Savannah isn't either. You'd think they were twins."

"Who's Savannah?" Lorelei asked.

"She's our cousin – Uncle Harrison and Aunt Sadie's daughter," Adele said. "She and Parthena are the same age."

Lorelei smiled. "So what does mending entail, exactly?"

"Sit down – we'll show you," Adele hurried into the kitchen, returning with a huge basket. "These are Father's and Jefferson's things." She pulled out a white work shirt with no collar and what looked like wooden buttons. She recalled a picture of an Amish man she'd seen in a book once. He'd worn a similar shirt.

Adele set the basket on the table in front of the sofa. There was a small rectangular sewing basket on top of the clothes pile. She threaded a needle, then passed the basket to Parthena, who did the same.

Lorelei stared at it. "So ... um, just thread a needle and find a tear?"

They exchanged a look, then stared at her. "You've never done mending either?" Parthena asked in shock.

"Well ... I hemmed an old skirt once, but I didn't do a very good job." She wasn't about to tell them she'd used Patsy's sewing machine.

"Well, that's something," Adele said. "Here – Jefferson's pants always need mending. You can practice on a pair."

She handed Lorelei a pair of worn … "Oh my gosh, these look like Levi's."

"Levi Stone?" Adele said. "Do you know him? He's our relation."

"On our Father's side," Parthena said as she got to work. "He married Father's cousin Fina."

"And he's *Jewish*," Adele added, as if telling her he was a unique creature, like a unicorn.

Lorelei stared at them a moment; her mouth half-open. "No, I, uh, don't know him. What I meant was these jeans are like … Levi Strauss denims. You know … from San Francisco." She had to think of the label on the back of her own Levi's at home. A home far, far, away …

"Jeans?" Adele said.

"That's what we call them where I come from." Good recovery.

"We just call them denims around here," Parthena said.

"Mr. Dunnigan calls them waist overalls," Adele added. "But I like the short version – denims."

Lorelei felt like she was in a history seminar. She smiled and threaded a needle, though it took her a few tries. If she kept busy and talked, maybe she wouldn't think as much about the reality of her situation. She was trapped here and had no idea what to do about it other than wait for Dallan and Shona to show up. And she had no idea what would happen then either.

They mended all morning, broke for some lunch, mended some more. She did her best to sew some patches and fix tears not only on Jefferson's denims, but Thackary's and Sam's too. She also realized she'd have to memorize certain names for different things. The denims vs. Levis incident was proof of that. Thank Heaven she had the excuse of being a city girl who didn't have a clue about ranch or farm life. That would serve her well as she tried to learn as much as she could about how these people lived their lives so she could blend in.

Belle came into the parlor and smiled. "How are you feeling, Lorelei?"

"Good," she said with a nod. "Much better than yesterday."

"Wonderful. Do you think you're up to a trip to town?"

"Why are you going to town?" Adele asked.

"We're all going. Mrs. King is casting the rest of the play, and I know you wanted to be involved this year."

Parthena jumped to her feet with a loud "Whoopee!"

Adele smiled as she stood. "Really?"

"Yes, but we must hurry."

"Is Father coming?"

"We'll meet him in town. And if we want to get there, take care of business and get back before dark, we need to leave soon."

"I'll go change!" Adele said happily, putting her needle and thread back into the basket.

"There's no need. Mrs. King won't care what you're wearing."

Lorelei glanced at her own dress. What were they going to do when they saw what she had on underneath it? No one saw her change yesterday. Did they even *have* underwear in the 1870s? She swallowed hard and hoped they didn't notice her blushing. The girls were excited, and she wondered if they didn't travel to town often. But Parthena and two of her brothers were just there. Was it the play that was causing all the excitement? And would Jefferson be coming? She hadn't seen him since breakfast and wondered what he'd been doing all this time.

"Are you sure you're feeling up to this?" Belle asked.

"I could stay behind," she offered.

"No, I wouldn't think of it. You shouldn't be alone."

Lorelei felt disappointed. Did the woman not trust her? Did Belle think she'd rob them blind while they were away? Or was she just worried about her health? "I understand," she finally said. "I'll be fine."

Belle smiled. "Good. My family looks forward to this every year."

Lorelei recalled Colin mentioning the play yesterday at the doctor's but didn't remember what he said. Her mind was so jumbled at the time; she was surprised she could remember even that.

The family filed out the back door to the barnyard where Jefferson and another man were hitching up the wagon. Lorelei watched in fascination. She'd never seen anyone do that before. As soon as they were done, Jefferson approached. "How are you feeling?"

"I'm all right. No need to worry."

"Glad to hear it." He glanced at the wagon as his siblings began to climb into the back. "I'll help you up."

She met his gaze, warm and comforting. "Thank you." She recalled the last trip she had in the same wagon and hoped fear didn't take hold again as they journeyed to town. The shock of recognizing the landscape around Canyon Park from her time was too much. That was less than twenty-four hours ago. It was as if she was functioning in a bubble, her mind hanging onto everything within her immediate surroundings: the people, the horses, even the chickens. They were living, breathing things. Therefore all this must be real.

She followed Jefferson to the wagon. His presence helped settle her nerves. He helped her into the back of the buckboard, his hands sure and strong. When he lifted her, she felt weightless. It wasn't a gym that kept him fit, but hard work. She smiled at the thought as he jumped in and sat beside her.

"Are we ready?" Belle called from the driver's seat.

A rapid succession of yeses was returned, and she got the wagon moving. Lorelei was a little apprehensive when they climbed the rise, but the horses did all right. She noticed smoke rising from the chimney of the cabin halfway up and pointed at it. "Who lives there?"

"Grandma Edith and Grandpa Jefferson. I'm named after him. Edith is his third wife."

"Oh?" Had he been divorced twice?

"His first wife died – I think her name was Mary - then he married Grandma Honoria, Father's mother, before they came west. Father was maybe twelve or fourteen at the time."

"And your cousin Honoria is named after her?"

"Yes." He smiled. "I know it's a lot to keep track of. There are more of us in Clear Creek than any other family if you count all the cousins."

Lorelei nodded – that was still the case in her time.

"We have relatives in England too."

She looked at him and smiled. "You do? Have you ever been there?"

He nodded. "Father and Mother went years ago. Honoria was real little, maybe two, I was just a baby. Neither of us remember any of it."

She laughed. "I've always wanted to go to England. It looks like such a wonderful place. There's so much history there."

He stared at her a moment. "Looks?"

"Oh, um, I've seen pictures."

He nodded in understanding. Another close call.

They bumped along and soon were passing the future Canyon Park. The road they traveled was a state highway in her time, the cut off to the park just up ahead. Out of curiosity, she had to ask, "Do you go into the canyon much?"

"All the time. Not in winter but when spring comes. We hold the town picnic down there every year."

She tried not to get too excited. How fascinating! "So, um, when did that start, the picnic in the canyon?"

He smiled. "Now there's a story. Right, Mother?"

Belle laughed. "Oh, no, not that story!"

"Tell it, tell it!" Parthena said with a laugh. Even Thackary smiled and looked at his mother with a hopeful gleam in his eyes.

Belle turned on the wagon seat as best she could while still keeping track of the horses. "That's where your father and I fell in love."

Lorelei grinned. "Really?"

"Well, a few things led up to it, but I won't go into that," she said. "The picnic itself was Grandma Waller's and Aunt Sadie's idea."

Jefferson touched her arm. "You met Grandma yesterday."

A tingle went up her spine at the contact and she smiled at him. "Yes, I remember."

"It was quite the affair," Belle said. "Colin and I shared our first kiss on the ride to the picnic."

"How sweet," Lorelei said without thinking.

"It was," Belle quipped, then whistled at the horses. They picked up the pace.

Lorelei grinned ear to ear. This was how families should be. The Cookes were happy, hard-working people that didn't take things for granted. They lived a simple life, everyone doing their part to make things run smoothly. None of them appeared to be independent like most people she knew, herself included.

Moreover, they were trusting, accepting of each other's faults. She shied away from others until she trusted them. It was difficult for her to get close to anyone, for if she did, they might be gone in a flash. Like her parents, then her first set of foster parents, then … her entire life in the 21st century. That was enough to give anyone issues, and she had her share.

How was she going to survive if she never made it back? What if the MacDonalds never returned for her? Kidnapping was a felony – they could go to jail for a long time. But what could she do about it? No judge would ever believe her. "Your Honor, they drugged me with aerosol cheese and stashed me in the 19th century …" They'd think she was certifiable.

"Something wrong?"

She looked at Jefferson. "No, just thinking."

He smiled. "Have you had any headaches today?"

She sighed in relief. The last thing she wanted was for him to think she was bananas. "No, it's fine."

"Good. I'd hate to think we've dragged you to this when you didn't feel well."

"To town?"

He smiled. "To the play."

"No problem," Lorelei insisted. "What's it like?"

He grinned. "Wonderful."

CHAPTER TWELVE

Josiah King was the town preacher but didn't look like any clergyman Lorelei had ever seen – more like an outlaw pretending to be a clergyman. He was tall with short dark hair and intense grey eyes. According to Jefferson, he'd been the only preacher in town since the church was built in 1858. His wife Annie had chestnut hair streaked with grey and a quiet, kind demeanor. They stood before her, looking her up and down with warm smiles. "Welcome," Annie said. "We heard yesterday was rough for you. You'll let us know if you need anything?"

Lorelei noticed Doc Drake sitting in a pew with his wife – Elsie, was it? That probably explained how Annie knew. "Yes, of course."

The doctor stood and headed over with an odd look on his face, as if he knew everything about her. Maybe he did. That made one of them. "How are you feeling today, Lorelei?" he asked when he reached them.

"Fine."

"No headaches, dizziness or nausea?"

"None."

He watched her a moment. "Good." He smiled at Annie. "Well, shall we start?"

"We're still waiting on quite a few folks." She motioned to the pews. "Why don't you all sit down? Josiah will give you some parts to read."

The preacher began to pass out sheets of paper. Lorelei took one and studied it. It was handwritten in wonderful cursive. Could she learn to write like that while she was here? People back home paid good money for calligraphy work ...

"All right, everyone," Annie called. "This afternoon we're reading for the parts of Joseph, the three wise men, King Herod, and a few others."

"Who got cast as Gabriel?" a man sitting in the back asked. He was tall and wiry, with salt-and-pepper hair and his front teeth missing.

Annie leafed through the papers in her hands. "Let's see, Willie ... that would be Cyrus."

"Cyrus?! Can he stand on a chair for as long as he's gonna hafta?"

"He assured me he's able. But I plan to have some of the children help him." She looked the Cookes' way. "Parthena, Thackary and Sam if they're so inclined."

"Do we get to dress up like angels?" Parthena asked with excitement.

"Of course. You'll be Cyrus's assistant angels."

Parthena and her brothers smiled at each other.

Jefferson leaned toward Lorelei and whispered, "Cyrus Van Cleet owns the hotel. He's getting up in years, so that's why she wants them to help. Besides, all my brothers and sister have to do is stand there and smile."

"How old is he?" she whispered back.

"Don't rightly know. At least seventy if he's a day. Poor man's liable to drop dead any time."

She looked at him. In her world that was nothing. But here, this Cyrus must be considered ancient.

"Belle, Elsie, are you doing costumes this year?" Annie asked next.

Belle raised her hand. "I planned on it."

"Me too," Elsie said.

The church doors opened and more people filed into the pews. She recognized the man from the mercantile – Patrick Mulligan, the same one from the photograph in her apartment. The woman with him, probably his wife, matched the picture as well.

"Ah, Paddy, Mary," Annie said. "Josiah has parts to read."

The preacher hurried over and gave them each a sheet of paper. Lorelei looked again at the one in her hands. It wasn't like any sort of paper she'd ever seen or felt.

More people came in and soon the church was almost full.

"How big is this play?" Lorelei asked.

"Not everyone is in it. Annie needs some folks for the choir," Jefferson explained.

"I see."

He shifted on the pew, his leg touching hers. Her belly did a flip and she put a hand over it. He looked at her, concerned. "I'm all right," she insisted. But the look on his face gripped her. No one had ever looked at her the way he was in that moment. He cared, he *really* cared. Her heart melted at the thought.

She looked around to distract herself. She didn't want him to care. She had no idea what would happen to her. From her viewpoint these people were all long dead. She couldn't let them – no, *him* – affect her like this.

"Colin, Belle, good to see ya here."

"Eli, Pleasant," Colin said. "What parts are you trying for this year?"

Lorelei studied the couple. The man wore a silver star on his vest – a lawman! She sat up straighter.

They were soon joined by another couple with two children, who sat in the pew in front of them. "Howdy, folks," the newcomer said.

"Tom, Rose," Colin and Belle greeted them.

"We all know what part Colin wants," Tom teased.

As if reading her thoughts, Jefferson bent his head to her ear. "That's Sheriff Tom Turner and his brother Eli. Eli's one of Tom's deputies."

"Colin, you have a guest, I see," the sheriff said.

Lorelei stared at them in awe. An honest-to-goodness Old West sheriff and deputy! For some reason, an image of Yosemite Sam popped into her head and she quickly pressed her lips together to keep from giggling.

"Tom, Eli," Colin began, "this is Lorelei Carson. She's a … friend of the MacDonalds."

"Dallan and Shona?" the sheriff said. "When were they in town?"

"They passed through two nights ago," Belle explained. "They wanted Lorelei to stay with us while they took care of some business."

"That so?" the sheriff drawled. He looked at his wife Rose. "We should have the Cookes to Sunday supper – whaddaya say, sweetheart?"

Rose had dark hair and blue eyes bordering on violet. A young brown-haired girl, maybe seven or eight, sat next to her, holding the hand of a younger boy. "Well, perhaps we shouldn't …"

Lorelei saw the worried look on the woman's face. What was wrong? Did they not want to invite the family over because of her? She slumped a little in the pew.

"Our guest has had a trying journey – she's under orders from Doc Drake not to overexert herself," Colin said. "But why not join us? We could dine in the main house. That way if Lorelei gets tired, she can simply go home."

She stared at him, her heart in her throat. Such a simple word. *Home.* Lorelei glanced around. These were families, friends who'd known each other for years. There was a sense of community here like nothing she'd ever seen or felt before, and she'd barely arrived. At the same time, she was eager to leave, to go back to *her* home.

"Welcome to Clear Creek," the other woman said. Her Southern accent was just like Major's next door. In fact, they looked alike. Were they related?

Lorelei smiled at her. "Thank you."

"You and Eli are more than welcome to come too, Pleasant." Belle offered.

"Why, thank you – that would be lovely." She smiled at Lorelei. "Have you known the MacDonalds long?"

A chill went up her spine. "No, not very long."

"They're fine people," she said. "A shame we missed them."

"Do you know them well?" she hedged. She might as well find out as much about her abductors as she could. Thing was, kidnappers usually didn't drop off their victims with nice families in the late 1800s.

"No, they're new to me, but Tom's known them for many years. So have the Cookes and quite a few others."

Her eyes flicked to Doc Drake and back. "And the Drakes?"

"Yes, along with the Brodys."

"Who are the Brodys?"

Pleasant nodded toward the church doors. A man and woman (who looked to be with child) were just entering the building with a child in tow.

Jefferson leaned her way again. "You'd never know it," he said as the man led his family up the church aisle, "but Mr. Brody's blind."

She did a double take as the family filed into a pew. "What?"

Jefferson smiled. "Like Pleasant said, welcome to Clear Creek."

WATCHING the residents of Clear Creek read for parts was in and of itself entertaining. To find out they'd been performing the exact same play (with a few variations here and there) for the last twenty years was downright astounding. Everyone in the church knew every part. Why they had to read for Mrs. King was anyone's guess, but the most obvious reason was that everyone was having such a good time. She'd never heard so many people laugh or seen so many smiling faces in one place.

She, too, laughed a few times, especially when Mr. Mulligan the saloon owner and Mr. Brody the blind hotel manager argued over who would play the tree this year. The part had been created specifically for a former Clear Creek resident, Andel Berg, who at the time had been the town blacksmith. Jefferson said he was as big as Mr. MacDonald, maybe broader. The part was perfect for him, and it was still referred to as the "Andel tree."

"How about you, Lorelei," Annie said during a break. "Would you like a part?"

She gaped. It was one thing to be horrified of heights, another of people. Getting up in front of others was simply not her cup of tea. "No, thank you."

"Why not?" Annie asked. "The play is in two weeks. That gives you plenty of time to rehearse."

"I really don't like being in front of crowds."

"You could always play a spectator in the audience,"

Jefferson said with a smile. "I've gotten away with it for the last three years."

His father glared at him. "Yes, you have, haven't you? Annie, give Jefferson something."

"Well, we don't have anyone to play the part of the camel yet."

"Oh, no, not the camel!" Jefferson said. "Besides, you need two people for that."

She looked at Lorelei and smiled.

"What? Me? No!" Her last word came out a squeak.

Annie turned back to Jefferson. "Front or back?"

Colin put a hand on his son's shoulder. "How about back?"

"What? Father!"

Annie bent to the pew so she could write. "So that makes Lorelei the front." She jotted it down.

"What?! Um, no. No, no."

Annie looked at her. "Unless you'd like to be the one stooped over."

Lorelei opened and closed her mouth a few times before inspiration struck. "But … it seems rather improper to be sharing a costume with a young man …"

Annie frowned. "You're right. Maybe I should ask Owen Kincaid."

Jefferson shrunk back in the pew. "Or have her and Adele do it –"

"Oh, no – you've gotten out of the play the last three years," Colin said. "It's your family and town duty to take a part this year." He looked at Annie expectantly. "Speaking of parts, have you cast Joseph yet?"

"Colin, you know we cast Joseph and Mary last."

"Yes, but today is the last day, is it not?"

Annie smiled at him. "True, but you'll still have to wait a little while longer." She went down the aisle to speak with

Grandma Waller and the old man with her – Grandpa Waller? They weren't trying out for anything, just watching everyone else and laughing.

"The camel," Jefferson groused under his breath.

"Is it that bad?"

"No, but I'd rather watch the play than be in it."

"I've never been in a play. Never wanted to."

"What? Never?" he said with disbelief. "But it's fun."

"You just said you'd rather not do it."

"When I was younger, I loved it. Now it's more fun to watch."

She looked away. She didn't want to make too much eye contact with him. When she did, it was hard to stop.

"You should take the front, like Annie said," he advised.

She thought a moment, then shook her head. Up on stage for hours with Jefferson's head level with her butt? No, no, no, no, no. "Who plays the donkey? You know, the one Mary rides on to the inn?"

He grinned. "Father and Uncle Harrison tried one year, and it was hilarious. Mrs. King was playing Mary and kept falling off. Since then, whoever plays Mary sits on a pretend donkey. It's kept at the livery stable during the year – Mr. Adams the blacksmith is in charge of it."

She smiled. "I can't wait to see it."

He gazed at her, cleared his throat and looked away. Was he trying as hard not to look at her as she was at him? Under different circumstances, she'd be flattered, excited even. But all things considered, what was the point?

The rest of the afternoon was full of friendly bickering over parts and Grandma's delightful cackles from the back of the church. Her husband, Lorelei learned, was Doc Waller, the original doctor in town. Doc Drake's wife Elsie was their niece.

She'd noticed Jefferson and some of the others spoke

carefully about Doc Drake, and she couldn't understand why. It was as if they were hiding something. Was he a criminal? Had something happened? Was he even a real doctor? That last thought was disturbing, to say the least. It was bad enough he was a nineteenth-century doctor without being a quack besides. Yet he was so peaceful and calming …

By the time they got to reading for the part of Joseph, Colin looked like he needed a chill pill. He had a determined gleam in his eyes that made Belle roll hers. "Now, Colin, don't be disappointed if Annie doesn't pick you this year. Just because *you* think it's your turn doesn't mean *she* does."

"Of course she does. She keeps track of all these things."

She looked at Lorelei and Jefferson and made a face. Lorelei giggled. It felt good. She liked these people – she was just afraid of liking them too much.

"And now for Joseph," Annie announced. "Josiah, will you start?"

"Josiah?" Colin echoed. "But he always narrates, or directs, or …"

"Colin," Belle said. "Quiet." She tucked a finger under his chin and physically shut his mouth.

He narrowed his eyes. "It's a conspiracy."

"Oh, for Heaven's sake, stop."

He faced front; his eyes glued to the preacher.

"Preacher Jo is really good," Jefferson whispered as the man began to speak his lines.

"He sounds like he is," she agreed.

"Father looks like he ate a bad apple."

Lorelei peeked past Belle at Colin, who watched the preacher like a cougar ready to pounce. "He really wants to play Joseph, doesn't he?"

"Yes, probably because Uncle Harrison isn't here. This is the first time my aunt, uncle and cousins aren't here for Christmas."

"Does it feel weird?"

"Weird?"

"Odd."

He shrugged. "A little. But more lonely than anything else."

She closed her eyes a moment. She knew exactly what that was like. "I understand."

He gazed at her and smiled.

"Doc Waller?!" Colin cried as the old man got up and shuffled to the front of the church. "But …"

"Colin, control yourself," Belle said. "If Doc wants to play Joseph, then let him."

Doc cleared his throat, held the sheet of lines before him, and with a dramatic sweep of his arm, began to read.

"Ohhhh," Colin covered his mouth with his hands and groaned.

Lorelei and Jefferson laughed into theirs.

And then … "Colin Cooke," Annie called.

"At long last," he said, stood and headed for the front of the church.

Lorelei, Jefferson and the rest of Colin's family watched as the man cleared his throat, gave Doc Waller a pointed look, then began to read his lines. "He's not bad," Lorelei commented. "I think the accent helps."

Jefferson's shoulders shook with silent laughter. "It does, doesn't it?"

When he was done, he returned to their pew with a satisfied smile. "I think that went rather well."

Belle eyed him but said nothing.

Colin glanced around, still grinning. "Why don't you read a part, darling?"

"Because I'm in charge of costumes. That takes up enough time and you know it." She narrowed her eyes. "I hope you're not already gloating. You don't know if you have it yet."

"Of course I do. After all, it *is* my turn."

Jefferson and Lorelei snorted.

"Quiet, you two," he warned. "Besides, fair is fair."

Lorelei smiled at him. She was having a good time. The Cookes were no different than … well, any other family she dreamed were her own. They were as far from what she'd had – foster families like the Browns – as they could be. She might be in the past, but she felt more at home here than she ever had in the 21st century.

It figured.

CHAPTER THIRTEEN

The reading of parts completed – along with the announcement that Colin *would* be playing Joseph this year, thus avoiding a scene – the Cookes left the church, piled into the wagon and headed into town. "Aren't we going home?" Lorelei asked.

"No – now we get to eat at the hotel!" Parthena said excitedly.

"You'll like the hotel," said Jefferson. "It's fancy, but don't let it scare you. It's not expensive. Cyrus keeps the prices low for all of us."

"What do you mean?"

"What he means is," Colin said, still proudly smiling, "the good people of Clear Creek are the ones that support the hotel, so he returns the favor by keeping prices reasonable. We don't get many visitors to town so he's not making money from the rooms."

"Cyrus makes most of his money off afternoon tea and the hotel restaurant," Jefferson explained.

Lorelei's face lit up. "There's afternoon tea?" She'd always wanted to sit down to an old-fashioned tea. Maybe now was her chance.

"Every day at four," Colin announced from his perch on the wagon seat.

"A town that has tea every afternoon at four? I've never heard of such a thing."

"Yes, I know, it's not something every town does," Belle agreed. "But given how many English we have here, then add in Bostonians like myself, my uncle Wilfred, Levi Stone and the Van Cleets, and all the Irish ... well, you get the idea."

"That does make sense," Lorelei said. "I bet it's wonderful."

"What will you bet?" Jefferson asked.

She smiled and rolled her eyes. "It's a figure of speech."

They parked the wagon across the street from the hotel and went inside. Mr. Brody sat behind the counter. "Watch this," Jefferson whispered to her as they came through the door.

Mr. Brody's eyes were fixed on them, though she knew he couldn't see. He slowly stood. "Is that you, Colin?"

Lorelei's jaw dropped. Jefferson smiled and winked at her.

"It is, Lorcan," Colin said.

"Congratulations on getting the part of Joseph this year. I'm sure ye'll do it justice."

The man was Irish – Lorelei hadn't noticed before. So that was what Belle meant by "all the Irish" – Mr. Brody and the Mulligans and probably some more she hadn't met yet. It wasn't surprising – she'd read Thomas Keneally's *The Great Shame* and knew that the Irish had spread out all over, even before the Potato Famine. Including her own Carson ancestors.

"Thank you. And congratulations at getting the part of the Andel tree."

"Aye, it's a grand part indeed. No lines. I just have to make sure I don't lose me leaves."

Everyone laughed, giving themselves away.

"Here for dinner, are ye?"

"Yes, the lot of us," Colin said.

Lorcan went still. Everything went silent. He tilted his head to the side. "Who's that with ye, Colin?"

Lorelei took a breath. "How did he know?" she whispered.

Colin motioned her forward. "Lorcan Brody, this is Lorelei Carson. The MacDonalds brought her to us for … well, they didn't tell us, but you know the MacDonalds."

Lorcan laughed as she went to the counter and stared at the blind man. His eyes locked right on her, and she took another breath and froze. "Aye – those MacDonalds are as tight with facts as most Scots are with shillings. Ye needn't be afraid of me, lass. Watching me miracle can be a little unnerving at first, but I don't argue with the Almighty for giving it to me."

She began to lift her hand but stopped herself from waving it in front of him. Wouldn't that be rude?

"Go ahead," Colin said.

Apparently not. But instead she raised her other hand.

"There's no need to surrender, lass. Me senses are good, but I don't dare wield a pistol."

She gaped at him. "How is this possible?"

Lorcan laughed again. "Ah, lass, this is Clear Creek. All sorts of things are possible. Now, Carson – a good Irish lass? Tell me, where do yer people hail from?"

"I … really don't know." Which was true enough.

Colin took her elbow and steered her toward the hotel's dining room. "We need to get seated. Ta-ta, Lorcan."

"Enjoy your meal," Lorcan called after them.

"Thank you, we will," Belle replied.

But before they even made it to a table, a plump woman with bright blue eyes and blonde hair going gray entered the dining room and headed straight for them. "Colin, Belle, it's so good to see you!"

Colin pulled a chair out for Belle as Lorelei and the rest took seats. "Good afternoon, Sally. We're here for dinner. What are the evening's choices?"

"Rosie's made two selections: roast chicken or beef stew." She looked at Lorelei and smiled. "Howdy, honey. You must be new in town." She glanced at Colin and Belle. "She a relation of yours?"

"I'm afraid not," Colin said. "The MacDonalds came through recently and left her in our care."

"Is that so?" Sally said, hands on her hips. She went straight to Lorelei's chair. "Welcome to Clear Creek, honey! Any friend of the MacDonalds and the Cookes is a friend of mine."

"Nice to meet you," Lorelei said shyly. My, but the woman was exuberant.

"Lorelei," Colin said, "may I introduce you to one of the finest cooks in Clear Creek if not the entire Northwest, Mrs. Sally Upton. Sally, this is Lorelei Carson."

"Good to meet you, Lorelei – and what a pretty name. Who wants coffee?" She took everyone's drink orders then hurried back to the kitchen. Lorelei wished Beatrice could be here to watch this. If only they had someone like Sally at Daisy's Café – it would sure liven the place up.

"What are you thinking?" Jefferson asked.

For the first time since sitting down, she noticed he was right next to her. Come to think of it, he'd been by her side since they left the ranch. "I like Mrs. Upton. She's jolly."

"That she is. And Father's right, she's an excellent cook – almost as good as Great Aunt Irene. Some people in town think she's better."

"Don't tell your great-aunt that, though," Belle advised with a smile.

"You'd best be forewarned, my dear," Colin said. "There's been a rivalry between Sally and my wife's dear Aunt Irene for decades."

"It's true," Adele said. "We love when they get into a fight because they start cooking all these wonderful things and everybody gets to judge whose is best."

Lorelei couldn't help laughing. "That's awesome."

The Cookes looked at one another. "I've never thought of it that way," Colin said. "But yes, I suppose it is … awesome."

Lorelei frowned. She'd slipped again. Her 21st-century idioms and sayings were different from those in 1879. She was beginning to feel so comfortable with these people that it was hard to remember to watch what she was saying.

"What are you going to have?" Parthena asked her.

She glanced around the table. "So there aren't any menus?"

"No, around here Rosie or Sally decide what they're going to make on any particular day," Colin explained. "There's usually only a few choices."

Lorelei's jaw dropped. If only it was like that at Daisy's! Not that it mattered now …

"Yes, most visitors are as shocked as you are," Colin said. "But it's a simple system and it works."

She recalled what Sally had said before about the two options. "I guess I'll have the roast chicken, then."

While they waited, they told her the story of Lorcan Brody, who'd lost his sight in a boxing match, came to Clear Creek and received a miracle. He couldn't see, but he could "feel" what was around him, including movement. If only she had internet access, she could look up what such a phenomenon was called. Because it had to have an explanation, didn't it?

She gave her order to Sally along with everyone else, then watched as other townsfolk filed in the dining room to eat. "Is this place usually full?" she asked Jefferson.

"A lot of folks are here tonight because they just came from the church like us. It's too late to start supper at home. Most folks have an early bedtime you know."

"I understand." She thought of her electric alarm clock. This morning she was awoken by the crowing of roosters. It was a simple thing, but it made her happy to hear them.

She didn't speak much as they waited for their meals, too busy studying the room. The Van Cleet Hotel was out of place in such a small town. Jefferson saw her gawking and explained. "Cyrus has a bit of money and spared no expense when he built this place. We don't get many guests staying in it, but that's okay. Everyone in town enjoys eating here and having tea."

"Why did he build it?" It didn't make sense.

"Because he could."

She smiled at him. "It must be nice to be that rich."

"Your family doesn't have a lot of money?"

She shook her head. "Remember? What family?"

"I'm sorry, that was rude," he said with a chastised look. "It's just that the dress you had on when Father and Mother brought you home, and you don't know how to milk a cow or feed chickens ... don't they do that in ... where you're from?"

She sighed and looked away. She'd always felt out of place, but out of time was a whole different story.

Belle came to the rescue. "Jefferson, you of all people know better."

Lorelei managed a smile for Jefferson. "I'll tell you what," she whispered. "When little ears aren't around to hear, I'll answer any questions you have, okay?"

"Thank you." Jefferson was blushing. It was adorable.

Speaking of little ears … "What happened to your family?" Parthena asked softly.

"They died in a fire." That, at least, was a truth she could share without frightening anyone. They had fires in the 1870s.

"Children, that's Lorelei's private business," Belle said. "If she wants to tell you, she can in her own good time, but not now."

Lorelei smiled in thanks. They'd been very courteous and hadn't pried into her background much. Which meant they trusted the MacDonalds more than she thought. But that didn't explain why the MacDonalds kidnapped her and brought her here in the first place.

Jefferson touched her arm. "Something wrong?" he asked with concern.

She glanced at his hand, then his face. "It's not easy getting used to here. And now. I'll be fine."

Thankfully, before anyone could ask more questions, their meals came. A younger woman helped Sally serve, and Lorelei was fascinated to find out she was a mail-order bride who'd married one of Pleasant Turner's *six* brothers. "My goodness, there are a lot of big families in this town."

"How big is your family?" Parthena asked, then winced. "Oops. Sorry."

"That's all right," Lorelei said. "I'm an only child."

They stared at her with a mix of sympathy and surprise.

Sally set her plate of roast chicken in front of her. "That's all right, honey. You're in Clear Creek now. Around here, everyone's your family."

THE MEAL FINISHED, the Cookes waited for dessert and coffee and visited with a few of the other patrons. Lorelei had never seen so many friendly people in one place in her life. They asked after each other, complimented one another, laughed, shared stories, and really seemed to care about one another.

She asked Jefferson a few questions during their meal and found out that Clear Creek had only about a hundred people living in the area. Most of the younger ones had never been anywhere else. The Cookes had traveled to England to visit a relation (a duke, of all things), and some others had visited Oregon City or Portland. That Harrison and his family and the Dunnigans had gone all the way to Washington Territory to spend Christmas with another family was the talk of the town.

Half the people in the dining room approached their table and asked how Colin and Belle were getting along without Harrison and Sadie. Lorelei wished she could meet them but wasn't sure if she'd still be here when they returned. When would the MacDonalds come back to get her? She hated the uncertainty, but what could she do about it?

"Are you ready to go?" Jefferson asked. He'd been unusually quiet during their meal and hadn't started talking a lot until folks came to the table asking after his aunt and uncle and what Christmas would be like this year without them.

"Yes. I'm ready." She smiled shyly. She liked how his voice softened sometimes when he talked to her. It made her feel special. There was a caring that was hard to miss. She could get used to someone caring about her – she'd always wondered what it felt like.

The family began to get up, and Jefferson pulled her chair out for her. Colin and Belle noted the action with interest. "Thank you," she told him and hoped his parents didn't disapprove. But they hadn't stopped him. Was it rude to do so?

Colin and Belle spoke with more people as the rest of

them headed for the wagon. Jefferson helped her in, sat next to her and smiled. "How did you like it?"

"The meal? It was wonderful. The best roast chicken I've ever had."

He rubbed his mitten-clad hands nervously on his legs a few times. "Sally's a good cook. Tea is nice too. We... should go sometime."

Her heart leaped in her chest. She had the distinct feeling he was asking her out on a date. "You want to have tea?"

He looked into her eyes. "Yes. I think it would be fine, don't you?"

A tingle went up her spine. "Yes," she said with a smile. Followed by her mind yelling, *no, no, you idiot! What are you doing?* If not for the circumstances, she could develop a whopping crush on Jefferson Cooke. Maybe she was anyway.

"I'll talk to Father and find out when I can take the wagon to town. We could bring Adele or one of the others along. After all, we can't go traipsing off to town by ourselves."

She shook herself. "We can't?"

"Of course not. What would people think?"

Her eyebrows shot up. "Excuse me?"

He looked at her like she was an idiot. "Lorelei, I know we're not courting. But people might think we're sweet on each other and then see us alone together and that's how the rumors start."

Part of her wanted to say, "Well, aren't we?" But he was right, they weren't. And in this time chaperones were commonplace; she'd forgotten that. "Yes, of course. Adele should come with us. Although then, you couldn't ask me about ..." She waved her hand to fill in.

He smiled. "I think she can keep a secret. Besides, I know she still has Christmas shopping to do and presents to make. She's bound to need ribbon or yarn from the mercantile. We can get what we need, have tea and go home."

"That sounds fine," she said as her heart sank.

"What's wrong?"

She bit her lip. The irony of it was too much. Of course he wasn't, as he'd said, "sweet on her." But a part of her wanted him to be. No one had ever asked her out in high school or junior high. She didn't connect with anyone until she met Jefferson. And all he wanted to do was have tea …

"Everyone ready?" Colin called as he climbed onto the wagon seat. Without waiting for an answer, he got the wagon moving. The ranch was only a few miles out of town – it took just under an hour to get there, but it would be dark by then. She wondered what the rest of the evening would entail.

When they reached the ranch, Belle, the girls and Lorelei went inside to get the fires going. They'd banked them before they left, and their foreman Logan Kincaid had come in and put a little wood on each one. Soon after, to Lorelei's surprise, they all began to get ready for bed. She'd been so exhausted the day before she hadn't noticed the time – not that there was a clock to confirm it.

"Would you like to borrow a book?" Adele asked as they entered the kitchen.

Thank Heaven! "Yes, what do you have?"

"I have a wonderful book I just finished. You've probably read it. *Alice's Adventures in Wonderland*."

Lorelei stared at her. "Actually, I've, uh… always wanted to read that one but never had the chance to." That was close – she'd almost said, "Seen the movie."

"It's in my room – I'll get it for you. Unless of course you'd like to read my newest book."

"Have you read it already?"

"No, but you're our guest. You're welcome to it."

Lorelei smiled. The gaping difference in manners

between her century and this one was astounding. "No, you read it."

"Thank you. I'll get your book and bring them both down."

Lorelei looked around the kitchen. "Are we reading in here?"

"No, silly, the parlor." She left her standing next to the stove

Belle put on a kettle to boil. "Would you like some tea?"

"Thank you." She went to the kitchen table.

Belle went to the hutch and took out some cups and saucers. "I'm sorry about your family."

Lorelei smiled and sighed. She didn't like talking about her family, and always felt a void in her heart where her parents should've been. But there was nothing. Even her memories of them were fading. "As they say where I come from, it is what it is."

CHAPTER FOURTEEN

Over the next week a routine developed. Lorelei would get up with the other girls, bring in water, wood and the morning's milking, and help Belle with cooking. She learned to separate milk from cream, make flapjacks, biscuits and bread. She especially liked making bread – Patsy had (will have?) a bread maker, and everyone in the house loved the smell when it was in use.

Unfortunately, one day Erwin and some of his friends were roughhousing, knocked it off the counter and broke it. Patsy, being Patsy, was so mad she told him she was never going to bake bread for them again, and she didn't. Lorelei figured it was because she was too cheap and/or too stubborn to buy another bread machine and certainly wasn't about to make it by hand.

The women made breakfast, cleaned up, then began the other daily chores – mending, darning, more baking, lunch preparation. And no sooner were they done cleaning up after lunch than it was time to start supper. But she had to admit the food was wonderful – she'd get fat if it wasn't for all the extra exercise she got from the chores. She was starting to feel great, with more energy than she'd ever had before.

"I asked Father about our trip to town," Jefferson announced as he entered the kitchen one afternoon.

Lorelei looked up from her mixing – she and Adele were making cookies. "Town?"

His eyes filled with disappointment. "Tea?"

"Oh!" She put the bowl down. "Yes, I'm sorry. We can go?"

He smiled in relief. "Tomorrow. Adele, can you come along?"

"For tea? Sure I can!"

A tingle went up Lorelei's spine, along with a sudden bout of shyness. He obviously hadn't forgotten about asking her to tea, though she had. "So it's all set, then. But … how well can you keep a secret, Adele?"

"You can trust me. Is this about your … big secret?"

Lorelei leaned back in alarm. "What do you know about that?"

"Only that I was pretty sure you had one."

"Well … yes, it is. Nothing illegal, of course, and your parents and Jefferson already know. But don't let anyone else know."

"Cross my heart," Adele replied and did.

Jefferson nodded. "What kind of cookies are you making?"

"Molasses." Lorelei looked at the crockery on the worktable. "I haven't gotten far. Adele is teaching me."

He smiled, joined her at the worktable and picked up a jar. "Here, I've made these many times growing up. I know the recipe by heart."

"You do?"

"Sure." He pried the lid off, poured molasses into the bowl, then motioned her to stir.

She did, her eyes never leaving his. Whenever he was

around, she felt so comfortable, so relaxed. "How much flour?"

He looked at the small flour sack on the table. "Two teacups full."

She smiled. She'd noticed early on there were no measuring cups or spoons in the house. Belle scooped out flour with either a large serving spoon or a literal teacup. Before she could reach for the flour, he plopped a cupful into her bowl, measured out another, then added a few pinches of salt and other ingredients. "You're good at this."

"I used to love helping Mother make cookies when I was young."

She smiled. To hear him refer to himself as young was odd. She expected to hear one thing, only to hear another. They might talk oddly, but it made her realize the Cookes were no different than people of her time, except for their impeccable manners.

Belle stuck her head in the door. "Adele, would you like to go visit Honoria about tonight?"

"Oh, yes!" Adele wiped her hands on her apron, took it off and was out the door in a flash.

Lorelei mixed the cookie dough, dropped spoonfuls onto a baking pan and put them in the oven. "What's happening tonight?"

"Oh, we're eating over there tonight," Jefferson explained.

She remembered the family mentioning they ate at the main ranch house a few nights a week. "Why haven't we done so?"

"Because of you."

"What?"

He shrugged. "We didn't want to overwhelm you. I told Mother and Father you'd be fine. Harrison and Sadie aren't here, and it would be much quieter than usual. But they thought you needed your rest."

"I'm not going to break, you know." She put the mixing spoon into the bowl and took it to the dry sink. "I feel fine."

"Then you should enjoy yourself tonight. You'll get to meet Grandpa Jefferson and Grandma Edith."

"Why haven't I met them yet?"

He shrugged again. "Like I said, Mother and Father..."

"Are a little too protective, I think," she finished. After all, she wasn't made of glass. But given what she'd been through, most people might have had a nervous breakdown by now. She had no idea why she hadn't, except that she'd been made so welcome here. And that with Jefferson she felt... more whole, as if part of her had been missing all this time. The feeling was growing too, and she wasn't stressing herself out by fighting it.

By the time Belle and Adele returned, Lorelei was taking the first batch of cookies out of the oven. "You made them yourself?" Adele asked in shock.

"I had help." She nodded at Jefferson, who sat at the table sipping a cup of coffee.

"What are you still doing in here?" Belle asked. "I thought you were helping your father in the barn."

"Logan and Owen are helping Father. I came in here and helped Lorelei make cookies."

Belle arched an eyebrow at him. "Baking cookies is not one of your chores, son."

"I was helping our guest. Everyone pitches in to do that."

Lorelei grinned at him. He was sly when he wanted to be.

Belle left to work on a dress she was mending for the Christmas play, which made Lorelei think. "If the play is only a week away, why haven't there been any rehearsals?" She began to spoon out the next batch of cookies.

Jefferson laughed. "Because we don't need many. We'll rehearse next week."

"That's not much time."

"It is when the whole town knows the play." He laughed as she put the next batch in the oven. "I know it by heart. I told you at the church, remember?"

She'd already forgotten about the tea, and now this. *Was* she starting to lose her mind?

"It's all right, I understand if you don't remember. You've been through a lot."

That was true enough. How did most people handle getting shot a century or more through time? Or was she the first?

Adele came back in. "When we go to town tomorrow, can I do some Christmas shopping at Dunnigan's?"

"I was figuring on just that," Jefferson replied. "Besides, I have some money and wanted to buy Mother her gift."

"I thought you already bought her a gift." Adele took a cookie and had a bite. "Mmm, these are just right."

"No, I haven't. Come to think of it, I haven't gotten you a gift either."

Her eyebrows shot up. "Did you draw my name?"

"No, I drew Thackary's, but I was going to get you a gift anyway."

Adele laughed. "Oh, thank you!" Then she turned thoughtful. "Am I going to be your chaperone?"

"Um, well … I mean …"

Lorelei snorted. Jefferson *was* nervous. The time period dictated a courting couple had to have a chaperone, lest anyone think something untoward happened while they were alone. He either didn't want Adele thinking the same thing or … "Yes, you're going to be our chaperone," she replied before Jefferson could.

"Finally! Why didn't you just say so?" Adele smiled at Lorelei. "I'd love to chaperone the two of you."

"It's not like that!" Jefferson said.

"It isn't?" Lorelei mock-objected. She followed it with a

sniffle, feeling positively giddy at this point. After all, Adele knew her brother better than she did. But was it safe to let her heart rule the situation? Did it not realize she was trapped in the wrong century and didn't know from one day to the next what would happen to her? She had to be logical about this and not give in to her emotions. And yet, she felt a lot better when she did – better than she could recall ever feeling before.

She wondered what it would be like if Jefferson had been transported to the 2010s and put in her or the Jensens' safe-keeping. He probably wouldn't know what hit him. But would he be attracted to her? Impossible to say.

Jefferson finally spoke but didn't answer her question. "Well, then … the three of us will go to town after lunch tomorrow, take care of business at Dunnigan's, have tea and come home."

Lorelei looked at Adele, who smiled in satisfaction. Maybe it was stupid to do this. But maybe it was about time she did something risky. "All right."

He grinned and backed toward the door, his eyes never leaving hers. He nearly bumped into the wall before grabbing his hat and coat off a peg, putting them on and leaving the house.

"My my, is my brother ever sweet on you," Adele cooed. "He's gone calf-eyed."

Lorelei couldn't help but smile back. "Calf-eyed? What does that … oh, I get it. Yeah, I think you're right."

Adele shrugged, left the kitchen table and joined her at the stove. "It was only a matter of time. How could he not?"

"I can think of a few reasons," she said automatically. But she'd always looked at things that way – the glass half-empty. It kept her from being as disappointed.

"How long do you think you'll stay?" Adele asked.

Lorelei shook her head. "I don't know. To be honest, I

don't know where the MacDonalds have gone or why they left me here." She shrugged and sighed.

"The MacDonalds are strange, everyone knows it. But they're good people, Lorelei. Most folks around here would tell you they'd trust them with their lives."

"That does make me feel a little better," Lorelei admitted.

"But even so," Adele went on, "Jefferson's my brother. I'd be much obliged if you didn't break his heart."

Lorelei's jaw dropped. "Excuse me?"

"If you don't hear it from me, you'll hear it from my parents sooner or later," Adele confessed. "Of course, you're both of marriageable age ..."

"What?!" Lorelei gaped at her. She didn't know what to say, so she tried the only logical thing she could. "But we've only known each other a week!"

Adele's eyebrows rose as she shrugged. "So?"

"So?! He can't possibly be thinking of dating ... I mean, *courting* me after just a few days!"

"Why not? If you were mail-order bride you'd already be married."

Lorelei held up her hands. "Marriage! Whoa, slow down ..."

"Why are you acting so strange?" Adele asked. "Don't people get married right away where you're from?"

"No! We believe in long engagements. Taking our time, getting to know each other ... sometimes for years."

"Years." Adele looked amazed, then glanced at the floor. "Are those shoes comfortable?"

Lorelei started. "What?" She looked at her feet. "Oh. Yes, actually, they are."

Adele smiled sheepishly. "May I try them on? I've never seen anything like them."

If it got the girl off the subject of Jefferson, courting, and

... *marriage*, then she was all for it. She went to the kitchen table, sat, and took off her tennis shoes.

It took longer for Adele to do the same. When she was done, she offered her own shoes to her. "We could trade for the rest of the day."

Lorelei looked at her serviceable work boots and cringed. Then again, maybe she *should* walk a mile in this girl's shoes, literally. Parthena wanted to hike out on the prairie and build snowmen. "All right, let's."

They proceeded to put on each other's shoes and Lorelei was surprised at how comfortable Adele's were. Of course, they didn't compare to her Converses, and she hoped Adele didn't grow attached to them. "Do they fit?"

Adele finished tying the tennis shoes and stood. "They're so... flat." She walked to the other side of the kitchen and back, a huge smile on her face. "But so comfortable!"

Lorelei did the same, sans the smile. "These are different. Sturdy." She cast a longing look at Adele's feet.

"Are these warm?" Adele asked.

"Not really. They weren't meant for snow. They're for ..." Was basketball even invented yet? "... for indoor wear."

"What kind of shoe is just made for indoors?" She paced the kitchen again. "I wonder if Mrs. Dunnigan can order them for the mercantile."

"No, they're ... well, that has to do with my secret." She was planning to let Adele in on it anyway – why not now? "Promise me you won't tell anyone? Your parents and Jefferson already know, but nobody else."

"I already promised, remember?"

That's right, she did. "Okay, sit down."

Adele sat. "So how did you get these shoes?"

"They're pretty common where I'm from. Or should I say, when I'm from. You see, the MacDonalds grabbed me from Clear Creek ... a hundred and forty years in the future. No, I'm not kidding," she added before Adele could ask.

Adele just stared at her, her mouth slowly opening.

"Don't ask me how they did it, or why – I don't know. Believe me, when they come back, I will be asking them. But I'm telling you the truth – I was born in 2001. And now here I am in 1879."

All Adele did for a minute was blink and breathe. Finally, she managed to whisper, "that's a big secret, all right." She paused again before asking, "Are you *sure* you're not loco?"

Lorelei laughed. "Oh, yes, I'm sure. It doesn't make sense to me, but it's either that or someone is playing a practical joke on me and spending millions of dollars to do it, and that makes even less sense. If you need proof, well, look at your feet."

Adele did. "Well, I've never seen shoes like this before. Whoever sewed them – that's better stitching than I've ever seen on anything."

"In my time, they have machines for that."

"Oh my." She bent down and touched the canvas. "Not much protection if you got stepped on."

"Stepped on?"

Adele looked at her. "Horses, cows …"

"Like I said, they're for indoor wear. Athletics, mainly, but people wear them for comfort too. People who work with horses and cows in my time, they wear big heavy boots."

"That makes sense." Adele was clearly in shock. Then she smiled and said, "I'm wearing shoes from the future?"

"Yes, you are. But I do want them back – they're almost the only thing I have from my time."

Adele nodded and they traded shoes again. "Let's find Parthena, clean up the kitchen and go build snowmen while we have time. Or … can you wear those while making snowmen?"

Lorelei grinned. "My feet might get a little damp, but I'll survive."

"Well, if you're sure ..." Adele headed into the hall.

Lorelei followed Adele to her bedroom and waited in the hall while Parthena put her knitting away. She was making a present for one of her siblings. Adele seemed to be taking it rather well. But she had a more pressing problem: Jefferson. To think she'd been worried about taking a liking to him. If what Adele said was true, what could she do, other than tell him to forget it? How did one let a boy down easy? She had no experience with boys, other than their rejection, and she didn't want to tell Jefferson to drop dead.

Besides, Jeff was no boy – he was a man. They were both of marriageable age, and in this century, people married young and quickly. Probably for survival reasons – it was just the way of things. She knew some people married for love even here, but that was an extra bonus if she remembered her history right. And deep down, she *wanted* Jefferson to be "calf-eyed" over her. Everything she'd dreamed of in a man in her own time, she was finding here in this one.

It wasn't fair.

Once again Lorelei told herself to stay strong and not get too attached. It could only end in pain – something she had far too much experience with.

CHAPTER FIFTEEN

"What do you mean there's no room at the inn?!"

Annie King pinched the bridge of her nose. "Colin, you don't need to scream."

"Oh?" he said as his eyebrows rose in innocence. "I thought it would have dramatic effect."

"The story's dramatic enough. We don't need ... histrionics."

He shrugged. "Oh, very well. I'll suppress my artistic tendencies."

Annie shut her eyes tight. She looked to Lorelei like she was counting to ten. This had to be the sixth time Colin had blown his lines - not messing them up, just adding to them.

"If that man don't do this right, Annie's liable to bust a gut."

Lorelei turned to find Grandma Waller, Mary Mulligan and – she couldn't believe it was really her name – Fanny Fig in the pew behind her. It was the latter who'd spoken, and she still wore a pinched expression and was shaking her head at Colin. "He was very excited to get the part," Lorelei said in his defense.

"Too excited, if you ask me. That man's going to make a shambles of this play!"

"He'll shape up," Grandma assured her. "I hope." She smiled at Lorelei. "How are you doing, child?"

Lorelei smiled shyly. She liked the old woman, who looked frail but was tough as nails. "Very well, thank you." She'd always wanted to say that to someone.

"Glad to hear it. Any word from the MacDonalds?"

"No, ma'am." She ran a hand over her skirt. She'd been wearing the same dress for days – people in the past apparently didn't change clothes too often. Thankfully, today she could get a new one at the mercantile after play practice. Belle was minding the store – she, Colin and the Mulligans were taking turns covering for the Dunnigans. Colin, mostly, which explained why Jefferson had to work more than usual. He'd even had to cancel their trip to town to have tea, much to her and Adele's disappointment. If all went well, they'd go tomorrow.

In the meantime, she watched him from a distance and spent as much time as she could with Adele and the other kids. They did chores together, cooked together, played games in the evening in front of the fire in the parlor, and occasionally – when the younger ones weren't around – Adele would ask her about "the future."

And the kids asked Lorelei to tell stories. They *loved* her stories. She had to change things, of course – replacing cars with horses and the like. But she still managed tales of a brave collie dog and the boy that owned her, of seven castaways stranded on a desert island, or of a family with a huge ranch in the Ponderosa region of California. Who knew that watching so many reruns of *Lassie, Gilligan's Island* and *Bonanza* would come in so handy? Oddly enough, they loved the *Gilligan's Island* stories the best. She could just imagine the looks on their faces if they ever saw a real television.

She made a mental note to try a different sort of story with them – if she could figure out how to word it. If she said, "A long time ago in a galaxy far, far away," would they know what a galaxy was?

"I think they need you, child," Grandma said.

She started. "What?"

"To fix the camel!" Fanny snapped.

Lorelei caught Grandma glaring at Fanny as she left the pew and decided to let them sort it out. She had a camel to mend.

"The neck seam – again," Annie commented, handing her a needle and thread.

Jefferson was standing in the back half of the camel, occasionally grumbling at Owen Kincaid in the front. Owen was sixteen and must be going through a growth spurt because every time he got into the costume, he seemed taller. Which meant that he split the seams holding the head to the neck and it had to be re-sewn. Lorelei, with no on-stage responsibilities and having proven she could mend a seam without stabbing herself to death, had quickly become the designated camel-neck repairwoman.

It gave her something to do, since even when Jeff wasn't in the camel, he'd sit next to his father, while she purposely sat on the other side of the church. When she sat next to him, her heart would race, and sometimes she'd even break out in a sweat. It had been especially bad when they'd attended church yesterday. True, she was attracted to him, no denying it. But she couldn't afford to get attached when eventually she would go home.

Home. She'd been in the past over a week. Did Mr. Jensen have the police looking for her? Did anyone question Patsy and Bob? Would they even care she'd gone missing? Or did time travel not work that way? She had so many questions for the MacDonalds when they returned …

"Lorelei?"

She gasped and looked at Annie. "I'm sorry, I was … thinking." She looked at Owen, who'd taken off the camel head and was blushing. "Maybe we should just add a few inches of fabric to the neck, make it longer."

Annie made a face. "It would be hard to get the colors to match."

"The colors don't match anyway." Jefferson replied, muffled by the fabric. Which was true – there were so many patches and add-ons that the camel costume looked like Frankenstein's next project.

"Why don't we make the extension red or black, so it looks like a collar?" Lorelei suggested. "And use some tougher thread, like … I don't know, maybe something for sewing shoes or …?" She was improvising – she knew next to nothing about thread types.

Annie tapped her chin. "That might work. Okay, boys, get out of there. And Jefferson, go to the mercantile and have your mother send over a yard by three inches of black canvas and some of the strongest thread she's got. We'll lick this one way or another."

Jefferson headed off at a run. Lorelei watched him go.

"What the …?" Annie said behind her.

Lorelei turned to find the preacher's wife staring at her Converse high-tops. Oh dear. "Yes, I hope to get a new pair of shoes today," she said with a shrug.

"I've never seen any like those before."

Okay, how to dissuade her from asking more questions? "It's a … long story. I'd rather not get into it." Lorelei did her best to look uncomfortable.

Thankfully, Colin saw what was happening and swooped in. "Is there any chance I could try again while we're waiting for the materials?"

Several people groaned. Annie gritted her teeth. "Colin, really," she sighed.

"Maybe I can help," Lorelei suggested. "Mr. Cooke, can we talk alone?"

"Um, all right." Colin walked to the far side of the stage – really, just a raised platform at the front of the church. In her time this church still sat at the edge of Clear Creek's restored Old Town, looking much as it did here, and was used mostly for weddings. Lorelei had attended a wedding here once, when her friend Julie's foster big brother got married.

Tears stung her eyes when she thought of Julie. She'd gone off to college in southern California in the fall. They were supposed to get together when Julie came home for Christmas break, but …

"Are you all right?" Colin asked.

Lorelei blinked. "Sorry, just … never mind. I was thinking – maybe you should try to downplay Joseph a little."

Colin shook his head in confusion. "Downplay? What does that mean?"

Lorelei frowned. How did one translate concepts gleaned from a lifetime of movie watching to an era where they didn't even *have* movies? Well, they did have stage plays – that was something. "I think Mrs. King wants you to show less emotion, not more. You could act like Joseph is a little bit in shock, or just so busy trying to get Mary to a safe place that he doesn't have the energy to get angry or loud."

"Hm. Would that work? How will the people in the back tell I'm doing anything?"

"I think it'll still come through. I know in my time, there are some actors who are very successful *because* they tend to be a little …" *Robotic* wouldn't make sense, hmmm … "… stiff. It works for the roles they take."

"I could do that." Colin didn't sound convinced, but he

did sound willing. "Just one try, please," he called to Annie. "I really do want to get this right."

Annie looked at Lorelei, who nodded. "All right. You, Fanny and Jefferson get in position." Fanny Fig was playing Mary; Jefferson Cooke the elder was the innkeeper.

They began, and Colin delivered his lines as deadpan as he could manage. It went off without a hitch, and at the end everyone in the church applauded. "That's exactly how I want it," Annie said cheerily afterward.

Colin went back to Lorelei. "Thank you for the advice. Who knew?"

Lorelei glowed at the compliment. "In my time, there's an expression – 'sometimes less is more'."

Colin laughed. "For someone who doesn't want to be on stage, you seem to know a lot about stagecraft."

"I've watched quite a few … performances." Never mind that they were on tape or disc rather than live on stage – she wasn't going to explain that with dozens of people around who weren't in on her secret.

Just then Jeff came back with the needed supplies. Annie turned direction over to her husband while she and Lorelei got to work on the camel's neck. Lorelei was still grinning from her successful assistance with Colin. If she'd tried suggesting anything to anyone in high school drama, she'd have been laughed right out of the room. It was one of the reasons she'd never been in a school play. But here in this place, with these people, she could almost be herself. No one judged her, no one made fun of her, there were no bullies.

She didn't know why she'd rubbed people the wrong way in her own time, only that the older she got the worse it became. Especially with people like Cindy Crankshaw and her friends. Even Erwin had become more and more irritable around her during her senior year of high school. At home he hardly spoke a word to her. But maybe that's because of

Cindy's bad influence. Boys weren't rational with someone they were playing tonsil hockey with.

Soon they had the new piece sewn in place and Jeff and Owen tried on the costume again. This time there was no danger of seam splitting – not only was the neck not stretched, but the added fabric naturally folded in on itself, looking just like a collar. Even Owen found it comfier.

Though there was another problem. "Owen, that's revolting!" Jeff groaned inside the suit.

"I'm sorry. I couldn't help it – it just came out."

Annie immediately realized what was going on but couldn't stop laughing enough to respond. Lorelei sighed. "Owen, did you, um ..." What was the 1870s term? She had no idea – she'd have to guess. "... break wind?"

"Yes, he did," Jeff answered before Owen could. "It smells like something died."

Now Lorelei was having to swallow giggles; Annie was doubled over. "Come out for some fresh air, Jefferson. And Owen, no eating beans until after the play – you don't want to make your back half ill."

"That probably was it," Owen admitted as Jefferson threw off the blanket that covered the middle of the beast, stood up and began gasping for oxygen. "Ma made a big mess of beans last night, and I was hungry, so I had three helpings."

Lorelei nodded. "That'll do it."

Annie finally regained her composure. "Owen, when you get home, tell your ma what Miss Carson said – no more beans this week." She shook her head and looked at Lorelei. "It happens at least once every year. The worst was when Wilfred and Cyrus were the camel several years ago. I think Wilfred did it on purpose the whole week – and twice during the actual play."

Now Lorelei broke up laughing. "That's so mean!"

"Cyrus had been beating Wilfred pretty badly at checkers,

I think, so it was Wilfred's revenge. Those two take their checkers seriously."

"Still ..." Though in a town as small and isolated as Clear Creek was in 1879, Lorelei could imagine things like checkers might be taken very seriously. Other than work, there wasn't much to do in town. She wondered if either of them played chess.

"All right, boys, let's get you back together. And Owen, if you feel it coming on, warn Jefferson and let him escape." Annie stifled a snort.

"Yes, ma'am," Owen said in some embarrassment.

As Annie brought the Wise Men on stage and had them practice walking the camel around, Lorelei went back to her pew. She couldn't remember having this much fun in high school. In fact, she couldn't remember when she ever felt like she belonged as much as she did here. The thought was sobering. Her life in her own era sucked, that was true, but after spending time with the Cookes she was beginning to realize just how much.

JEFFERSON DID his best not to trip and pull Owen down with him. Not that he hadn't earned it by breaking wind right in his face, but it was certain to tear the costume. "A little warning?" he complained as he stumbled over a step, or something.

"I ain't supposed to talk," Owen replied.

"Well, give me some way to know." There was only a little light because it was daytime, but Jefferson was bent over and covered by the suit and a blanket. In a dimly lit church on the night of the play, he wouldn't be able to see anything.

They fell silent as one of the Wise Men continued to lead them around. Then Owen tapped twice on Jefferson's hand, which was holding Owen's belt to keep them together. "Step," he whispered.

Knowing it was coming made navigating a lot easier. The next time, Owen tapped without talking, and Jefferson had no problem. "I think we're getting this," he hissed.

"All right, places everyone," Annie called out. "Owen, you and Jefferson stand over here."

Owen walked them to wherever it was she indicated and stopped. "How are you doing back there?"

"Fine, seeing as you're not blowing leftover beans on me."

"I said I was sorry!"

"Why did you take this part, anyway?"

"From what I was told, 'cause Mrs. King wouldn't let ya do it with the girl you're courting."

"We're not courting!"

"Ya wish ya were."

Jefferson *did* wish he was courting Lorelei Carson. But he wasn't sure he was allowed to, what with her being from the future and all. The MacDonalds and his parents hadn't said they couldn't … but what if the MacDonalds came and whisked her back to the Clear Creek of two-thousand-whatever? He couldn't just leave everything and catch a ride with them – and besides, what little she'd told him of the future sounded so strange. He would be setting himself up for heartbreak when she left, and who needed that? "You aren't supposed to talk, Owen."

Owen laughed like a loon.

"What's going on?" Colin asked.

"Nothing." Jefferson gave Owen's belt a yank.

Owen stopped laughing, but not teasing. "Jefferson Cooke's sweet on somebody …" he whispered.

"Maybe. But no girl's sweet on Owen Kincaid."

That shut Owen up. Which was the idea. But that just left Jefferson thinking about Lorelei. She was amazing – smart and strong, and with a sweetness about her he couldn't explain. Did she even know it was there? He sensed she was unsure of herself, even though it seemed like she could learn anything. And she was frightened so much of the time; he could see it in her eyes. Part of that was because the MacDonalds hadn't told her she was coming here. Why hadn't they told her, or Father and Mother? What was she doing with them in the first place?

He didn't know the MacDonalds well, but he did know strange things happened whenever they came to town. His mother told him about the time they brought friends that were stranger, like years back when a big Negro man and his wife were with them. He couldn't remember their names, but would never forget how others described what they looked like – the man had to be seven feet tall, and his wife six. The last time they showed up was when Amon Cotter married Nettie Holmes and helped the new couple build their first cabin. The man was always laughing a lot and slapping people on the back. Hard. He shuddered at the memory.

"Are you okay back there?" Owen hissed.

"I'm fine."

"I didn't mean to rile you up. Well, not too much."

"It's okay. I guess you're right – I am kind of sweet on her. I think she might be sweet on me too."

"I wish some girl was sweet on me," Owen sighed. "I wish there were more girls around. It's just your sisters and cousins, and … I'd feel odd courting one of them. They're like my sisters and cousins too."

He smiled at the concern in Owen's voice. "I know what you mean. But you're not old enough to get married yet – there's plenty of time. Someone might move here with a daughter. You might go somewhere else. Maybe even send for a mail-order bride – it's worked before."

"With purt near half the town," Owen chuckled. "Or

maybe I should ask the MacDonalds to bring me one." They both laughed at that, earning another warning to hush.

When practice was finally done, Owen unbuttoned his half of the costume, ducked out of the head and let it fall. "Whew, I'm glad that's over."

Jefferson straightened, a hand to his back. "Me too." He pulled the brown sheet off him and ran a hand through his hair.

Owen gasped. "Wow, your face is red!"

Jefferson rolled his eyes. "Yours would be too if you were the back half. Want to trade?"

"No!"

Jefferson took a deep breath and smiled. "Coward."

"No, smart. Besides, I figure you'd give me *your* leftover beans if you had the chance." Owen gathered up his half-costume. "Where do I put these?"

"The office. Annie will take them to the parsonage later." Jefferson was watching Lorelei speak with Mrs. King about some other costume. He still couldn't get over how beautiful she was. So pure and untouched, like a doll in a brightly colored box. A gift he was just starting to open.

He pulled his gaze away. He shouldn't be thinking these things. The MacDonalds would come and he'd never see her again.

"Jeff," his father called.

He turned. "Yes?"

"Since we're all done, why don't you take Lorelei to the mercantile so she can get some clothes?" He joined him on the platform and gave him some money. "This should be enough. Your mother is there, she can help her pick something out."

He nodded, then thought a moment. "Could we get some tea at the hotel if there's time?"

"Hmm, I suppose that would be all right. You'll come back here straight after tea, though – no dawdling?"

Jefferson's heart began to race. "Yes, sir."

"Fine, but just in case ..." He glanced around. "Grandma!"

Jefferson's eyes went wide. *No, not Grandma Waller!* Having Adele accompany them tomorrow was one thing, but Grandma? He wouldn't be able to ask Lorelei about herself with Grandma around. Worse, she would *encourage* them to court! Everyone knew what a horrible chaperone – and romantic – she was! What was his father doing? Unless ...

"Yes, Colin?" Grandma shuffled down the aisle toward them.

"Jeff and Lorelei are going to the mercantile, then for a cup of tea at the hotel."

She smiled at Jefferson and winked. "That's nice."

"Would you like to join them?" his father asked.

"I'd be delighted! Don't worry, Colin, I'll keep a close eye on them."

Jefferson glanced Lorelei's way. She was still speaking with Annie. How were they going to handle this? They really shouldn't court, not if the MacDonalds were just going to take her away again. And they couldn't talk about the future with someone who didn't know Lorelei was from there.

But Father knew that too. If he was asking Grandma, that hopeless matchmaker, to go with them, did she already know? Hmmm ...

CHAPTER SIXTEEN

"How about this one?" Belle held up a red calico dress with tiny blue flowers on it and the bodice and collar trimmed in lace. Most importantly, it wouldn't hang off her like a flour sack. "Prairie dresses," as Lorelei had come to call them, were comfortable but shapeless. The ready-made "Sunday clothes" in the mercantile weren't like that.

"Try this green one on too," Belle continued. "I think it would look lovely on you. Aunt Irene ordered these from Portland."

Lorelei examined the green day dress made from sturdy cotton. It was pretty and it would last. "I don't want to spend all the MacDonalds' money," she told Belle.

"Nonsense, you have nothing. They left us with enough for you to get a few outfits." Belle looked at Lorelei's feet. "Might I suggest some shoes too?"

"Please." Lorelei was tired of answering questions about her anachronistic Chuck Taylors.

"You can use the storeroom." Belle handed her both frocks and went hunting for footwear.

Lorelei took them, went through the curtain, stopped and stared at the stairwell leading up to the Dunnigans' apartment. *Her* apartment. She swallowed hard. "Belle?"

"Yes?"

She peeked at her through the curtain. "Your aunt and uncle live up there?"

Belle came through and stood next to her. "Yes, it's a cozy little place. I lived with them when I first came to town, but you already knew that. What's the matter ... oh, that's right. You lived up there ... or live up there when ..."

"Yeah." Lorelei nodded slowly. "It's pretty cozy in my time too."

Belle smiled. "Very, would you like to see it?"

Lorelei took a breath. "Could I?"

"I don't see why not. I'm sure Aunt Irene and Uncle Wilfred won't mind." She disappeared into the storefront but returned within seconds. "I've got the key." She started up the stairs.

Lorelei followed, her heart in her throat. For some reason she wished Jefferson was with her, but he'd escorted Grandma to her house so she could get something.

Belle unlocked the door and pushed it open. "After you."

Lorelei fought against tears. What was she doing? She'd managed to hold herself together this past week by immersing herself in the Cookes' daily activities and telling herself she should enjoy it while she could, convincing herself her situation was a blessing, not something to be terrified of. But below that she was terrified by the surrealistic scenario.

"Lorelei?"

She met Belle's gaze, forced a smile and stepped inside.

To see the apartment now was exhilarating and sad at the same time. The furniture was placed differently. The chairs in front of the windows with the table between them in her apartment were against a wall instead. A sofa sat in front of the windows, a little coffee table in front of it. There were no pictures of Paddy and Mary Mulligan on the wall yet, nor even of the Dunnigans. But there would be in about ten years.

"This is the kitchen," Belle stepped into the hall. "There's no dining room, but they don't need one."

Lorelei followed her, took one look at the cookstove, the table and chairs, the gingham curtains in the windows, the hutch, and sighed. "It's wonderful."

Belle laughed. "I'm glad you think so."

The dry sink was in the same place as the modern one, but the table and chairs were in front of the windows, not against the wall. When she got back, she'd change it to this. She hoped she'd get back. Or was she forever stuck in this century?

"Down this way are the bedrooms."

Lorelei stared at the large bedroom. In her time half of it was her bathroom. "How do they get water?"

Belle laughed. "From the water pump out back, how else?"

"Oh, yes. I wasn't thinking." The old couple had to haul their water upstairs every day? Wow.

Belle led her to the other bedroom. "This is the room I stayed in when I lived with them. Well, in the old building. It burned down."

"It did?" she said in shock.

"Yes, this is the second mercantile. It's much bigger and better than the first one."

She nodded as she noted the armoire – the same one as in her apartment! She stared at it in awe, then looked for … yes! The washstand was there too! "This is still there."

"Really?" Belle joined her at the armoire. "Uncle Wilfred bought it for my aunt last Christmas. She loves it." She opened it and smiled. "It's so nice; I'm a little jealous. And you say it's still in here?"

"Right in this spot too. I half expect to see my own clothes hanging up here." Lorelei sighed, fighting back homesickness. As nice as it was here, part of her still longed for her own time when most people hated or ignored her. It was all what you're used to, she supposed.

"Most don't have drawers – that's why I love this one," Belle went on. "I keep hinting at Colin, but so far, nothing. Though Christmas is just a few days away. Speaking of which, we need to prepare things for the tree."

Lorelei continued to stare at the armoire. "I like Christmas trees."

"So do I. I'd better make a list of everything that needs to be done." She went to a writing desk, took out some paper and a pencil and began to jot things down.

Lorelei's eyes went wide. "Belle, could I have a piece of paper and something to write with? I need to make a note to myself. I ... forget things sometimes." True enough, but that wasn't what she wanted it for.

"Certainly." She pulled out another sheet of paper and handed it to her. "You can use the desk. I can finish my list downstairs." She stood. "There's pen and ink in the drawer. And while you're up here, you can try on the dresses."

"Thank you."

"You're welcome. Close the door when you leave, will you? Then I'll lock it."

Lorelei nodded, opened the top drawer and took out a fountain pen as Belle left. "Wow." She found the inkwell, opened it and grinned. "This is so cool." She dipped the pen in the ink, stared at the paper a moment, then began to write.

"DID YOU MAKE YOUR LIST?" Jefferson asked when she came downstairs.

She glanced at Belle and back. Belle must have told him what she was doing upstairs. "Er … yes." She patted the pocket of her dress for good measure.

Belle headed for the curtain. "I'll lock it back up while I'm thinking about it. You're not the only one that forgets things, Lorelei. The older I get, the worse I become." She disappeared behind the curtain.

Jefferson smiled. "Did you pick out a dress?"

"Oh!" she said in surprise. "I left the dresses up there – be right back!" She hurried behind the curtain and up the stairs to the back bedroom, plucked the dresses off the back of the chair and began to leave, taking one last look at the armoire as she did. With a smile, she headed back downstairs. "The red one is great, but the green is okay too."

Jefferson glanced at the mercantile doors. "We'd better hurry or we won't have time for tea with Grandma."

"You're having tea with Grandma?" Belle said in surprise.

Jefferson shrugged. "Father asked her to chaperone us."

His mother glanced between him and Lorelei. "Did he?"

"Mother, it's only tea. Besides, what else can we do with our extra time?"

"I can think of plenty that needs to be done around here." Belle eyed him a moment. "But all right, have your tea. I'll pay for those for you, Lorelei, and bring them home with us. Wait – the shoes!" She rushed over to another shelf and pulled two boxes off it. "Try these on – just have a seat over there."

"Thank you." She hurried over to Jefferson, who was standing right by the chair his mother had indicated and sat down to try the shoes. Both pairs fit fine, though she instantly missed the comfort of her Chuck Taylors – these shoes were stiff and unyielding. But they probably would protect her from horses' hooves, as Adele had hinted, and the thick leather would last a lifetime. Still wearing one pair, she repacked the other and brought it back to Belle. "Both will do."

"Lovely." Belle put the Converses in the empty box. "I'll take care of these if you like. You two had better check on Grandma. Oh, and Jeff?"

"Yes, Mother?"

"Take my wagon home when you're finished. I'll ride home with your father and the others. They're coming here after play practice to help me with a few things."

Jefferson gave his mother a nod then headed for the door without a word. Lorelei grabbed her coat and followed. She caught Belle watching them as she closed the door behind her, then hurried down the porch steps. Jefferson was walking away as if he was fleeing something. Whatever was wrong with Jeff, she wanted to know.

She hurried across the snow and mud-covered street, careful not to let the hem of her dress get wet, and finally caught up with him at Grandma's porch. "Why did you leave so fast?" she panted. "What's wrong?"

"Nothing." He turned away and knocked on the door. "Grandma said she was getting something for you."

"For me?"

He nodded but still didn't turn around. Lorelei felt like smacking him upside the head! Why was he acting so strange? Of course, she was the outsider, the one that didn't know what was what around here, but that was all the more reason for Jeff to explain things.

Grandpa – no, *Doc* – Waller let them in, and they waited at the bottom of the stairs for Grandma. Lorelei stared at Jefferson's back, his broad shoulders and long legs. He had the "V" shape girls referred to when comparing boyfriends. If he ever came to the 21st century, he could become a fashion model if he wanted.

"Here we are." Grandma came downstairs, holding a small vial. "I knew I had some left."

"What is it?" Jefferson asked.

She joined them and held it up. "Something the MacDonalds gave me. I want you to have it, child." She handed it to Lorelei.

She stared at it; her cheeks hot. She shouldn't be thinking about how nice Jefferson's jean-clad derriere looked, nor the rest of him, for that matter. Yet the more time she spent with him, the harder it was becoming to ignore her growing feelings.

"Go ahead, take it," Grandma urged.

Lorelei took the vial and studied it. It was full of green powder. "What is it?"

"Medicine. They bring it to me periodically – clears the head and makes you feel like new. I thought maybe you might need it more than I do."

"Drugs?" she said in shock. "They're giving you drugs?!" Oh great, this figures! Not only were the MacDonalds kidnappers, but dealers too?

"Drugs?" Grandma said innocently. "You mean medicine."

"Yes, of course, but ..."

"Child, why are you so upset? This is the finest herb mixture I've ever had."

Lorelei stared at the vial, then at Jefferson. "How much does she know?" she whispered.

"Child, I've known Dallan and Shona for twenty years," Grandma scolded. "They can't keep secrets from me any more than anyone else in town can. You came from the future Clear Creek. Don't ask me how, but they have their ways."

Well, that settled that, though it took Lorelei a few

seconds to get her voice working again. "And they ... knocked me out with some 'medicine' before they brought me here. That's why I reacted the way I did."

"I know, and don't think I didn't give them a good talking-to about that. They could've just asked you. But you're here now, and we're glad to have you. That stuff is safe, I promise."

Lorelei smiled. Clearly Grandma knew what she was about. "I'm sorry if I upset you."

"Well, we'll call it a misunderstanding. The MacDonalds could've handled it better, I think. But they've never given us a reason to distrust them before, and I'm not about to start now." She nodded at the vial in her hand. "That's all I have. If you get a headache, feel dizzy, any of that, just mix a teaspoonful in a glass of water and drink it down. You'll sleep better too."

Lorelei stared at the old woman. If Shona had given it to her, Grandma must need it a lot more than her. "No, I can't. You keep it."

"I insist."

She put the vial into Grandma's hands. "No. She gave it to you for a reason. I'm fine – I've been fine for days."

Grandma smiled at her. "Well if you're sure." She nodded, turned and went back upstairs.

Jefferson sighed in relief. "Grandma can be stubborn as a mule. What you did was kind. I know she needs whatever that stuff is – Mrs. MacDonald brings her some once a year."

Lorelei gaped at him in disbelief. "That little vial lasts her all year?"

"It must. Everyone knows the MacDonalds bring herbs and medicines here for Doc Drake and Doc Waller to use. But they make a special batch for Grandma."

Lorelei stayed quiet as Grandma came down the stairs again and they left the house. *Who were the MacDonalds?* Time travelers, landowners, dealers in herbal medicine ... where (and when) did they come from? And what were they trying to do?

She decided not to think about it – it just made her feel overwhelmed and confused. She didn't want to fall into a state where she couldn't think straight – she'd had enough of that the first few days here. She had to keep her head, and that meant doing normal everyday things like the dishes, cooking, bringing in wood and having tea with a man she'd become far too attracted to and an old lady who got her prescriptions from time travelers ... she put a hand to her head. That part wasn't going to help!

"Are you okay?" Jefferson asked as they reached the hotel.

She shrugged helplessly. "Yes and no."

He opened the door for Grandma, let her go inside then stopped Lorelei before she could follow. "You can talk to me, Lorelei. You can trust me – I'm here for you."

Her heart melted at the gentleness of his voice, the concern in his eyes. He was being as sincere as anyone could be. She wanted to throw her arms around him and hang on until she woke up and discovered it was all a dream. But her dream was looking into her eyes, imploring her to say something. "Thank you, Jeff."

He stepped closer. They were almost touching. "Remember what Doc Drake said?"

She shook her head, her gaze fusing with his.

He leaned toward her, so close she could feel the brush of his breath on her cold cheeks. "Don't be afraid, Lorelei. Please don't be afraid."

Her jaw trembled and she swallowed hard. "Oh, Jeff ... that's easier said than done."

CHAPTER SEVENTEEN

Jefferson wanted to take Lorelei in his arms and hold her. She had that look in her eyes again, the frightened one that tore his heart out. She did her best to keep it hidden, looking away when she thought no one would notice. Sometimes she wiped her eyes or nose. She had a funny way of twisting a strand of her hair with her fingers when she was nervous, and he caught her more than once staring at the prairie from the window at the end of the hall. She was so … lost.

But he had no idea how to help her. What do you do for a girl who was born a century after you? The MacDonalds were responsible for her sadness, her fear, everything she tried to hide from everyone. But he knew, even if the rest of his family didn't. He knew because when she was frightened, he felt it as if it were his own. But he had nothing to be afraid of – he had his family, his health. There was nothing out of the ordinary to cause him or anyone else alarm … except her.

"Let's sit at that table in the corner," Grandma said. "I think we'll need some privacy."

They walked over and Jefferson pulled a chair out for

Grandma, got her seated, then did the same for Lorelei. He smiled when he noticed she'd waited for him this time. He'd tried to do it at home a few times, but she always sat before he had a chance.

"Thank you," she said softly as she scooted her chair closer to the table.

"You're welcome." He sat himself. Grandma had picked a smaller table that only seated four, where most in the dining room could hold six to eight. Very cozy.

"Well, hello!" Sally said cheerfully as she approached their table. "Here for tea?"

"We sure are," Grandma said. "Got any pie this afternoon?"

"Yes, apple. And the usual other goodies." She turned to Jefferson and Lorelei. "How about you? Would you like anything in particular to go with your tea?"

"Do you have chocolate cake?" Jefferson asked.

"Sure do!" Sally made everyone smile.

Jefferson smiled too. "What else do you have?"

"Oh, honey, we got cake and pie and cookies and scones. Take your pick or have a little of this and that."

Lorelei's smile widened. "Anything chocolate."

"One slice of apple pie and two of chocolate cake. Be right back with those!" She hurried back to the kitchen.

"She'll bring out a tea cart with more goodies than we want," Grandma said. "She always does."

Lorelei smiled again, and Jefferson's heart swelled. How could such a simple thing as a smile entrance him so? He did his best not to let his eyes roam over her, but she was so beautiful. She'd kept her hair in two thick braids tied with red velvet ribbon since her arrival, and he wondered how it would look loose and flowing down her back. Her eyes were the prettiest he'd ever seen, and he liked the way they slanted slightly upwards. High cheekbones, a lovely mouth.

And best of all, her voice. Did she have any idea that every time she spoke his limbs grew weak? It first happened a couple of days ago, and since with increasing frequency. It was all he could do to get through play practice.

What in the Sam Hill was wrong with him? Was he … falling in love? But how did one know if they were? Besides, falling in love was all about a man's heart, not his body. Or maybe it was all connected. Even his heart felt funny when she was around. Like it wanted *out*. As if given the choice, it would leave him and go to her, merging, becoming one …

"Jefferson!"

He yelped and jumped in his chair. "What?!"

Grandma frowned. "I said, tell your father when you see him that Doc and I accepted Belle's invitation to join you on New Year's. You'll probably see him before she does. I'll bring a pie."

"Oh, uh, yeah," he said, then blew out a quick breath and glanced at Lorelei. What was she doing to him?!

Sally came back into the dining room, pushing a tea cart. "Here we are!" She began to lay everything out on the table: cups, saucers, plates, a teapot and a tray filled with slices of cake and pie, scones and some cookies. "You let me know if you need anything else." She turned and went to greet an older couple just coming into the dining room.

"Well, if it isn't Cutty and Imogene." Grandma waved them over. "Jefferson, fetch another chair. Lorelei should meet them."

"More relatives," Jefferson explained. Dadgum, would he ever get a chance to just talk to her one-on-one?

"Oh." Lorelei studied the couple as they approached. Jefferson could tell her smile was forced – he didn't "feel" it as he had earlier. Maybe she was as frustrated as he was.

"Grandma!" The old man gave her a hug, then turned to Lorelei. "And who is this?"

"This is Colin and Belle's house guest, Miss Lorelei Carson," Grandma said. "Lorelei, this is Cutty and Imogene Holmes. They live several hours ride out of town. Needless to say, we don't see them as often as when Imogene lived out at the Triple-C years back and Cutty lived at the men's camp. Once they got hitched, that was the end of that."

Lorelei smiled again. "It's a pleasure to meet you."

Jefferson knew he should look at the Holmeses, but his eyes were glued to Lorelei. He sensed it was all she could do to hold herself together. And it was probably his fault for dragging her here. She needed help, lots of help – he knew it with every fiber of his being and had known it almost since she arrived – almost as if he could read her thoughts. But he didn't know *how* to help, and that made being near her downright unbearable.

Cutty and Imogene sat and began to visit with Grandma. The extra chair at the table meant Jefferson had to scoot closer to Lorelei. He poured her a cup of tea, reached for the sugar bowl, spooned some into her cup and gave it a stir without even thinking.

"My my," Imogene said. "I dare say I can't get Cutty to give me such service."

"Pah!" Cutty scoffed. "I do plenty."

"True, but not with *that* look in your eye."

Lorelei blushed as Jefferson's ears turned to flame. Caught! "I was only being polite," he insisted.

"Is that so?" Grandma grinned at Lorelei. "As an aside, did you know that Cutty and Imogene write books together?" She gave Jefferson a pointed look. "They're considering writing a romance."

Lorelei sank lower in her chair.

Cutty snorted as his eyes darted between them. "Yep, and I'm sure it'll scandalize the town."

"Cutty!" Imogene smacked him in the chest. "Don't say such things."

"Well, either the book will or young Jeff here." Cutty winked at Lorelei.

Jefferson made sure to look at the table. His distant cousins were older, and he usually enjoyed their company, but oh, not right now. He didn't want Lorelei to think he was sweet on her and run away.

But of course, he *was* sweet on her, definitely. And if these three could see it, not to mention Owen, who else had? He'd just figured it out, but this wasn't like anything he knew of – he didn't have any experience with women.

Thankfully their three elderly chaperones started to talk about the Christmas play and Uncle Harrison's trip to Washington Territory, basically ignoring he and Lorelei. "They're English?" Lorelei whispered.

"Yes, very."

"I like their accents. I've always liked accents."

He smiled – did she like his too? His was very slight, but it was there. "Imogene is a distant cousin. And Cutty's real name is Thackary – my brother was named after him."

She smiled again, and his heart warmed. How did that happen? He swallowed hard. "He was badly burned years ago. Imogene helped nurse him back to health, they fell in love and the rest is history."

Her eyes filled with admiration. "That's awesome."

He leaned as close as he dared. "You always have such an interesting choice of words."

She blushed. "Thank you. I guess the language changes a little over time."

"I guess so." He then asked in a low voice, "Where did you go to school?"

"Clear Creek High School," she whispered. "A public school – free to attend. Go Cowboys!" She stopped and thought before adding, "Schools in my time have mascots … um, symbols that represent the school, usually animals or something. But Clear Creek High's is a cowboy."

"That kind of makes sense," he mused. "Since our ranch is still around, and you said our family is still pretty important …"

Then she looked at him, their eyes locked, and for a moment he felt … no, it went beyond feeling. It was more like he *heard* her say something, without her opening her mouth. It was unclear, distorted, like the time he yelled at Sam and Thackary when they were underwater in the swimming hole. They yelled back but none of them could understand more than a word or two of what the other was saying. What he could make out was "I wish …" Wish what, though?

"Do you ever think of leaving Clear Creek?" she asked softly. "Seeing other places?"

He gazed more deeply into her eyes, surprised no one had scolded him yet. But Grandma was busy telling Imogene and Cutty about his father's failed attempts at livening up the part of Joseph in the play. "I'd like to. Someday."

"When?"

His eyebrows rose at the question. "I don't know. I'm not even sure I'd know where to go."

She closed her eyes momentarily, breaking the contact, and turned toward Grandma, taking a sip of tea as if it could wash away the fear he sensed rising in her again. When would it stop? What caused it? And more importantly, why could he feel it? Maybe he was hearing his own thoughts and not hers. Seriously, how could he hear hers? That was impossible. But then, so was traveling to the past, yet here she was.

And he found he believed her about that, believed her implicitly. There was no question in his mind that she was exactly what she said she was: a girl from the 21st century stranded in the 19th. It went beyond her odd use of the language and strange shoes and her recognition of Mr. Mulligan, went beyond any physical evidence. He knew it like he knew to breathe – too deep in his heart and mind to even find its roots.

He'd mostly wanted to finagle information from Lorelei, what her time was like and how people lived and had they found men on the Moon yet or not. But the longer he sat next to her, the more questions he had about what was happening to *him* when she was near. Did she feel it too? Who could he talk to about this? Did he dare even try? Land sakes, people would think he'd gone loco or something.

So he continued to sit and pretend none of this was happening, but there was no denying it. He kept it to himself, but was that the right thing to do? Should he discuss it with Lorelei, or would it frighten her? She seemed upset after he told her not to be afraid, that he was there for her. But he felt so strongly about it that if he didn't say anything, he worried his heart would burst.

But for now, he could watch and learn. Maybe he'd find an answer on his own. At least no one would think he'd gone 'round the bend, including Lorelei. But how was he going to stop this, whatever it was, from growing? He hadn't slept well recently and wasn't touching Rosie's delicious cake now – he had no appetite. He'd heard when a man falls in love, he has a hard time eating and sleeping – was that the reason?

Jefferson shoved his plate away, picked up his teacup and took a sip, while watching Lorelei out the corner of his eye. He'd figure this out eventually. He just hoped for his sake it was sooner than later.

LORELEI COULDN'T STOP her heart from pounding. Grandma was enjoying her visit with the Holmeses. The only thing she could think to say at the time was how she liked listening to their accents. What she'd really been thinking was how she liked listening to Jeff, but she couldn't tell him that.

Ever since he stopped her at the doors of the hotel and told her not to be afraid, her heart was doing all sorts of weird things. Something happened in that moment, but what? How could there be a connection like this between them, when she was from another century?

At least he seemed to believe her – most people wouldn't. H.G. Wells' *The Time Machine* wouldn't be published for another sixteen years – she knew that from the book report she wrote on it in Mr. Frank's English Lit class. She was still annoyed he gave her a B instead of the A she thought she deserved. But she didn't think anyone had ever addressed time travel before then ... and here she was, living it. Better no one else know, lest she be locked up as a lunatic. That six people did already seemed like too many for comfort.

But that didn't distress her right now as much as her reactions to Jeff. She tried to make sense of the way her mind and heart seemed to be separating, as if part of her wanted to stay here, in 1879, with him. Jeff helped. He calmed her. He made her feel ... cherished, as if she was the only person in the world he cared about. The way he looked at her, his closeness ... and when he told her not to be afraid, she thought she might die of happiness. Something in her made her want to never leave him.

But would she be willing to get stuck in this place forever? Never to see her own world again?

She stole little glances of Jefferson as he watched Grandma speak with his other relations. She'd never had a boy speak to her the way he did. She never wanted one to, not really. When they had, it was usually some kind of prank Cindy or Heather had set up. But the mean girls from school weren't here. No one she knew was here to tell these people what a loser they thought she was.

She kept sipping her tea, just to give herself something to do. What if she did stay? What if she never went back?

Her eyes drifted to Jefferson, who was quietly listening to his elders' conversation. He'd hardly touched his cake. He must not have been as hungry as he thought. She'd devoured hers – chocolate always helped when she was stressed. And right now, she was as stressed as they came.

What was she doing, thinking of staying? Was she crazy? How could she survive in a place like this? They didn't call it the Wild West for nothing. And having to live with no internet, no running water, no flush toilets? She knew from history class that Clear Creek didn't get *electricity* until around 1909 – was she willing to go the next thirty years without it?

But what if she had help? What if the Cookes and Jefferson were willing to teach her everything she needed to survive? They'd already started, and she'd been learning quickly. They didn't think she was loony – or at least didn't let on. Maybe she could even help them by letting them know about coming events. Her knowledge of the 1880s and 1890s was spotty at best, but she knew more than they did.

And Clear Creek had its share of weirdness already that people seemed to tolerate – Lorcan Brody and his extra sense, for example. Or the way they treated Doc Drake, as if he had special healing powers. Maybe she could be just another of the town's lovable freaks. It certainly beat being an *unloved* freak in her own time. And few people in this time period believed in witches, or not enough to burn them at the stake.

But even if she wanted to stay, that didn't factor in the MacDonalds. What did they plan on doing with her when they returned, if they returned at all? She still didn't know why they took her in the first place. Everyone here trusted them, true, but lots of people trusted Hitler at one time. That wasn't enough.

She swallowed hard. Should she stay? Should she leave? Could she leave? Where would she go? The questions kept coming harder and faster until she thought she might scream.

That's when Jefferson reached over, took her hand from her lap, looked her in the eye and whispered, "Lorelei, stop. Whatever it is, just stop."

CHAPTER EIGHTEEN

Lorelei froze. How did he know?! She glanced at Grandma and her friends, now talking about the Christmas play.

Jefferson reached for a scone, drawing her attention. He took a generous bite as if forcing himself to eat it. Maybe he was trying to act as if nothing had just happened. But something had. If she only knew what. She sometimes did wear her heart on her sleeve – could he see how her thinking was starting to overwhelm her and make her panic? Yes, that had to be it.

But what if he really did know?

She made herself finish her cake, then poured herself another cup of tea.

"I'll take a refill," Grandma shoved her cup and saucer toward her.

Lorelei poured her tea with a smile then looked at Imogene and Cutty. The latter was studying her intently. Did he know something? Was she an open book to everyone here? If she was, would they accept what she was, or lock her up and melt down the key?

"I'll have some more, too," Cutty said, his eyes still on her.

She nodded as he held out his cup and saucer for her. She glanced at Jefferson, who was staring at Cutty much the same way Cutty was staring at her. It was beginning to feel a little like a standoff in … well, an old Western. Showdown at the Van Cleet Hotel.

She finished pouring and set the teapot down. "Mrs. Holmes, did you want any?" The question broke the tension and Cutty smiled at his wife.

"Yes, please," the old woman said. "How was the cake?"

"Fine." Lorelei had barely tasted it.

"Jefferson, didn't you like yours?" Imogene asked next.

He looked at his half-eaten cake. "I wanted a scone too. I can take this home if I don't finish it."

"Sally always outdoes herself at teatime," Grandma said. "It's amazing we don't all look like pot-bellied stoves."

Jefferson smiled, his shoulders shaking with silent laughter. It made Lorelei feel better.

The tension gone, she did her best to relax and enjoy the rest of their tea.Again, she reminded herself she should enjoy this strange adventure while she could. There was no way to escape it, but she could still have fun.

When the tea was over, Jefferson once again did the gentlemanly thing and went behind her chair to help her up. He did the same for Grandma. She would miss these people's good manners when she went home. *If* she went home. That thought gave her an icy feeling in her stomach and her hand automatically went to it.

Jefferson was at her side in an instant. "Are you all right?"

NO! I am NOT all right, she wanted to scream. *I'm from the future. I was kidnapped and brought here and I. Don't. Know. Why!* She licked her lips then smiled at him, ready to say, "I'm fine."

But he spoke first. "You don't have to shout," he whispered.

She blinked at him. "What? I didn't say anything."

He leaned toward her and whispered more quietly, "You said no, you weren't all right, you're from the future and were kidnapped and brought here and you don't know why. You just about screamed it."

"But ... I didn't say a word ..." No, no, she would *not* faint!

"Then how did I hear you?"

She stared at him, wide-eyed. "I don't know." She closed her eyes. "Now I really don't feel good."

He stared at her intently, then glanced at Grandma. "I think I'd better get her home. She's a little tired."

Lorelei knew when to play along. "I guess I didn't get enough sleep last night," she said with a chuckle.

"You sure you don't need anything?" Grandma reached into her pocket for her special medicine.

Lorelei smiled and waved her off. "No, I'll be all right. I just need some rest."

They said goodbye to Cutty and Imogene who were staying at the hotel for the night, then took Grandma home. By the time that was done it was time to return to the ranch, and Lorelei was glad for it. Now she really *was* feeling tired.

"Can we talk?"

That was the last thing she wanted Jefferson to say. She shut her eyes tight, as if that would make everything go away. Of course it didn't. Of course she was stressed – she was fourteen decades away from home and had been given no chance to prepare for it, she was having to keep that huge secret from almost everyone around her, the boy she found she liked was suddenly able to read her mind (!), and she never knew when her abductors would whip back in, tear her away from the nice boy and his nice family and drop her back into her depressing life.

She didn't say that. No need to make Jefferson suffer even more for her troubles. Instead she said, "Um, sure."

He nodded, breathed – had he been holding it? – and said, "I'm sorry you're going through all this."

She could've melted into his arms in that instant and sobbed like a colicky baby. She wanted to. But not in the middle of Clear Creek That Was. "How do … how did you know what I was thinking back at the hotel?"

Jefferson shook his head. "I don't know. I just … did."

"What's happening to us?" Lorelei shivered, but not from cold. Were they an "us"? Could they be?

Jefferson was quiet until after they reached the wagon, helped her onto the seat, got up himself and began driving out of town. The rest of his family had taken another wagon home. "I don't know that either."

Lorelei nodded sadly. "Boy, when the MacDonalds get back here, I have some questions for them!"

To her surprise, Jeff laughed. "I think we all do. I know Father wants to sit them down and ask a few."

Now she laughed. It felt good. Her situation was bizarre, but at least she wasn't alone. She had Colin and Belle Cooke, and Adele, and Grandma and Doc Drake. And most of all Jeff, who she'd totally fall for if she'd met him in her own time. Who she was falling for despite meeting him here. Yeah, she could admit that to herself. "I guess tea at the hotel didn't go the way you hoped."

"It sure didn't. I was figuring I'd be asking you about what life was like in 2019 and who'd be elected president next year."

"Honestly, I'm not sure who's president now."

"Rutherford B. Hayes –"

"Yes – 'Old 8-and-7,' right?"

He laughed again. "That's him."

"I remembered that from U.S. History class in school."

Okay, so after Hayes came … hmmm, 1880, 1880 … "James Garfield is the next president. From Ohio. But he got shot and didn't last long. *Gets* shot. You know what I mean."

"Oh my. Why did someone shoot him?"

She racked her brain. "I think they'd been passed over for a political appointment. His vice president took over – Chester Alan Arthur, and the only thing I remember about him is that he had these big muttonchop sideburns." She drew her fingertips across her cheeks to illustrate.

"Huh. I guess he isn't much of a president?"

"No. All the presidents between Lincoln and …" He wouldn't know Teddy Roosevelt – not for another twenty years. "… and the end of the century are just so-so. Sorry."

"Aw, that's too bad. Are they any better in your time?"

Lorelei wasn't sure how to respond. How would he react to a president who was black? Or one who was a real estate developer? Or one who'd gotten caught with a woman under his desk? She finally settled on, "Some are, some aren't. It's kind of complicated."

When they reached the ranch, Jefferson whispered, "Meet me in the barn."

Her heart began to race. "Okay …"

"If anyone asks where you're going, tell them you're fetching some wood. I'll bring some in too. It's part of evening chores anyway."

She nodded. She'd brought in wood before supper before. Sometimes you had to chop some, which meant it took longer. She shivered at the thought of being alone with him, even though they'd been alone the entire ride back to the ranch. Belle must trust her son to have let them ride home together alone. Still, what would the rest of the family think? No wonder chaperones were such a big deal in these times – you never knew what could happen.

Jefferson helped her down from the wagon. His hands

were so warm that when he removed them from her waist, she could still feel them. It was an odd sensation, but she liked it. Something was happening between them, and though she didn't know how, she was getting a good idea of what. If she was right, it would only make it worse when the MacDonalds came back for her.

They were coming back for her, right? Unfortunately, the only way to double-check was to ask them, and they weren't around to ask.

As soon as Jeff left for the barn, she hesitated. Things were getting even weirder, and that was saying something. She headed for the door, stopped, saw no one around. "I'd better get some wood for supper," she said to help.

"I can help," Thackary said, coming around the corner of the house.

"No, I'm fine. Besides, I think Jefferson went to chop some. Between the two of us we'll get the evening wood in."

"Okay," Thackary said, sounding disappointed. He trudged up the stairs and went inside.

She breathed a sigh of relief and went out to the barnyard. Jefferson was already chopping wood in the woodshed by the barn. He must have figured it looked better – anyone could see them there but wouldn't be able to hear them.

"What do you want, Jeff?" Using his nickname helped calm her raw nerves. The thought that he might tell her something she didn't want to hear loomed over her. Whatever he had to say, she hoped she could take it.

He studied her face before his eyes flicked over the rest of her. "Who are you?"

Her heart sank. "You know who I am. Lorelei Carson."

"No, who are you really? Where did you come from? Why are you here? Why …" He stopped and looked away. "Why am I able to … to know when you're scared?"

She sighed. "I'm not lying to you, Jeff. I really am from the

21st century, from Clear Creek then. As to why I'm here or how you can read my mind or my heart or … I really don't know. No one's told me."

"I know. But it's so hard to believe. Especially when …" He looked at her again, eyes full of pain, and waved his hand between them. "It's like I've gone plumb loco! But everyone acts like I'm normal, I'm fine – it's like only I know I've gone 'round the bend … and I'm not sure what to do about it."

She sighed. "You and me both. I don't know what it all means. I am sorry for scaring you … for being scared and making you sca …" She put her face in her hands. "The English language wasn't made for messes like this."

"There's another language that is?"

"I don't know. Ask the MacDonalds."

He groaned and set down the hatchet he was holding. "It keeps coming back to them, doesn't it?"

She nodded, lifting her face out of her hands. "They made the mess. Only they can fix it."

Now he looked hurt. "Is that what's happening between us? A mess?"

She shook her head. "Bad choice of words. Sorry."

Jeff came to stand in front of her. "Lorelei, this has been going on for days. I haven't said a word to anyone except you. I thought it was just me, but this afternoon at tea I thought I'd have to leave the hotel, it was so strong."

And here she thought she was the one in the hot seat. Now *he* was telling *her* the weird stuff no one would believe. She went to the chopping block and sat. "I don't understand this at all."

"Neither do I. That's why I wanted to talk to you. To see if … you feel it too."

"Feel what?"

"Feel *me*."

She stared at him hard, as if that would help. But it did

remind her of the calming effect he had on her with his voice, the tender looks he gave her, his presence. He touched her heart in ways no one ever had. "Now that you mention it … yeah. Though it's not the same."

He raised one eyebrow. "What do you mean?"

"I mean … I feel … I think I feel something from you or that is you or – see what I mean about language? – but … yeah. Only I don't feel your fear. I feel your peace, your … faith? Your … it's like you're telling me everything will work out all right."

That lifted his other eyebrow. "I am? Because I'm scared out of my wits." He chuckled nervously.

"But I'd never guess that. When I'm around you, when you're talking to me or looking at me, it's like, it's like I'm being wrapped in a blanket. I feel … protected, safe, no matter how stark raving terrified I feel otherwise. I can't explain it, Jeff – it just happens … is it okay to call you Jeff?"

"Yes. I like it." He paused, swallowed, as if steeling his nerve. "I like you."

"I like you too." But she couldn't miss the despair in her own voice. "I don't know what to do about it, though."

He looked as sad as she felt. "Yeah."

She sat and he stood in silence for a minute, thinking their own thoughts. Finally, she stood, knowing she had to do something. The wheelbarrow sitting to the side gave her an excuse. "I'll load the wood, you chop it?"

He smiled, as if she were giving him a break too. "Good idea." She went to the wheelbarrow while he came over and took up his hatchet again.

As she tossed wood into the barrow, she knew she'd made the right move. She was numb all of a sudden. Too much had happened in too short a time, and she – *they* – had too few answers for it. Some light physical labor was just the tonic to take their minds off it. Though not entirely – nothing could do that.

The wheelbarrow was halffull, and she was gathering more pieces when he stopped her with a hand on her arm. "Huh?"

"Don't tell anyone. It was hard enough to tell you."

"You know I can keep a secret." She smiled.

He smiled back. "Yeah."

"Though ... maybe we should tell your parents. They're in on it too, and ... well, they're your parents."

He nodded judiciously. "I'll have to think about it." He half-turned to go back to the chopping block, then stopped and turned back. "I want us to be friends."

Her heart sank to her toes. The "friendzone" was the kiss of death in her world. It meant someone wanted you around but didn't want you for anything more. "*Just* friends?"

Apparently not, as he blushed almost purple. "Well, I mean ... I ... not ... awww ..."

She covered her mouth to keep from laughing. "Sorry, I didn't mean to put you on the spot ... er, to embarrass you. But ... yes, I would like us to be friends. And maybe ... if ..." Drat, now she was blushing.

"Yeah, maybe. If."

Before she knew it, her arms were around his waist and she was burying her head in his chest. "I'm sorry," she sobbed. "I know I shouldn't be doing this, but if I don't ..." Then she stopped hearing, stopped seeing, as something permeated every fiber of her being. A glorious peace filled her, banishing all fear and trepidation. She needed this. She needed him.

Why? her mind asked. *Who cares?* her heart replied.

"It's all right, Lorelei, everything's going to be all right," he said against her hair. "You don't have to be afraid."

They shouldn't be embracing like this. Even she was

familiar with the general decorum of the period. But she couldn't let go if she wanted to.

He held her tighter and something deep within her responded, as if it was diving into him. Like a dam breaking, she began blubbering like a baby in his arms.

"Shhh, it's okay," Jeff whispered. "You're okay. I'm here."

Lorelei's body shook with racking sobs as everything she'd kept hidden from the world poured out of her. She was helpless to stop it. And it didn't matter. Only being with Jeff did.

JEFFERSON FELT his first tears fall. How could they not when the woman in his arms wept so desperately? He held Lorelei as tight as he could without hurting her, and she cried as if he were squeezing poison from a deep wound. It had to be done. He didn't know how he knew that, but he just did. It was instinct – he was doing something he'd always known how to do, but never knew he knew.

Was it strange? Yes, but what had happened since she arrived that wasn't?

Who was she, this beautiful young woman who'd been dropped into his life from another time? Why did his heart demand he do something to protect her, keep her safe from the fear that threatened to tear her apart? Were they both going loco? He didn't know. Right now, he didn't care. He felt a peace he'd never known while holding her. Was she giving it to him? Was it something new? Would there ever be an end to the questions?

"Jefferson?"

He looked up, his cheek resting on top of her head, and saw his father by the woodshed, a lantern in his hand. So another question: how much trouble was he in?

"Jefferson, what's going on?"

Jeff squinted against the light, tried to let go … and couldn't. "She's scared." He was more than a little nervous himself.

His father watched them a moment. "Perhaps we should send Major for the doctor."

Lorelei, still crying, managed to reply. "I don't think there's much he can do …" She wept some more.

Jeff sensed she'd emptied herself of the worst of it but didn't want whatever was left to take hold of her again. Again, he didn't know how he knew; it was just there, like his own heartbeat.

Father fidgeted, like he felt there was something he should be doing but had no idea what. Which made two of them. "Bring her into the house," he finally said.

"I will." But he couldn't move, only hold her tighter. The thought of pulling away made his blood turn to acid. What was this? He tucked a finger under Lorelei's chin and brought her face up to look at him. "I'm taking you into the house now, okay?"

She sniffed back tears, reached a hand between them and wiped her nose on her sleeve. "Okay," she whimpered.

His father stood patiently as, one arm still around her, he held her hand with the other and steered her toward the house. He didn't know what to tell his parents. They would ask why she was crying, and he didn't want Lorelei to have to explain it. He didn't want to try either.

His father led the way, the lantern lighting a path through the snow. Maybe she needed sleep – she'd said she was tired. Maybe everything had caught up to her.

"My goodness, what happened?" Belle asked as they brought Lorelei into the kitchen.

"It's all right, Mother," Jeff said quickly, hoping his own

tears had dried enough not to be noticeable. "Today was a bit much for her." That was at least part of the truth.

"I'm going to send for Doc Drake," his father said again and headed for the door.

"No!" Jefferson and Lorelei said in unison. He looked at her as his throat grew thick. Whatever was connecting them tightened another notch – and it hurt.

Father held up his hand. "He knows … where she's from. I'm thinking we might want to talk this out, since we're the only people beside the MacDonalds who know."

"And Adele," Lorelei managed. "But I really just want to rest."

His parents exchanged a look. "He has a point, Lorelei," Mother said. "Maybe there are things we need to talk about."

Jeff nodded. It made good sense. But he wasn't going to press her, not in the shape she was in. "Lorelei, if you want to talk, we're here. And we can get the doc too."

She glanced at Jefferson, then Father, and swallowed hard. "Thank you, but I just want to go upstairs. I'd like to be alone right now if that's okay."

"Of course," Belle said gently. "I'll bring you up a supper tray."

Lorelei smiled weakly. "Thank you."

Jeff began to guide her out of the kitchen when Father stopped. "Belle, why don't you take her upstairs, see if there's anything else she needs?"

"Good idea," Mother said as she pulled Lorelei out of his hold.

Jefferson almost doubled over at the separation. It hurt all over, like getting run over by a wagon. Whatever this was and however it was happening, it couldn't be ignored. This wasn't normal, and no one in Clear Creek would understand.

Well … maybe not no one.

"Jefferson. A word, if you please?"

Jeff sighed. He knew he'd have to face his father and his questions, and he wasn't sure he had answers. But maybe a talk would help. And as soon as he had the chance, he'd ride to town and speak with Doc Drake or Grandma Waller. The doc knew miracles, and Grandma knew the MacDonalds – maybe one of them could explain all this.

CHAPTER NINETEEN

"Adele and I could prepare you a hot bath," Belle offered when they entered the bedroom.

"Yes, that would be nice." Lorelei sat on Adele's bed. "I'm sorry I fell apart."

Belle sat next to her. "I understand." She took her hand and held it. "I know the circumstances are strange. I don't claim to understand them myself. We've known the MacDonalds for many years and have always found them to be trustworthy, but this ..." She shrugged.

Lorelei frowned. She was spent, yet at the same time felt so much better, like a huge weight had been lifted off her inside and out. Confession was supposed to be good for the soul, but it was more than that and she knew it. "I don't want to think about that now." She looked at Belle. "Please?"

Belle put her arm around her. "Just know this. When Dallan and Shona left you with us and told us to care for you, that, to us, means in every sense of the word. You can talk to me if you wish."

The woman's kindness was like a healing balm on a bad wound. Only this particular wound had somehow just been cleansed by Jefferson and stitched up besides. "Thank you. But I'm too tired to talk right now. Sorry."

"Don't be. I know how it feels to have a good cry. And from the looks of you, you just had a great one."

Lorelei smiled. "I did."

"I hope my son handled himself."

Lorelei met Belle's gaze. "He was a perfect gentleman."

Belle smiled. "I'm sure he was. What I meant was that Jefferson, like most men, can't stand to see women cry. They don't know what to do."

Lorelei thought of Jeff's tight embrace, his voice, his words, the thing that reached down deep within her and extracted her deepest fears … "He gave me what I needed at the time. It helped."

"I'm glad to hear it." She gave her a hug and got up. "I'll have Adele and Parthena start heating the water for your bath."

"Belle?" Lorelei's heart warmed at the tender look on the woman's face. "Thank you."

Belle smiled at her. "You're welcome." She turned and left.

Lorelei took a deep breath and lay on the bed. It was as if everything within her had been poured out during her cry until there was nothing left but a blissful numbness. But what was now empty, she sensed, would need to be filled. With what, she had no idea. She couldn't think – she was too tired, the result of more than just a good cry. It had been a cleansing.

"Jeff …" she said without thinking. She looked at the door. He'd rescued her in that woodshed, but how? And from what? She just knew it was bad and … old. Something that had been lurking in the deepest recesses of her heart, something bitter. But after years of not liking the person she looked at in the mirror every day, was it any wonder? Now her heart felt empty, ready to be filled with … what?

She lay there and stared at the ceiling until she realized she wasn't afraid anymore. The fear was really gone. She smiled just as something deep inside "clicked," fell into alignment. "Jeff?" She didn't know why she spoke his name again. It just happened.

Lorelei ...

She sat up, eyes the size of platters. She'd heard him, she knew it, but not with her ears. She swallowed hard. "What the heck?" She sat very still, seeing if she'd hear her name again.

Nothing. She breathed a sigh of relief and fell upon the bed. How could she hear Jeff call her name ... not in her head but in her heart?

Lorelei lay there and puzzled over it until she couldn't keep her eyes open any longer and drifted into a dreamless sleep.

The next morning at breakfast it was all she could do not to stare at Jeff across the table. They'd shared something – he'd held her, comforted her, and was there for her in ways she couldn't explain. She still had no explanation for whatever happened between them in the moments she stood sobbing into his chest. She wanted to ask him about it but couldn't with the entire family sitting at the table. She'd have to wait for an opportunity with just him, or at least without the younger Cookes around.

But as soon as breakfast was done, he'd be off to do his chores and she'd have to help with hers. That was one thing about the 1870s she'd quickly grasped: the work was *never* done.

She ate her eggs, potatoes and bacon and tried not to look at him, but it was hard. Now that she'd been held by him and had cried her heart out in his arms, there was no going back to the way things were before, no "just friends." Even her attraction to him had changed – now he was just there. In fact, he was *everywhere,* as if they were now two parts of the same person. Weird.

"I want you girls to hurry to get everything done before play practice," Belle said as she began to clear away the dishes. "We have only two more and I'd like to get there early to check on everyone's costumes."

Lorelei's eyebrows rose. "Only two?"

"Yes, Christmas Eve is just three days away."

She stared at Jeff, who smiled reassuringly, and relaxed in waves. "Oh. I didn't realize." Her eyes locked with his and her chest swelled. It was as if she'd known him forever. She didn't care if she was blushing – she couldn't take her eyes from his. Something was different about him now …

"Jefferson, your father would like you to help him in the mercantile today," Belle announced.

He flinched in his chair. "What?"

"Yes, he needs to do inventory. Logan and the hands can handle things around here."

"But who's going to drive you and the others to town?"

"Logan is perfectly capable," his mother replied. "So am I, for that matter."

Jeff gave Lorelei an apologetic look. *I'm sorry I won't be here for you today.*

She returned the look. *It's all right, I'll get along.*

He smiled and nodded in acknowledgement. He knew. Wow, they'd just done that. He *could* read her mind – and now she could read his. Whatever happened last night was powerful stuff. Did this happen to everybody, only nobody talked about it? Or was this something unique between them? Either way, it was trippy.

He gave her one last look – *see you later* – before he left the table, gathered his coat and hat and went out the back door.

She sighed and began to help clear off the breakfast

dishes. Her heart was light, no longer weighed down by fear or her own self-loathing. She felt brand new, and she liked it.

"You look better this morning," Belle commented as she took the dishes from Lorelei. "We never even got you into that hot bath. Sleep must have done you wonders."

Lorelei smiled. "Yes, it did." But it wasn't sleep that had her looking and feeling this way – it was Jeff. Now more than ever, she thought that staying in this century might not be so bad. So long as she was with Jefferson Cooke.

JEFFERSON KNOCKED on the door of the doctors' house. He hoped Doc Drake was in.

The door opened. "Why, hello, Jefferson," Mrs. Drake said. "What can I do for you?"

"Is your husband home, ma'am?"

"Yes – is there anything wrong?"

He glanced down the street at the mercantile. He told his father he needed a break from doing inventory and wanted to take a walk. "No. Yes. Really, I'd just like some advice."

"Okay," she said as her eyebrows rose. She too looked at the mercantile. "Is your father working?"

Jefferson took off his hat and twisted it in his hands. "Yes, ma'am."

Her eyebrows rose again, and he knew what she must be thinking: *What is it that you can't talk to your own father about?*

"Please, Mrs. Drake, I don't have much time."

She stepped aside. "Come in." She turned to the stairwell. "Bowen?"

"Yes?" came the reply from above. Doc Drake appeared at the top of the stairs. "What is it, Elsie?"

"Jefferson would like to speak to you."

"Oh, of course." He started down the stairs. "Is this about Miss Carson? Is she all right?"

"Yes, sir. I …" He glanced at Elsie and back. "… well, can we talk in private?"

Elsie smiled. "Why don't I go fix you both a cup of coffee?"

"That would be fine." Doc came downstairs and motioned Jefferson to follow him. They filed down the hall into the kitchen where Elsie was at the stove, then continued to the patient room beyond.

As soon as Doc closed the door, he brought the two chairs in the room together and indicated Jefferson should sit. "Now what's on your mind, son? Don't tell me something's ailing you?"

"Well, I'm not sure."

"Oh?" Doc Drake stood as if to examine him.

"I'm not sick, if that's what you think."

Doc sat again. "Really? Then what is it?"

Jefferson sighed. "It's about Lor … Miss Ca … Lorelei."

Doc's head tilted to one side. "What about her?"

Jefferson wiped his palms on his pants a few times. "Doc, do you know why the MacDonalds brought her here?"

Doc sat back in his chair. "No, son. I don't know any more about that than you do."

"Do you trust them?"

He nodded but said nothing.

"Why?"

Doc seemed to contemplate that. "Do you trust the wind?"

"What?"

He shrugged. "You can't see it, I know, but can you trust it's there?"

"Well … you see it in the trees, and can feel it in your hair and …"

"Exactly. Dallan and Shona are like the wind. You know they exist. You see them when they blow through town, you see and feel the effects of their passing through. Then they're gone, everything settles and some things have changed. Look at Rufi Cucinotta and C.J. Branson. They're married now."

"Because of the MacDonalds?"

Doc smiled. "Indirectly. If they hadn't come to town with their friends looking for that bird last summer, would C.J. and Rufi be married now?"

"I couldn't say."

"Let me put it this way – when the MacDonalds blew through last summer, they created the circumstances that put Rufi and C.J. together a lot. The result was they fell in love and got married."

Jefferson stared at him, his heart thundering in his chest. "And this time they brought Lorelei."

"Yes." The doctor suddenly smiled. "Jefferson? Are you sweet on Lorelei?"

Dagnabit, how did the man know? Wait a minute – this wasn't *that.* This was something way beyond that. This was …

Doc continued to look at him, the way a hawk zeros in on a mouse. It wasn't a bad thing, he knew – it was when the doc closed his eyes that things … oh no! He closed them! Doc wasn't just known for miracles of healing, but for knowing a man's mettle. Doc Drake was a lot like Lorcan Brody in that he sensed things about people. The town was blessed to have these men among them. But Jefferson was nervous as to what the man might find in him.

Doc finally opened his eyes and stared at Jefferson in shock. "What's happened to you?!"

Jefferson was too surprised and confused to lie about it. "Well, shoot, Doc, if I knew that, I wouldn't be here asking you!"

Doc snorted in laughter, then stared at the floor in puzzlement. Finally, he said, "It's as if ... hmmm. You know, I'm not sure myself. What I can tell you, son, is that circumstances have brought Lorelei Carson to you. Now, what are you going to do about it?"

Jefferson's eyes widened. "I don't know what to do."

Doc smiled. "What does your heart tell you, Jefferson?"

He swallowed hard and fought the urge to get up and leave. Maybe he should have gone to Preacher Jo instead. But then, he'd probably give him the same sort of advice – and worse, Preacher Jo didn't know Lorelei's secret. Doc Drake did.

The problem was ... "But if I follow my heart, and the MacDonalds come back and take her away ..."

Doc nodded. "That is a risk. But let me suggest something ... if the MacDonalds brought her here *to you* – if that was their reason for bringing her here – do you think they'd take her away *from you?*"

Jefferson froze, his eyes wide. Could that be?

"I'll let you think about that one for a minute. How about that coffee?" Doc opened the door and waved at Elsie. She brought them each a cup, set them on the hutch next to a basket of bandages, then smiled at Jefferson. "Would you like some cookies?"

He could only stare blankly at her – his mind was otherwise occupied.

"Yes," Doc answered for him. "A small plate, if you please." She smiled again and returned to the kitchen, and Doc took his cup and sat. "Have you spoken to your father or mother about this?"

Jefferson shook his head.

Doc smiled. "Have you spoken to Lorelei about this?"

That shook him out of his deep freeze. "We, uh ... well, something happened and ..."

"What happened?" Doc said sternly.

"Nothing bad!"

"I didn't say it was."

Jefferson swallowed again. "I held her, that's all I did. She was crying, sobbing, and I kept holding her is all."

"But?"

"But I can't stop thinking about her. It was bad before, but now it's almost unbearable. It's like … like I have to be with her. I … just being here in town when she's not is …" Jefferson sighed, unable to go on.

Doc smiled. "And does the young lady feel the same way?"

"I couldn't say."

"Then you need to find out and see where it goes."

Did Doc think he was falling in love with Lorelei and nothing more? Though he *was* falling in love with her. It was all the unexpected extras with it that had him confused. He knew people could fall for each other quickly – his own family history provided several examples. But this need, this feeling that his heart was being ripped out of him … he hadn't heard any stories like that. "Doc?"

"Mmm?"

"When you met Mrs. Drake … did you feel like you were being torn apart? Because that's how I feel."

Doc gaped. "No … no, I couldn't go that far." He thought for a moment. "Maybe it has something to do with her being from another time. Maybe when the MacDonalds come back …"

"… We could ask them," Jefferson grumbled. "Yeah, I think a lot of us have a lot of questions to ask." He shook his head. "They've done a lot of good for us, I know, but they sure left us in a real pickle this time."

"Yes, I suppose they did." Doc took a sip from his cup and handed the other one to Jefferson. "Here. You could use the pick-me-up."

Jefferson took it and had a long drink, draining half the cup. "If someone had told me even a month ago that I'd fall for a girl from way in the future, I'd have told them they were loco. Now I'm not sure I'm not."

"You're not, I assure you. The situation is loco. But we'll all do the best we can – and I have faith it'll come out right. That's how things are around here."

Jefferson smiled. "Thank you, Doc, I think I understand."

"Do you?"

"Yes sir." Jefferson knew what to do, at least for now. He'd leave the stuff he didn't understand for later. For the present, he'd follow his heart's first instinct – to be with Lorelei Carson, to be there for her. He'd talk with his parents about it. And when the MacDonalds came back, he'd fight like a tiger to not lose her.

CHAPTER TWENTY

Lorelei didn't know what happened between when Jefferson left the ranch that morning and when he arrived at play practice that afternoon, but something certainly had. The look on his face was one she'd always hoped a boy would have when he saw her, and now here it was. In the wrong time, maybe, but who was she to argue?

This morning had brought both relief and angst. She still couldn't figure out what had happened between them, and still couldn't stop thinking about it. She felt so much better than she had since she'd arrived here – now – but was worried she'd freak out again, and this time when there were outsiders there to see it.

Outsiders. Now there was a concept. Mentally she'd drawn a circle for her own safety, enclosing the people who knew she was from the 21st century and excluding those who didn't. The circle had begun with Jeff and his parents – Parthena and Sam had witnessed her outburst, but apparently were too young to understand it – then expanded to include Dr. Drake. She'd let Adele in, and Grandma Waller had barged in on her own. She felt like she shouldn't stretch it any further, but was happy with it at this size. Her own little support system …

"Ready to get into your costume?" Annie asked Jeff and Owen.

Both of them nodded and headed for the office, though Jeff was watching Lorelei as he went.

Annie followed his gaze. "Yes, I see." She made a funny sound, as if she was trying not to laugh. "Lorelei, keep an eye on the seams. Though why do I have a feeling I don't have to tell you that?"

Lorelei shrugged, realizing she was grinning like a madwoman. Yes, she'd be watching Jeff wherever he went. She just hoped he would be watching where he was going – they couldn't afford him or Owen getting injured with the play three days away.

As she prepared needle and thread, she tried to imagine what it might be like to date Jeff in her time. Would they eat at Daisy's Café? What about coffee at the Java House? Or maybe spend an afternoon at the bookstore or library? Did he like books, she wondered? What about going to a movie – would that freak him out? Well, that would make them even.

She laughed to herself. Yesterday was weird, no doubt about it. But this afternoon she was feeling less like a freak and more the way an eighteen-year-old girl should feel when a cute guy was looking at her the way Jeff did. *Like he was in love* … though that seemed unlikely. No one fell that quick, did they? Well … maybe. Love at first sight was a thing – maybe love in a week or so was too.

And what about her own feelings? The desire to go back to her own time was there, but it didn't overwhelm her as it once had. Despite the physical labor, she rather liked it here, which was more than she could say for where she came from. Now she was pondering whether she could live in this time, maybe fall in love, get married, all the things she'd always dreamed of.

Jeff and Owen exited the office in their costume, moving almost smoothly. And no seams looked like they were about to burst. Good. Maybe she could just relax through this practice. She couldn't see where Jeff was looking, but since he couldn't see out the back end anyway, it hardly mattered.

Heat shot through her, but not like a crush or a passion. More like knowing she already belonged to him. Done deal. End of story. It gave her a confidence she hadn't known before. Maybe it was because she was the only one around he could be with even if she did live in this century. Adele had told her that there were no single young women in Clear Creek near Jefferson's age except for those related to the Cookes.

She smiled at the thought as she watched Annie adjust the blanket over the camel's back. Wasn't there a Bible verse about two people coming together to be one? "A man shall leave his mother and father's house and become one with his wife" or something like that? Just like it took two to make one camel. It was a silly comparison, but she'd take it.

They rehearsed their scenes, laughed at Colin's not-so-subtle attempts to add lines where he shouldn't, and enjoyed Annie calling him out on it. "Now Colin is just being Colin," Grandma explained from the pew behind Lorelei. "He won't do that during the actual play – he just likes keeping things lively."

Lorelei just nodded. She kept being distracted by Jeff's thoughts toward her: *I like you. I wish I was with you in this getup instead of Owen. Do they still have Christmas plays in your time?* And she responded: *I like you too. That wouldn't be proper, and you know it. Yes, they do – complete with two-person camel costumes.* She couldn't stop smiling if she tried.

But as much as she was enjoying this, the possibility of

being yanked out of this situation as abruptly as she'd been dropped into it nagged at her. She wasn't promised a happily ever after – the MacDonalds hadn't promised her anything. She couldn't make plans because she wasn't in control of this – the mysterious Scot and his dazzling wife were. And they'd kept her – and, it seemed, everyone else – in the dark.

She thought of the cabin just inside the tree line at the base of the mountain. Should she go back there? Could she glean some clues? Was that the way home? And where did she want her home to be? That was the real question – because when it came down to it, what did she have to go back to?

"Lorelei," Belle whispered.

"Yes?"

"We're getting the Christmas tree tomorrow."

Her heart leaped. She loved Christmas trees! "You are?"

"Well, Logan is getting it. He and his boys get ours when they fetch theirs."

"That's nice of him. But don't you like going to get one?"

"I haven't gone in years. But you could go with them, and Jefferson with you. Logan won't mind so long as there's room in the wagon. Or we could use the sleigh."

Her jaw dropped. "You have a sleigh?"

"Well, we have a wagon we put sliders on."

"Sliders? Oh, I think I get it." Lorelei smiled. "A sleigh ride through the snow to get a Christmas tree. Count me in!" Of course, the tree wouldn't be the main attraction – Jeff would, if he decided to come.

Belle grinned. Did she sense why Lorelei was excited? If so, she didn't seem to mind. "I'll let Logan know as soon as we get back to the ranch. We'll only need one horse for the sleigh, so that won't be a problem either."

Lorelei giggled. "A one-horse open sleigh?"

Belle gave her a funny look. "You know that song?"

Lorelei leaned over and whispered, "It's still popular."

"Well. How about that?" Belle shrugged again.

"Owen, don't you dare!"

Lorelei faced forward, along with everyone else at Jeff's outburst, and laughed at Jeff's distress. Could this get any better? Despite all the weirdness of the day before and her circumstances, she'd never been so happy. How romantic! She wasn't going to sweat it, wasn't going to chastise herself for falling for Jeff Cooke. She just wanted to enjoy this little slice of Heaven that had been handed her on a silver platter. Or in her case, a cracker covered in squeeze cheese.

It was hard to be angry with the MacDonalds now, when they'd brought her here to where she could fall in love. Whatever strange thing bound them together was only growing stronger, and she couldn't ignore the heady feelings she had when he was near. It was like the front and back of the camel coming together to become one. You never knew you were just one half until you were whole, and your world was turned upside down. No one would know what she was talking about if she tried to explain it, but she understood.

And so help her, if the MacDonalds tried to split them up, Lorelei would raise Cain to stop them. She knew that deeper down than anything.

JEFFERSON'S MIND was full of ideas. Doc had made him think, hard. Lorelei had specifically been sent to stay with his family by the MacDonalds, to care for her, protect her. He was now taking that to heart, wondering if, just maybe, they'd brought her to *him*.

She was different, as who wouldn't be from 140 years in the future? How different would he seem to someone from 1739? But they shared something he couldn't explain. Did he dare allow his heart free rein? He'd avoided it before, too wrapped up in trying to understand what was going on. There were still so many unanswered questions, still no idea what the MacDonalds wanted or planned.

But all he could do for now was follow his heart, and his heart wanted *her*. So he would pursue her, make her his. Besides, if he didn't it could be a long time before he ever got another chance at a wife. If the MacDonald wind had blown C.J. Branson and Rufi Cucinotta together last summer, it could do the same with him and Lorelei. He could court her, do things properly ... and hope he could hold on long enough to do that. The need to be with her was overwhelming and he wasn't sure how to bank that fire.

He'd kept his distance easily enough for the first half of play practice, when he was stuck following Owen's rear end around. Now he was sitting with her in front of Grandma and Mary Mulligan, and Mother on the other side of her, watching the rest run through their parts. It wouldn't look good for him to pull her onto his lap, but he was still tempted.

"When do you think we'll get the tree tomorrow?" she asked, excited at the prospect.

He smiled at her tone of voice and the sparkle in her eyes. Mother had already mentioned hauling out the sleigh and going with Logan and his boys. "After the morning chores are done. With any luck, we'll be back in time for lunch, but I'd rather we take lunch with us."

"I can't wait."

He smiled again. "I like the decorating best."

"Me too, but I've never gone to cut a fresh tree. We always got them from tree lots or bought one from the Boy Scouts."

His brow creased. "Boy scouts?"

Her eyes widened slightly, and she leaned toward him to avoid being overheard. "It's an organization for city boys to learn ... well, farming and wilderness skills. There are Girl Scout clubs too. And sometimes they sell Christmas trees to raise money for their activities."

"Makes sense. City folk can't run off into the woods to fetch one as easily as we can." He turned to her. "Do the boys and girls get them?"

"You know, I'm not sure. I was never a Girl Scout."

She was suddenly nervous, he could tell, but didn't know why. He glanced around the church and didn't sense any danger. Was it something he'd said? And why was he looking for trouble anyway? It's not like outlaws were going to swoop in on play practice and snatch her away from him.

But someone might. He thought again about what he'd do if Dallan MacDonald showed up to take her off. He wasn't going to let him, nossir. Maybe he could get Preacher Jo to marry them before that happened. He smiled at the thought, though it felt like he was going too far with it.

He spied her hand next to his on the pew and swallowed hard. He wanted to hold it, hold her. But he didn't dare with almost half the town there.

"Something wrong?" Lorelei asked him.

"No, I was just thinking about tomorrow." Unable to help it, he turned in the pew to face her. "We could take some cookies to snack on. In fact, I'll tell Mother we should take a lunch with us."

"And you could take me along with you," Grandma quipped from behind them.

Their heads swung to her. "Grandma?" Jefferson said.

"What, I don't have ears? Do you really think your pa will let you take a pretty gal like this alone on a sleigh ride?"

"Logan and his sons will be there," he pointed out.

"In another wagon. And for all you know it will only be Logan, and how much chaperoning can he do when he's got trees to chop down?"

"All the more reason he takes his boys with him," Jefferson argued.

"Owen's the only one big enough to get the job done. Him and you." Grandma leaned closer and whispered, "I'm not trying to spoil your fun. In fact, I'm trying to help it along. Anyone can see you two are sweet on each other."

Lorelei faced forward and sunk in the pew.

Jefferson winced. "I ... I wasn't planning ..."

"I know, but things happen. And Fanny Fig saw the way you were looking at her as well."

She had him there. If Fanny knew, then within a day everyone in town would.

"Pick me up at nine," Granny added. "I know Logan passes through town on his way to the tree line."

Jefferson looked at Lorelei, who shrugged helplessly – what else could they do? – then back to Grandma. "All right, we'll be at your house at nine in the morning."

"Good," Grandma smiled and winked.

Jefferson sighed. Maybe this wasn't such a good idea after all. When Grandma Waller got it in her head to help love along, she was pretty clear about it. But after yesterday, he and Lorelei didn't need help – they needed a good set of brakes. The feelings he was dealing with were more powerful than anything he'd ever experienced. He loved his parents and loved his siblings. He even loved some of the folks in town, Grandma being one of them. But this was beyond his usual comprehension of love. This felt more like survival.

Well, he'd decided to stop battling himself and let his heart free. He just hoped and prayed it wouldn't be the biggest mistake of his life.

As soon as chores were done the next morning, Logan helped Jefferson get the sliders onto the small wagon they used with them, and Jefferson hitched up the horse. With Grandma with them they'd barely have room for a tree, but he'd make it work.

"You sure you want to take the little wagon?" Logan asked. "We can all fit in the big one."

"You didn't see the look on Lorelei's face when I told her about the sleigh. I can't disappoint her."

"No, guess not." Logan reached for some harness hanging on the barn wall. "I'm going to hitch up the other wagon. Susara made us sandwiches to take in case we're out there longer than expected. Be sure you bring enough blankets to keep the women warm."

"Yes, sir, I will. And I asked Mother to make sandwiches too."

Logan smiled, took the harness and left the barn.

Jefferson went to a stall to fetch Powder, Father's dapple grey gelding and one of their driving horses. He was glad he told Mother to make sandwiches. Besides, Logan's wife was right. They could be out there longer than expected any way, and he wouldn't want Lorelei or Grandma to get too hungry. He hitched up Powder, then went into the house to see if his Mother had anything else they might take to munch on.

As soon as he walked in, she handed him a bag. "For your excursion," she said.

He opened the bag and smiled. "Wonderful, thank you."

"No, Susara brought them by a minute ago. There's enough for everyone so I didn't have to make any." She went to the worktable and picked up another bag. "Here's my contribution. Molasses cookies."

"Thank you, Mother."

She returned to the worktable to chop up some potatoes. "Take good care of Grandma out there. I don't know why she insisted on going." She stopped chopping. "Actually, I do know. Jefferson Cooke, you'd better be on your best behavior."

"Mother!" He looked nervously at the hall. "Lorelei will hear you."

"She needs to be too."

"Mother!"

"Jefferson, I know you're a grown man now, but there are some things your father should have told you about."

Jefferson froze. "Motherrrrr ...," he groaned.

"Courting is all fine and good, but we don't know enough about Lorelei or what Dallan and Shona's plans are. For all we know, they'll come knocking on our door tomorrow and whisk this girl away and ..."

"Not if I stop them." He said it before he could think to stop himself.

Mother wheeled to face him. "And how will you go about that? How will you stop a man a head taller than you and twice as wide?"

"I don't know. But I will if I have to." He was unnerved by the determination in his own voice. "I want to court her, Mother. I ... I *have* to court her."

Mother was stunned. She slowly moved toward the nearest chair and sat down. "What are you saying?"

"I don't really know how I know that," he replied. He felt as confused as Mother looked. "But I know it. I gotta do this. I need to, she needs me to."

"Well." She didn't add to that for a minute. "You sound very sure. If you say so, I'll trust you on that." She sighed. "You're all grown up, and I don't know when it happened."

He went over and put his arms around her. "I'm right here, Mother. Just taller and a few other things." He knew there was more to it now, but he didn't know how to talk about that.

"Are you sure about this?"

"More than I've ever been about anything."

She smiled in resignation. "Then you need to speak to your father soon."

He nodded. "I will. Maybe at Christmas. He's caught up with the play right now." He kissed her on the cheek. "Can you fetch Lorelei for me while I put some blankets in the wagon?"

She smiled. "I will."

He left and went to fetch blankets they used for trips to town in the cold, his smile quickly vanishing. He'd set things in motion now that he couldn't stop. His mother knew, Grandma knew, and if Fanny Fig had her way the whole town would know he was courting Lorelei.

Jefferson smiled. Let them.

CHAPTER TWENTY-ONE

"Bye-bye," Elsie called from the porch. "Have fun!"

Jefferson, Lorelei, Grandma and Doc Waller waved back as the sleigh set off. Now they had two chaperones, but Jefferson didn't mind. No one – namely Fanny Fig – could say he wasn't doing things properly when he had a young lady with him, and even if Grandma was lax in her chaperoning duties, her husband wasn't. Jefferson wouldn't be surprised if Doc whipped out a measuring stick to make sure he and Lorelei kept a proper distance.

Fortunately, the wagon was small and cramped with the four of them. Even better, Doc and Grandma were sitting facing backward behind them, the best way to fit everyone when they put a tree in. They'd have to place it across the wagon bed to make it fit, but it would do.

Once they left town, he let Powder break into a trot. There was enough snow on the ground to move with ease, but not so deep it would give the horse trouble.

"Whee!" Grandma said as the sleigh sped up.

Doc laughed. "One would think you've never done this before."

"I've never done it in this rig," she said. "It's smaller than the one Logan takes."

"Logan?" Jefferson said. "You've gone to the tree line with Logan before?"

"Of course, if I can catch him in town. Doc and I used to go with him and your father and uncles back in the day. Those were good times."

"Have you heard from your Uncle Duncan lately?" Doc asked.

"No, not since he wrote in the fall."

"Is that the duke in England?" Lorelei asked.

"Yes. He was here last summer. We had a good visit."

"An interesting one is more like," Grandma laughed.

He knew what she referred to: the infamous hunt for a rare bird everyone in Clear Creek thought was just a strange-looking chicken. The Turners found it and sold it to August Bennett, who'd had it for years until the MacDonalds showed up in town with Uncle Duncan, Aunt Cozette and some strangers who were looking for it. Those strangers were the oddest people Clear Creek had ever seen … hmmm. Were they from another time too?

He pushed the thought aside. He didn't want to think of the MacDonalds, exotic birds or anything but spending the day with Lorelei. With any luck he'd catch a private moment with her and tell her his intentions. She'd either say yes or no, but he was pretty sure she'd say yes. It felt like there wasn't another option, not for his heart. Then it would just be a matter of doing that – provided a Scotsman the size of an oak tree didn't get in the way.

They talked of the play, the weather, and Uncle Harrison and Aunt Sadie's trip to Nowhere to visit the Weavers. He wondered how his cousins were getting along. Finally, they spotted Logan's wagon far ahead, just entering the tree line. "Oh, there they are!" Lorelei said, looking around. She'd been looking around a lot. "It's so beautiful out here. I can't believe it."

"Not too hard to believe the good Lord knew what He was doing when he made it all," Grandma said behind them. "But I do have to admit, I never tire of taking it in."

"Me neither," Doc agreed.

Jefferson smiled at Lorelei. "Are you having a good time?"

"The best. This is great!"

His chest warmed. He liked seeing her happy. Her smile made his heart swell almost to bursting.

They continued on to the tree line, where a small track led to Amon Cotter's cabin. They'd leave their wagons and horses there and hike into the trees behind it to a spot where there was new growth. Amon had cleared an area for horses, but it never got used and the pines and firs reclaimed it. It would be a handy spot for a few years, until the trees grew too large to use for Christmas.

Lorelei looked around again. "I think I've been here."

"Yes, you have," Jefferson said. "Father told me this is where the MacDonalds had him and Mother meet them to fetch you."

She fidgeted, glancing around. "I thought this place looked familiar."

A shiver ran up his spine and he began to sense her agitation. "Everything all right?"

"Yes, I'm fine. But ... well, it reminds me of ..."

She didn't need to finish the sentence. He looked at her and thought, *It's all right.*

Her gaze met his and her shoulders relaxed. *Thanks.*

By the time they reached Amon's cabin, Logan and his son Owen had a fire going in the cabin for Doc and Grandma. "It's a shame Amon built this place then never got to use it," Grandma said as Jefferson helped her out of the wagon. "Nice place. Big too."

"Where did he go?" Lorelei asked, still subdued.

"England, to help my Uncle Duncan. I think I told you that, remember?"

"I don't recall. Sorry."

He thought a moment. Maybe he hadn't told her. Ever since Lorelei arrived, he'd been muddled at times. She did that to him.

Logan came out the front door. "I'm going to have to tell Cutty the place needs some cleaning."

"He's the one that joined us for tea, isn't he?" Lorelei said.

"Yes – Amon married his daughter Nettie," Jefferson explained. "They live on the Jones ranch about an hour and a half from here. The Joneses help them keep the place up so when Amon or any of the others come visit, they can use it."

"I see." She stared at the cabin warily – probably remembering how the MacDonalds had press-ganged her here – and shivered.

He took her hand. "Come on, it will be warmer inside. You can stand by the fire and wait with Doc and Grandma."

"Sounds good to me," Grandma said. "We can get lunch ready for these rascals. They'll load the trees on the wagons, we'll eat, clean up, then head back."

Jefferson would rather take Lorelei with him to pick a tree, but she was cold, and he didn't want her trekking through the snow. "She's right – you'll be much warmer in the cabin."

She looked at it and swallowed hard. "If you say so." She didn't seem convinced.

"C'mon, Lorelei," Grandma wrapped an arm through hers. "Let's go stand by the fire. You can tell me what it's like where you're from. I hear that place has really grown."

She gave Jefferson a helpless look, clearly wanting to go with him too. But this was best – he didn't want her shivering with cold the entire way back to town. "Stay with the

Wallers, honey." His eyes widened at the endearment, but it slipped out before he could stop it.

She was just as surprised but smiled and blushed as Grandma dragged her off.

Grandma headed toward the front door. "Don't forget the canteen! I know for a fact there are no glasses in this house."

Jefferson smiled. No one seemed to mind his slip of calling Lorelei "honey", least of all Lorelei. He gathered what he needed and headed for the cabin. The sooner they got the trees, the sooner he could spend time with her. The cabin was the perfect place to grab a private word. He could offer to show her around, provided Grandma or Doc didn't beat him to it. If so, he'd have to come up with something else. No matter what, by the end of the day he wanted to let her know how he really felt.

LORELEI STOPPED at the threshold of the cabin door. *Uh-oh,* she thought, *this is where I came in.*

Thoughts roiled in her head of the party, the MacDonalds, that stupid spray cheese on the stupid cracker. If she stepped inside, would the past week and a half disappear? Would she be at the party again in her own time? Would Jefferson disappear from her life forever? Would she be sent to another century into the past, when this area was uninhabited except by Native Americans and beavers?

"What's the matter, child?" Grandma asked. "You look as if you've seen a ghost."

She forced a smile. "I'd rather not explain, Grandma."

The old woman nodded. "Well, let's go inside before I freeze to death."

Lorelei stepped inside and looked around. The ceiling was no more than nine feet high here, but the living/dining area was still large. The kitchen at the other end wasn't walled off as it was in the future - no pass-through, no modern appliances next to the old cook stove.

Doc went straight to the stove, took a piece of wood out of a nearby bin and put it in to burn.

"Let's sit over there," Grandma said. Lorelei escorted her to the table and pulled out a chair for her. "Thank you, child."

Jeff entered the cabin and joined them. "Here's the food." He met Lorelei's gaze and stepped toward her. "We'll be back before you know it."

They locked gazes and her heart leaped in her chest. She wanted to hear him say it again, say *anything* again. He could talk about cattle breeds and make her heart buzz and her stomach somersault. But the way he'd said *honey* – it was like a drug, and she was hooked. "Hurry back."

"We will." He strode out of the cabin.

"Well, he's a might smitten, wouldn't you say?" Grandma quipped.

Lorelei smiled. The old woman didn't waste any time. "I hope so," she gushed, then covered her mouth and giggled.

"Oh, child – looks like he's not the only one!" She opened the bag of cookies and took one. "I think you two will be the talk of the town."

Lorelei opened her mouth to protest and stopped. So what if she was? Isn't this what she wanted? She could have a life here with a man she was falling for, and a family – his family. They were wonderful people. Work would be hard, and she'd miss electricity until it arrived in thirty years, not to mention all the tech that went with it, but here she was happy without it.

There was just one hitch – the MacDonalds and their intentions, whatever those were. She remembered the Scot's voice the night she was taken. When he told Shona to take them to Clear Creek, it was a command. She might have been drugged, but she heard and *felt* what he said. If he tried to take her away from Jeff … no. She didn't care what they wanted. If they tried to separate them, she'd tear their eyes out.

Wow – where did *that* come from?

"Something bothering you, child?" Grandma asked softly.

Lorelei relaxed the claws she didn't realize she was making with her hands, took off her coat and hung it over a chair, her back to the stove. "Yes."

"Jefferson?"

She glanced between Doc and Grandma. "Yes and no." She stared at the fire in the hearth at the other end of the room.

"Sometimes it helps to have a listening ear," Doc said. "And lookie here, you have four!" He motioned to Grandma and himself. "We have the time if you do."

She put a fist to her mouth to fight back tears. She needed to tell somebody. But there was a concern she needed to address. "I … it's …" She frowned and looked at Grandma, waving a finger between her and her husband. "Does he know …?"

Grandma looked surprised. "You don't think I keep secrets from my husband, do you? Of course, he knows. And he's a doctor, so he knows how to keep things to himself."

Lorelei nodded. That made seven – eight if Doc Drake had told *his* wife. The circle was getting too crowded. "Okay. Had to check."

Grandma stood, went over and wrapped Lorelei in her arms. "It's going to be okay."

Lorelei sniffed back the tears before they could fall. "I'm sorry, I'm just not sure what to do."

"No one ever said young love was easy," Grandma soothed. "And in your situation, it's that much harder. But we were all young once. You'll get through this, just like we did."

Lorelei smiled weakly as she pulled away, turned a chair around and sat in front of the old couple. "Did you have to worry about a Scottish couple popping up out of nowhere and breaking up your relationship?"

Doc frowned. "No, I'm afraid you've got us there. But I'll tell you this – if they try, they're going to have to go through me."

"Us," Grandma corrected.

"Awww," Lorelei sighed. She couldn't remember anyone going to bat for her like that. The Wallers were so kind, so real – nothing phony about them – and she knew, absolutely *knew* that they'd keep that promise. Whether it would do any good ... well, only time would tell.

"Lorelei, we know what true love looks like," Grandma said. "And you and Jefferson have it by the bushel. I don't think the MacDonalds will try to split you two up. In fact, I'm thinking that might be why they brought you here."

Lorelei stared at them. "You really think so?"

"Have you ever been in love before? With anyone from your time?"

"No."

"Ever felt like you were close to anyone back then? Or forward then, I suppose."

Lorelei chuckled at the phrasing. "No. I've always been on the outside looking in."

Grandma nodded. "So maybe you belonged here all along. Maybe you were born in the wrong place, and the MacDonalds were fixing it."

That hadn't occurred to her. "Huh."

"Sarah," Doc said. "Maybe you ought to tell her."

"Tell me what?" Lorelei asked.

Grandma sighed. "Maybe it will explain some things. To all of us. Lorelei ... we've known the MacDonalds a long time. Twenty years now. When Duncan Cooke and his wife

Cozette were courting. According to Duncan, Dallan was the one that made that happen."

"He did?"

"Yep. Might fine looking folks, the MacDonalds are, wouldn't you say?"

"Well, I suppose …" The couple was striking, though what did that have to do with anything?

"So how old would you guess they are?" Doc added.

Lorelei shrugged. "I … they seem pretty young. Shona doesn't look much older than me. Maybe 21, 22? And Dallan, I'd say thirty at the most."

"That's our guess too," Grandma agreed.

Lorelei glanced between them – what were they trying to say?

"We've known them for twenty years and haven't seen a gray hair or wrinkle on either of them," Doc said. "And they're not the only ones …"

"Doc, that's enough," Grandma said. "Can't you see you're scaring the poor child?"

"No, keep talking," Lorelei insisted. "I want to hear this."

"No one in town talks about it," Doc went on. "Maybe they're too afraid of the answer, whatever it may be. And the MacDonalds have brought nothing but good to Clear Creek and to us, so we're not about to look a gift horse in the mouth. But those folks are from … well, they're way beyond us normal folks. They're not just time travelers. They're something else too."

Lorelei snorted. "I know *that*. The time travel alone was a dead giveaway."

"My guess is they know things we probably don't want to know. So don't you think that if they're going to drop you back in your distant past without warning, they have a very good reason for it? And if they're good people – and I can vouch that they are – don't you think they might be doing it for your benefit?"

"But … then why didn't they just tell me that?"

"Would you have believed them?" Grandma mused. "Or would you have run the other way?"

Lorelei felt her stomach settle. That was a really good point. "Are you sure they won't …?" She couldn't even say it.

"Oh, we're pretty sure. Why would they go to all this effort just to hurt you?"

Another good point. Again, she felt like a burden was being lifted off her. If they could trust the MacDonalds – and given the medicine Grandma received, they were trusting them with their lives – couldn't she? "I suppose you're right. Ugh. I feel like an ingrate when you put it that way."

"Oh, pish tosh," Grandma replied. "No sense beating yourself up over it. We've known them for decades – you've only known them for a couple of months?"

"Not even that."

"Well, there you go," Doc said and blew out a long breath. "Well, now that that's taken care of …"

"What?" Grandma said. "It doesn't solve anything."

"Maybe it does," Lorelei mumbled. "I mean, I don't know how to get home. But I do know what I can do while I'm waiting. Because …" Should she say it? Yes. Yes, she should. "… because I'm crazy in love with Jefferson Cooke."

Doc exchanged a quick look with Grandma. "Yeah, we kind of knew that."

"And he can read my mind."

"I'm sorry, what?"

CHAPTER TWENTY-TWO

By the time Jefferson and the others returned to the cabin, Lorelei had given Doc and Grandma a rundown of her life over the last few years and a full sketch of what was happening between her and Jeff. They listened quietly, with an occasional nod or two, their eyes widening when she described the whole mind-reading business. Lorelei skipped over explanations of 21st-century technology – things were complicated enough without that.

"Don't worry, Lorelei," Grandma eventually said as she peeked out the window. "Doc and I will help you and Jefferson. But you'd better speak with the young man."

"I intend to." Lorelei looked out the window and saw Jeff tying the tree down across the sleigh. Logan had two in his wagon. "I just have to find the right opportunity."

Doc shook his head. "No, you need to grab the *soonest* opportunity."

She smiled. Gosh, it was nice to have allies! And yes, she had to tell Jeff how she felt, or she'd burst! "Thank you."

"I'm sure Grandma and I can find a way to keep Logan

and his son busy for a short spell. But don't waste time, you hear?"

"No, sir, I won't." She smiled, quickly smoothed the skirt of her blue day dress and tried not to panic. She'd never told a young man she loved him, let alone the way she felt about Jeff. She knew he felt the same, but did he? In her heart she knew they were already together, but did he know it? What if this was all in her head? After all, she'd been moved through time – what did that do to a person, exactly?

"Ah, that feels nice," Logan said as he entered the cabin followed by Owen. Jeff brought up the rear. From the kitchen, Lorelei and Grandma watched them cross the big room to the dining table. Owen took one look at the sandwiches Grandma was taking out of the bags and sat, his eyes on the food. It made sense – being the front end of the camel *and* a woodsman besides had to burn calories. Logan sat across from him.

Jeff joined Lorelei at the stove. "Mighty cold out there. It's a good thing you stayed inside where it's warm."

She smiled shyly. Talking with Doc and Grandma about the MacDonalds had made her hopes soar. She felt a little more sure of things now.

He smiled. "You're awful quiet." He glanced at the table and back. "Would you like a sandwich?"

"Yes, thank you."

He went to the table, fetched two and handed her one. They bit into them at the same time as their eyes locked. It was warm by the stove, but his gaze was warmer. There was something magical in that moment. Did he sense it too?

He swallowed and smiled. "Did you look around the place yet?"

"No, I spent the entire time talking with the Wallers."

He nodded. "Uh, I could show you around if you like."

Her heart leaped in her chest. Perfect! "That would be nice. I'd love to see it."

He grinned. So did she. They were so busy smiling at each other, they didn't notice the others staring at them until Logan cleared his throat. "Ahem. Jefferson, shouldn't you be getting Grandma and Doc back to town?"

Grandma waved him off. "Oh, let them look around – this place needs to have folks move around in it. Besides, someone should check the rooms and make sure no critter's been making a nest where it shouldn't." She smiled at Lorelei.

Lorelei smiled back as a tingle went up her spine.

"She's got a point, Logan," Doc said.

"Hmmm, very well. Take a look around and make sure nothing's homesteading in here. We'll let Sheriff Tom know, and he can tell Cutty and Imogene. I hear they're in town for a few days to watch the play and visit. That'll save them having to check on it themselves."

"Best we do it now," Jeff said. "Logan's right, I do need to get Doc and Grandma back before it gets too late."

They finished their sandwiches and began the tour. "Amon Cotter came to Clear Creek some years back. I couldn't tell you where he's from – Logan or Doc might know." They reached the staircase. "Anyway, he lived at the men's camp."

"I've heard that mentioned before," she said. "What exactly is it?"

"Well, when Cyrus Van Cleet built his hotel, before I was born, he brought wagon trains of supplies from Oregon City to Clear Creek – lumber, tools, everything, including the workers."

"Wow."

He smiled. "Cyrus also had the men build themselves a big bunkhouse outside town. When the hotel was done, some of them stayed and worked around town or on the farms, wherever there was work to be had. That's when folks started calling it the men's camp. It was a place a man could stay while he worked in the area, saved himself some money, and got his own place or moved on."

She smiled. "What a great idea."

"It worked out for everyone. The place is still in use, though there's only a few men there now."

"Fascinating." She looked up the stairwell. "What's up there."

"I'll show you." He glanced at the other end of the long room before he took her hand and led her up the stairs.

When they reached the second floor, she felt nervous, but it quickly disappeared when Jeff gave her hand a squeeze. She breathed a sigh of relief. Being in the cabin wasn't going to mean she'd suddenly be back in the 21st century. It had probably been a silly thing to worry about, but then, a month ago she would've said time travel was impossible. You never knew.

"There's just bedrooms up here." He went to the nearest door and opened it. "See?"

She peeked in. This wasn't the same room she'd woken up in nearly two weeks ago. "And no one else has lived here but Amon?"

He joined her in the doorway, turning slightly so they'd both fit. "No one," he said softly.

She turned and looked up at him, so close she could smell his scent – leather, wood smoke, fresh air, evergreens and him. She drew a shuddering breath. "Why … doesn't anyone live here now?"

He looked at her. "I told you. Amon owns it. The Jones family might use it now and then, but it's his to do with as he pleases."

She swallowed hard. Had he gotten closer? They were

touching now. She realized one of his arms was around her, the other moving to join it. "Jeff?"

"Lorelei," he whispered. "I … I've been meaning to …"

"Me too!" she blurted.

He drew back. "What?"

"Talk to you. I've been meaning to talk to you." Her heart was racing so fast it was becoming hard to breathe. The man was intoxicating! She hoped her knees didn't give out. She'd seen enough romance movies to know it could probably happen in real life.

"You want to talk to me?" he said, looking worried.

"Yes … but maybe you should go first." Maybe he'd tell her he just wanted to be friends. But if so, why did he have his arms around her, and why was his face drawing closer to hers?

"Lorelei, I don't know how to say it, so …"

When his lips touched hers, it was like getting hit by lightning. She couldn't move, couldn't breathe, couldn't think. She could only exist and receive. It was the sweetest, most wonderful moment of her life. Her first real kiss.

She didn't know how long it lasted. She didn't care. All she knew was that in that moment, Jefferson Cooke had managed to tell her everything she needed to know, and what she wanted to tell him too.

He broke the kiss, his arms drawing her closer. "I'm not sorry I did that."

"Neither am I," she replied, not holding back her enthusiasm. Wow – this put every movie lip-mash she'd seen to shame!

He gazed into her eyes and smiled. "Did you like it?"

She nodded vigorously.

"Me too." He rested his forehead against hers. "I've had that kiss penned up for a long time. It's been screaming to get out and find you. I couldn't keep it from you any longer, Lorelei."

Tears filled her eyes. It was the most romantic thing she'd ever heard. "I'm glad you set it free."

He smiled. "So am I, honey."

Her smile faded as a tear slipped down her cheek. "So what do we do now?"

He stared at her a moment then smiled. "Well, I'm not right sure. I mean, I think you know how I feel about you now."

"And you know how I feel about you. If I didn't have to be a lady, I'd kiss you until I turned blue."

Jeff's eyes went wide, and he blushed magenta. "Oh my ... really, honey?"

"Sorry. Lost my cool there."

"Lost your ...?"

"I, uh, went loco for a second?"

"Oh, okay. Yeah, I understand that."

She looked into his eyes and her heart skipped a beat. Whatever was connecting them tightened another notch. *Oh, Jeff ...*

"I heard that," he said softly.

Her jaw trembled. "I know. I ... felt it in my heart. I'm sorry, that's the closest I can come to describing it."

He drew in a shuddering breath. "That's a good description. It ... doesn't happen in our heads. It's here." He pointed at his chest.

She nodded. "Like our hearts are speaking to each other. You just ... know what's being said."

He nodded as his eyes fused with hers. And in that moment, it was as if his heart was joining with her own at the same time. Lorelei closed her eyes and let her heart speak to him, just to see if it would. *Is this as strange for you as it is for me, talking like this?*

Yes, it is. But I like it.

She opened her eyes. *Me too.* She drew him in for another kiss, and there was no more to be said for a while by heart or voice. Jeff pulled her closer still as he took the kiss and added some variations on it. Her knees went weak and she tightened her arms around his waist to keep from falling. Not that she would the way he was holding her, but no sense taking chances.

When he broke the kiss this time, his breathing had picked up and he looked at her like a starving man looks at a sandwich. He'd had a taste of her and clearly wanted more.

Jeff ...

We have to stop, I know. Someone's going to come looking for us. He made a face as if bracing himself, then let go of her and stepped back into the hallway.

"Ouch," she said, and she wasn't kidding. When he stepped away, she felt like someone was trying to rip her sternum out for a second. The need to hold him again was overwhelming. *Wow, it's true.*

He tilted his head. *What is?*

She looked into his eyes. It was now or never. *Love really is powerful.*

He grinned. *Do you mean that, honey?*

She was back in his arms in an instant. *Jefferson Cooke, I LOVE YOU!*

I knew it! I knew it! He picked her up and swung her around. *And I love you too, Lorelei Carson!*

She looked into his eyes once, then kissed him, hard. *This is crazy, just crazy.*

Maybe it is, but I still love you.

But I'm not even from this century*!*

I don't care. You're here now and that's all that matters to me.

But ... That broke the spell, and the kiss. "But if the MacDonalds ...," she began hoarsely, using her voice again.

There was steel in Jeff's eyes now. "If they try to take you away from me, I'm going to fight them. I don't care how big he is or how powerful they are – they're not taking you away from me."

That knocked the breath from her lungs. It was the kind of declaration women dreamed of – he was really ready to go to war for her. "Same here," she finally whispered.

"I'll speak to Father after Christmas." He let go of her, took her hands in his and kissed them both. "As soon as we have his blessing, I'll speak with Preacher Jo and we can be married."

She looked into his eyes and smiled. "Christmas is only two days away."

"Yes, honey. And it'll be the most wonderful Christmas of my life. Because you're here, Future Girl."

She smiled again. He loved her! He really did. And that nickname ... it made her feel so special. Not like a freak, but like a priceless treasure. He knew her secret, and he reveled in it.

Still, what if that blasted Scotsman showed up in the meantime? That was a problem no matter how she looked at it. But at least she was sure of one thing: she and Jeff were in love. She'd enjoy it and worry about the rest later. "And I'm glad I'm here with you, my Old West cowboy."

To both Jeff and Lorelei, that seemed to call for another kiss. And this one was the sweetest kiss yet.

Lorelei couldn't keep the smiles from coming on the trip back to town. Doc and Grandma turned into chatterboxes, telling about the day they met and their subsequent attempts at seeing one another. Grandma had been sort-of-engaged to another man – well, she was being hounded by her mother to marry him. It was the stuff of romance novels. Which only served to make the cloud Lorelei was walking on bigger and fluffier.

But there was still another cloud, a black one, looming over her: what would happen when the MacDonalds showed up? She still wasn't sure why she was dumped here by them in the first place, but if they dropped her off, they meant to pick her up. That was one reason she liked Jeff's plan so much – if she and Jeff were already married, it might be harder for the time travelers to take her away from him.

Harder, but maybe not impossible. Like the Wallers, she was afraid to ask herself too many questions when it came to the MacDonalds. Because if they could travel through time, what else were they powerful enough to do?

Jeff took her hand as they neared the outskirts of Clear Creek. Once they dropped Doc and Grandma off, they'd be alone. She smiled at the thought. But Logan and his boys would also be passing by town on their way back to the Triple-C. Would they stop and wait for them so they could drive home together?

Sure enough, that was exactly what they did. But no matter – they could have a private conversation even if someone was sitting right next to them, or in this case, keep their voices low. "This has been the best day ever," she sighed.

"I agree. And more good days will come, you'll see."

"Jeff? Are you sure your father will give his blessing?"

"Let me deal with Father. He's not like my Uncle Harrison – he doesn't worry so much."

"And your uncle does? What if he tells your father we shouldn't marry?"

"Uncle Harrison won't be home until shortly after Christmas. By then we might already be married."

Well, that was a thought. Uncle Harrison the worrywart might have to just accept it and cope. Still, she was from another century – who knew how that would affect things? "Say your father gives his blessing but wants to wait until the MacDonalds come back to tell them our plans? What if they interfere?"

Jeff went silent. That black cloud was still hanging over them. Finally, he said, "They'd better not."

He sounded so sure of himself, though he had no idea what he'd be up against. Then, neither did she. But like him, she'd fight like a wildcat to stay with him. The thought of losing him hurt more than any idea about what the MacDonalds could do.

For now, Lorelei just wanted to enjoy the next few days, spend Christmas with the Cookes and soak in the joy of being with Jeff. That was enough to think about for now.

CHAPTER TWENTY-THREE

Decorating a tree in 1879 wasn't the same as in 2019 - no untangling Christmas lights, replacing bulbs, plugging the mess into a wall and hoping it didn't trip a circuit breaker. At Bob and Patsy's house, tripping the breaker was a holiday tradition. But in the Cookes' home, things were much simpler.

"Parthena made that one," Jeff explained as Lorelei held up a pretty angel made from twigs and white feathers. It reminded her of a fairy more than an angel, but the workmanship was astounding.

"It's very pretty," she said. "Where should I hang it?"

"Anywhere." He pulled a star out of the small barrel he'd been digging through. "Ah, here it is."

She smiled. It was amazing how something like Christmas bound people together through the centuries. She felt so at home here, as if she'd lived with the Cookes forever. "Does your father put it on the tree?"

"No, we take turns. It's Sam's job this year."

She remembered getting a black eye from Erwin one year over who would put the tree topper on. Was she twelve, thirteen? She couldn't remember. What she did remember was Bob breaking up the fight and putting it on himself. She didn't want to go back to that kind of life, not ever. Instead she'd focus on how to keep this one. She pushed the thoughts aside and began to hum – humming always calmed her. She'd been so discombobulated since she came here, she hadn't thought to sing to herself.

Jeff smiled. "You have a pretty voice."

She blushed and reached for another ornament. They were all simple and delicate. "Thank you." She felt comfortable enough to keep humming, though usually she only did it when she was alone.

"What's that song? I've never heard it before."

She stopped. "Oh, um, it's ... well, it's from my time. You wouldn't know it."

"I like it, though." He turned to her as Parthena and Thackary entered the parlor. "Hum it some more."

"What?" Parthena asked.

"Lorelei is going to teach us a song," Jeff said with a grin.

Lorelei almost dropped the ornament. "Oh, uh, no, I really shouldn't." She glared at him for emphasis.

He took the cue. "Okay, maybe not."

That set the younger ones off. "Aw, I want to learn the song!" "Pleeeeease?"

Lorelei hung the ornament, while thinking furiously. "No, I only know, like, half the words ..."

Jeff handed Thackary some ornaments to distract him. "Put those on the other side of the tree."

Thackary headed that way. "You sure you won't sing it for us?"

"Maybe another time – if I can remember the rest of it." She sent Jeff a pleading look.

Thankfully Jeff understood and nodded back. He handed some ornaments to Parthena. "You go over to the other side."

Lorelei sighed in relief. Maybe it wouldn't have done any harm to teach the kids "Mary, Did You Know?" a hundred and some years in advance, but she really didn't want to take any more risks with her secret. She looked over at Jeff, who was watching her boldly. "Like what you see, Cowboy?" she mouthed. Was it okay to flirt in the 1870s? Who knew? As long as they didn't get caught.

"Yes, I do," he mouthed back and smiled. "I can't wait to make you my bride."

Her heart melted. He looked so happy, so in love – and good enough to eat. She'd have to be especially careful – 21st-century girls were clearly more aggressive than their 19th-century counterparts. She wanted to wait until after the wedding anyway, but around here it was absolutely required by society. She couldn't afford having anyone think she was hot to trot.

Lorelei took a deep breath, mimed fanning herself with her hand, and got a chuckle from Jeff for it. Yes, she'd be all right, provided she exercised some self-control – and the MacDonalds didn't nuke the whole thing when they returned.

IT WAS all Lorelei could do not to fidget as Owen and Jeff took their position on stage. She wasn't up there, but she was still invested in their performance – and that of their costume. But there had been no split seams since they added the extra fabric to the neck, so she was cautiously optimistic. "There are so many people here," she whispered to Annie King.

"Yes, it's a full house every year. We even get the folks who live a half-day's ride from town – they'll either stay at the hotel or camp out in their wagons for tonight. And the

Joneses and Holmeses often go to Amon's cabin and spend the night there."

A chill went up Lorelei's spine at mention of the cabin. "I see."

"Well, I need to get to work. Enjoy the show." Annie left the pew and went to the edge of the stage, while Lorelei joined Belle a few feet over. Everyone was in place, even Cyrus Van Cleet. Parthena, Sam and Thackary stood around him to help him keep his balance on the chair. He was a wiry man with wispy white hair and a kind smile. She'd met him and his wife Polly during play practice. If she ever did make it back to 2019, she'd never look at the Van Cleet Library the same again.

She wouldn't look at any of the town the same way. She'd met Tom Turner, the man depicted in a statue in City Park. Colin was there too, along with his brothers. Not to mention Dunnigan's Mercantile, or Mulligan's Bar & Grill, or Canyon Park … it was one thing to know places had historical roots, but now she was seeing the roots as they were being put down. It was an education, as much as learning to bake bread or riding in a one-horse open sleigh with a freshly cut Christmas tree and a real live cowboy.

But now it was time to concentrate on the play and prepare for singing Christmas carols and enjoying the refreshments afterward.

Colin performed his part perfectly, much to Annie's relief. Lorcan did a fine rendition of the Andel Tree. Tom Turner narrated the play with unusual warmth and heart. And Fanny Fig did her best as a rather pinched-faced Mary. At least she didn't give Colin the evil eye like she had during rehearsals.

When it came time for intermission and the first round of refreshments, Jefferson introduced her to some of his other relatives and the "Jones boys," as they were called around town. But Seth and Ryder Jones were grown men with sons of their own, having married two of Jefferson's second cousins. They would indeed stay in Amon's cabin that night, then head home in the morning.

The second half of the play went as smoothly as the first, but Lorelei was eager for it to end. Tomorrow was Christmas, followed by Jeff talking to his dad about marrying her. Any apprehensiveness she'd had about the MacDonalds messing it all up was gone, or at least well locked away. She knew that Jeff would fight for her, and the Wallers, and she herself. Nobody was going to take away her man. Besides, who knew when – or if – the MacDonalds would ever return?

"That was the best play yet!" Parthena said on the way to the wagon later. "I want to be an assistant angel again next year."

"I want to be Gabriel," Colin said jovially. "Then you can keep me from falling off a chair."

"I want to be the camel," Thackary said. "Sam can be my hind end."

Sam frowned. "I don't want to be nobody's hind end. I want to be the innkeeper."

"You're too young – I'm afraid you'll have to pick another part," Belle said when they reached the wagon. "Do we have everyone?" She looked around. "Lorelei? Where's Lorelei?"

"Right here." She'd been floating on a cloud of pre-marital bliss since the previous day, and sometimes it distracted her from … well, everything.

"Oh, good," Belle said worriedly. Now why would that be? The woman didn't think she'd just, *poof*, disappear, did she? Or maybe she did. Did Belle know something she didn't? Were the MacDonalds coming? Oh no! She hoped not!

She fretted over that the entire ride home. Were they showing up tomorrow to take her? No, no, no – she wouldn't let them take her from Jeff. She'd have to come up with a plan if they tried. Was there somewhere she could hide? A weapon she could use?

She looked at Jeff sitting on the other side of the wagon bed and shook her head. She was being silly, worrying like this. Everything would be fine. He would talk to Colin the day after tomorrow, Colin would give his blessing, they'd meet with the outlaw preacher, and in a few weeks (or days) she'd be Mrs. Lorelei Cooke. She just wished she could invite the Jensens. Well, and rub Cindy Crankshaw's nose in it. But you couldn't have everything.

They returned to the ranch, unhitched the wagon, got the stock settled and gathered around the Christmas tree. Sam stood on a chair and put the star on top, then Belle and Colin lit the candles that had been placed carefully on the tree's branches that afternoon. Lorelei was fascinated by the clips on the candle holders, having never seen them before – in her time, it would be considered a fire hazard.

Thank goodness the tree was so fresh. Thoughts of it going up in smoke and burning the whole house down flashed across her mind as she watched. But now that the tree was lighting up, she saw why folks in the past, this one included, used them.

The family stood back when Belle and Colin were done and admired the soft warm glow of the tree. "It's the most beautiful thing I've ever seen," Lorelei said in awe.

"It always is." Colin put his arm around Belle and looked at Lorelei, who was standing between him and Jeff. "Merry Christmas, Lorelei."

She smiled, but before she could say anything, the rest of the family echoed him with a chorus of "merry Christmas, Lorelei."

Her jaw trembled. "Thank you. That … was a nice gift."

"That's not your gift," Parthena said. "Mother made you mmpfff!"

Jeff narrowed his eyes at his sister before removing his hand from her mouth.

"Sorry," Parthena gave her mother a sheepish look.

Lorelei looked at the floor. "I don't have any presents for anyone ..."

"Nonsense," Colin replied. "You've already given my son great happiness."

Lorelei's jaw dropped and she looked at Jeff, who was grinning hard enough to split his head open. *You know,* she thought at him, *I think your father's going to give us his blessing.*

CHRISTMAS MORNING, the Cooke family awoke to snowfall. It was beautiful and Lorelei watched the big fat flakes come down from the bedroom window.

"Are you going to wear your new green dress today?" Adele asked as she went behind the changing screen to put on her clothes.

"Yes. I think it'll be perfect for today."

"It doesn't accentuate your waist as much as the blue day dress, but it's still lovely on you."

"Thank you." Lorelei turned from the window, went to the armoire and pulled out the dress.

"Would you like me to style your hair today?" Adele stepped out from behind the screen. "You've been wearing it the same way almost since you got here. And those ribbons are beginning to look ..."

Lorelei looked at the ribbons Shona tied onto her braids to hide the rubber bands. It seemed like ages ago. "Ratty?" she volunteered.

"Frayed and ugly." Adele went to the dresser and picked

up a hairbrush. "Though I suppose they do look like rats have been chewing on them. Let's fix them quick. As soon as chores and breakfast are done, we get to open presents."

Lorelei smiled, pulled the ribbons from her braids and quickly removed the rubber bands, sticking them in a pocket of her green dress as she picked it up. She had other things she'd rather do than explain them to Adele – maybe another time. "Let me put this on first, then you can tackle my hair."

"Tackle?" Adele laughed. "For Heaven's sake, it's not that bad. I don't have to wrestle it to get it to do what I want."

Lorelei smiled. "Don't be so sure." She went behind the screen and changed, then let Adele do her hair before she washed her face and got a good look at herself in the mirror. "Should I be wearing my hair down like this?" As she recalled, young girls in this era wore their hair down, but women didn't. Was she wrong?

"You're not married," Adele said as she ran the brush through her own locks. "Besides, your hair is so long and beautiful."

Lorelei turned. She did have long hair, almost waist length. Patsy was always trying to get her to cut it, but she never gave in. "Your hair's long too."

Adele finished tying it back with a ribbon as she'd done for Lorelei. "Yes, but not as long as yours. Now let's hurry – I want to see what's under the tree!"

They went downstairs to a houseful. Honoria was there with her bulging belly and her husband Major. Jefferson and Edith were there too, and the ranch hands. Belle and Honoria were already setting food on the table buffet-style, while Parthena went around pouring coffee for everyone. "About time you two came down," Grandpa Jefferson barked. "Merry Christmas, Adele!"

"Merry Christmas, Grandpa." She kissed him on the cheek, then Edith.

"And Merry Christmas to you, young lady," he said to Lorelei.

"Merry Christmas, Mr. Cooke."

"Well, don't just stand there, come here," he ordered.

She went to him and he grabbed her into a hug. "And here's to many more Christmases!"

Edith hugged her next and kissed her on the cheek. "We're so glad to have you with us." She motioned to the table. "There's plenty to eat, so have your fill."

Lorelei looked at the spread. It was true. There were fried potatoes, ham, bacon, sausages, pastries, boiled apples, and Belle was just setting a huge bowl of scrambled eggs on the table. "What happened to chores?" she whispered to Adele.

"The hands must have already taken care of everything. They don't come into the house until they're all done – ours included."

She smiled. "They certainly gave you a nice present, didn't they?"

"We'll be sure to send them off with lots of cookies!"

Colin and Jeff came in the back door. Jeff took one look at her and smiled. "Merry Christmas!"

And around the room it went. Lorelei had never heard so many "Merry Christmases" in one house before. Soon they were standing in a large circle around the entire kitchen, hands joined. Colin cleared his throat, said the blessing, then to Lorelei's surprise, everyone hugged everyone else. She took it all in, her throat growing thick at the sight.

She couldn't help sending up a silent prayer. *Oh please, I don't want to leave this place. I don't care about having to use an outhouse, hauling water, chopping wood and all of that. I know it's not my own time, these people are not my own, but I don't* have *a people. Please, I want to stay...*

Lorelei had no idea if God heard her. She'd never been much of a churchgoer except when Bob and Patsy dragged her to a Christmas or Easter service. But she attended one service at this Clear Creek's little church and would like to attend more. She just had to make it through the next few days. Jeff had to talk to his father. They had to talk to Preacher Jo. Everyone had to hope no time travelers came by to toss a wrench in the works. This was starting out as the best Christmas she'd ever had, and she didn't want it to end.

CHAPTER TWENTY-FOUR

Lorelei held up the scarf. "It's lovely. I don't know what to say."

"I hope you like the color," Belle said. "I kept thinking of the beautiful dress you were wearing when …" She smiled. "… we first met."

Lorelei smiled weakly in return. "I'm sorry I don't have anything …"

"You needn't worry. We know your situation. And as my husband said, you've made Jefferson so happy."

Lorelei blushed. "And he's done the same for me."

"I guess that means it's my turn." Jeff stood, a small wrapped box in his hand.

"Oh, you didn't."

He took her hand and pulled her away from Belle. "I wanted to." He gave her the gift.

She smiled. "Thank you."

"Open it."

She tore off the wrapping and string and opened the little box to find a delicate silver bracelet with a tiny heart charm dangling from it. "Oh, Jeff …"

His face lit up. "I picked it out myself, then sold it to myself."

Her face screwed up. "What?"

"The day I helped Father with inventory at the mercantile."

"Oh," she laughed. "Thank you – it's lovely."

"You're lovely." He leaned closer.

"Ooooh!" Parthena called. "They're gonna kiiiiiss!"

"Parthena!" Adele scolded.

Lorelei wanted to kiss him, but not with his entire family watching, and getting a private moment anytime today was unlikely. A heartfelt smile would have to do. But it didn't matter. They were together, surrounded by laughter and love. What more could she want?

The day progressed and Lorelei found herself caught up in the celebration of the holiday. And she did get a moment with Jeff when she accompanied him to the woodshed to gather some for the house fires after supper. "What a wonderful day this has been."

"It sure has." He stopped, spun on her, grabbed her around the waist and kissed her quickly but firmly. "And it just got better."

"Whoa there, cowboy," she laughed. "I'm as eager as you are, but if we get ahead of things your parents will flip out!"

He pulled away a little but didn't loosen his hold. "You sure do have some funny expressions in your time. Or do you mean they'll throw you out?"

"Well, I meant they'll get angry. But they might throw me out too if they think I'm leading you into sin or something."

"We wouldn't want that," he said with a smile.

"We certainly wouldn't. I love you too much to lose you."

Me too.

His heart's words melted into her own heart, warming her all over. It was such a strange phenomenon, yet at the same time, was so natural. So much of this was strange, but the more time went on, the less strange it became. *I just hope I don't end up disappointing you.*

Now he did release her. *Honey, how could you ever disappoint me?*

It took her a few seconds of picking up wood to figure out why she'd said that, or rather, her heart did. *I told you my parents died when I was young.*

Yes, I know. Jeff set up a log on the chopping block and grabbed the hatchet.

So when they died, there were no relatives to take care of me. You have Cookes around you for miles, but there were no other Carsons.

He split a log with one easy blow, then lined up one of the halves. *Did you end up in an orphanage?*

No, but ... maybe in something worse.

I can't imagine anything worse than an orphanage. WHACK!

She stared at him a moment. This form of communication was almost second nature at this point. She understood full sentences. Time for a real test. *Well, in my time they have what's called "the foster system." The state pays families to take in orphaned kids, or kids that can't stay with their own families for some reason. That means I had someplace to go, but if the foster family decided I was too much bother or we didn't get along or they just got bored with me, they'd send me back and the caseworkers – the state employees – would have to find another family to put me with.* She passed him another log and waited to see if he'd respond the way she hoped. Did he get the whole thing?

That's terrible. Did you get sent back?

She drew in a shuddering breath and nodded. He did! *Five times. And the last family I was with, for six years, wasn't the nicest. And they had a son who was just mean to me. A total brat.*

She swore she could feel his heart seizing, even as he kept

chopping away. *I'm so sorry you went through that. I know my family won't send you back, I promise.*

Thank you. But it's not just that. She began loading the wood into the wheelbarrow. *It's that ... I didn't have examples to follow of a good marriage, being a good wife, raising children. I did my best, and some of the foster parents weren't awful, but ... I worry that I won't know what I'm doing, that I'll be a terrible wife, that I'll mess up everyth–*

Stop it!

Funny – a yell sounded even louder when it was inside your heart. *What?*

Stop it. You're not going to fail. You'll be a great wife and mother. And anything you don't know, you can ask Mother or Aunt Sadie or Mrs. Kincaid or Edith or Grandma or any of the women in town for help. I don't know what your *Clear Creek is like, but in this one we help each other.*

Lorelei stopped and took a deep breath. "Really?" Her voice sounded strange to her ears.

He swallowed hard and stared at her. He was as unnerved as she was at carrying on such a lengthy heart to heart conversation. "Of course," he said. "We couldn't survive out here if we didn't."

She shuddered. If the MacDonalds did show up, this was one thing she'd demand they tell her about. How could they possibly communicate this way?

"Lorelei?"

She smiled at him and thought about what he'd just said about survival. A very good reason indeed. No wonder she loved this place – people really did care about each other, even if it was just because they'd die if they didn't. But she knew it was more than just survival. *I love you, Cowboy.*

Jeff grinned at her as he split another log. *I love you too, Future Girl.*

"Lorelei, Jefferson! Hurry up with the wood!" Belle called

from the house. "We're going to sing Christmas carols! And it's way too quiet over there!"

Lorelei and Jeff both chuckled. Nothing improper was going on, but what were they supposed to say – "we were just reading each other's minds"? "We'll be back in a minute!" Lorelei yelled back. She grabbed another armful and dumped it into the wheelbarrow.

Jeff helped her gather up the rest. "I think we have enough. Let's go."

They each picked up one arm of the barrow and began rolling it toward the house. Lorelei felt a little tired from all the hard work, but hey, it was a great workout and she didn't even need to pay a club membership. She was going to build up some terrific arm muscles. One more benefit of the 19th century.

She just hoped she'd be allowed to stay and got a few explanations to some things besides.

THE NEXT DAY was another load off Lorelei's mind. "Did you honestly think I'd say no?" Colin told her and Jeff incredulously.

"Well ... you never know," she replied. "I mean, me being from ..."

Colin pulled her into a suffocating hug. "Of course you two have my blessing! My dear daughter-to-be, I wouldn't care if you were from the future or the past or you arrived on an elephant from Siam – it's obvious you and Jefferson are made for each other. That's all that matters."

Jeff scratched behind his ear. "But what if the MacDonalds come and try to take her back?"

Colin pulled away and let Lorelei breathe again. "Then

either we'll send you with them, or I'll be giving them what for. And so will your mother, I'm sure."

"And the Wallers," Lorelei added. "They promised."

"So that settles it, then," Colin declared. "'What God has put together, let no man put asunder' and all that. Tomorrow, we'll go into town, speak to Preacher Jo and make all the proper arrangements. Oh … a wedding dress might take a while to make. How strongly do you feel about wearing white, Lorelei?"

She almost laughed. "I'll wear denims and a work shirt if you want. All I care about is being with my cowboy." That put a grin on Jeff's face she would've kissed off if his father hadn't been there. Boy, she *needed* chaperones right now!

But over the next two days, they couldn't make it into town. A pack of coyotes were sniffing around, which meant all hands were busy making sure they didn't bother the stock. Even Belle went out to join the other cattlemen, leaving Lorelei, Adele and Parthena to make the meals. But Lorelei's suggestion the first night – grinding up beef and forming it into patties to grill – meant that they surprised the family with hamburgers for dinner. It was a little frustrating not to have American cheese to put on them, Lorelei thought – the "farmer's cheese" they had just didn't do the trick.

And on the third day, they'd barely cleared the afternoon chores when Parthena came running through the front door, yelling like Indian braves were chasing her. "Mother, Mother! Uncle Harrison and Aunt Sadie are home!"

Belle came down the hall, a huge smile on her face. "Come, Lorelei – meet the rest of the family."

Lorelei set the mending she was working on aside and followed Belle onto the front porch. She immediately looked for Jeff, but he was nowhere to be seen. Probably still on coyote patrol.

The man driving the wagon was very obviously Colin's brother – brown hair graying at the temples, about the same height but leaner, brown eyes instead of hazel. His wife had sable hair and big blue eyes – she looked almost Mexican. Like Belle and Colin, they were a handsome couple. In the back of the wagon, two teenage boys and a girl about Parthena's age sat amongst the luggage.

"Belle!" the man called, with the same British accent as his brother. "I know it's late but Merry Christmas!"

"Welcome back!" Belle replied.

Harrison Cooke spotted Lorelei and smiled. "Good afternoon." He looked at Belle. "I saw Colin at the mercantile. He told me you have a house guest?"

"Yes, we do. Come meet Lorelei." Belle took her hand and descended the porch steps.

Harrison helped his wife off the wagon seat as the boys climbed out and helped their sister. "Aunt Belle!" the girl cried and hugged her. "We had the best time! Clinton got kissed by a girl and Max …" She glanced at the older boy and saw his glare. "… uh, never mind." She hung her head and went to stand by her mother.

Lorelei welcomed the distraction and studied them some more. The middle one, Clinton, didn't look very happy about being kissed. His brother Max seemed positively dour.

But the girl made up for both of them in enthusiasm as she made a beeline to Parthena. "Wait until I tell you what Mrs. Dunnigan did!"

Belle's eyes widened. "Oh, dear. What happened to Aunt Irene?"

"Nothing," Harrison assured. "She's fine, just tired. She did a lot of cooking."

"Oh, I see. I'll go into town and see her tomorrow." She glanced at Lorelei. "You can come too, you and Jefferson."

Lorelei smiled and nodded. It was strange meeting more

Cookes – she was still getting used to all the ones she'd already met. And she knew there were plenty more – all of the mail-order-bride cousins and their families. "Cooke-town," indeed.

She watched the family reunion continue as Honoria came out of the main house to greet her parents and siblings. The Cookes' love for each other was so real, so tangible, just like her love for Jeff. She hated that Jeff was so busy the last couple of days – they'd barely had a chance to talk, verbally or otherwise. But then, sometimes there were coyotes or other dangers that threatened their stock and trade. It was no different than if he were an executive on a business trip. Every century had its annoyances.

But tomorrow ... well, coyotes or no coyotes, tomorrow they needed to go to town and talk to that preacher. She was tired of waiting, and suspected he was too. *I LOVE YOU, COWBOY!* she shouted in her head, her heart, her very soul. She had no idea if he could pick up her signal when they were far apart. This whole heart to heart communication thing was new to her – certainly it never happened to Meg Ryan or Amy Adams in the movies.

She got no *I love you too, Future Girl* back, so she filed into the house with the rest of the family as Harrison and his brood went to the main ranch house.

The next few hours were a bustle of activity, as the entire clan would be having supper together next door. Lorelei had only been in the main ranch house a few times, but the kitchen was huge. No wonder the Cookes gathered there for meals – they'd never be able to cram everyone into Belle's kitchen, at least not as comfortably. Christmas was proof of that.

She helped carry bowls of mashed potatoes over, then came back to fetch fresh-baked loaves of bread. Colin brought a platter of sliced ham, while Adele and the other kids carried this and that. But there was no sign of Jeff, and her stomach began to churn – was he all right? Was he getting cold feet? Had he finally decided she was crazy?

And why couldn't she stop worrying and just enjoy this?

Lorelei shook her head. Jeff would probably be back for supper, with some thrilling stories of coyote warfare. Everything would be all right. Everything would be all right. Everything would be all right …

WHEN JEFFERSON finally dragged in from a long day helping Logan move part of the herd – and keeping watch for coyotes that, thankfully, never showed up – Lorelei was already in bed. She heard him trudge up the stairs and fought the urge to speak to him in the hall, but no, if he was coming in this late, he was exhausted. Let him get his rest and catch him tomorrow. *I love you, Cowboy,* she thought. But the thought wasn't just in her head, but her heart.

Love ya too, Future Girl. Ugh.

She smiled and drifted off to sleep.

In the morning she got up early in hopes of seeing him at breakfast, but once again he'd disappeared. "More business with the herd, I'm afraid," Belle told her. "But be ready to go to town after the mending's done. We'll visit my aunt and uncle, see if they need any help at the mercantile, then come home."

Lorelei sighed. "I was hoping he and I could speak with Preacher Jo."

"In a hurry?"

"Uh … yes." She laughed.

So did Belle. "Don't fret – Preacher Jo will still be there once the herd is taken care of. I'm a little more worried about Aunt Irene and Uncle Wilfred right now. They're in their seventies and don't get around as quick as they used to, and they just got back from a long trip."

"That's true." Lorelei smiled and took a sip of coffee. She'd finish it, then clear away the dishes. She liked the routine of breakfast, dishes, mending and so on. There was a rhythm to each day and the ranch ran like a well-oiled machine. She'd miss this if … no, don't even think it. She had to stay positive.

A few hours later they were off, just her and Belle – sure enough, Jeff was out in the far reaches of the ranch again. "Didn't Adele or any of the others want to come along?" she asked Belle.

"No, Adele's far too interested in what happened to Max and Clinton while they were away." She rolled her eyes. "Apparently Savannah said more than she should last night after supper. Now Parthena and Adele want to know how much of it is true."

"What did happen?"

Belle smiled. "It appears that Maxwell has fallen in love."

"Okay. What's wrong with that?"

"Max is sixteen."

"Oh. I guess that's a little young to be married, but not to have a crush … er, an infatuation."

"I suppose. Harrison and Sadie told us some details last night, but they didn't want it to be a huge topic of conversation."

Lorelei recalled Belle and Colin speaking with Harrison and Sadie for a time after supper but didn't know what they were talking about. That was about the time she wanted to know what had happened to Jefferson – Major had filled her in.

When they reached town, they went straight to the mercantile, parked and went inside. An old man was behind the counter, and Lorelei recognized him immediately – Mr.

Dunnigan himself. He gave them a big smile. "Good morning!"

"It's almost lunch time." Belle gave him a hug over the counter.

"And who is this young lady?" Mr. Dunnigan asked.

"Lorelei Carson, at your service, sir." She extended her hand.

The man shook it. "Well, it's a good thing you're here, Miss Carson. Doc and Grandma Waller were in here earlier. They'd like to speak with you when you have a moment."

Before she could answer, she heard someone coming down the stairs. The curtains separating the front and back of the building were shoved aside – and Lorelei gasped. Mrs. Dunnigan looked like she'd just stepped out of the picture! So this was the original owner of her apartment. Except that she wasn't sure it was hers anymore … oh, never mind.

"Well, don't just stand there gaping at me!" the woman snapped. She turned to Belle. "Is this her?"

"Yes, Irene, this is our guest Miss Carson."

Mrs. Dunnigan scrunched up her face, narrowed her eyes and looked Lorelei up and down like a Marine drill instructor preparing an insult. "Kinda skinny, ain't she?"

Lorelei's eyes went wide. Belle had mentioned that her aunt could be brusque, but holy cats …

"Well, if Jefferson's smitten," she went on, "then what's a person to do about it? He's of age."

Lorelei smiled at that. "Smitten" hardly seemed to do it justice.

Mrs. Dunnigan turned back to her. "And what about you, young lady? Are you sweet on him?"

She swallowed hard. "Well, ma'am, we are planning to be married. I wouldn't agree to it if I wasn't."

"Huh. Sparky little thing, aren't you?" She turned back to Belle. "What are you and Colin going to do about it?"

"They already have our blessing. I was hoping Jefferson could come with us to talk to Preacher Jo, but he's busy on the ranch today. Coyotes."

"I hate those varmints," Mrs. Dunnigan grumbled. "Well, if you're sure about this girl, I won't object. Where are you from, Miss Carson?"

Of all the things she could've asked … Lorelei racked her brain for a good lie.

Thankfully, Belle interceded with a good truth. "The MacDonalds brought her to us to take care of."

"Oh." Mrs. Dunnigan must have decided not to meddle in the affairs of MacDonalds, because she immediately changed the subject to how the mercantile had done in her absence. Lorelei couldn't blame her for that. She decided to go look at a shelf full of books, just out of curiosity.

A couple of minutes later, Belle called to her. "I'm going to be here for a while. Why don't you go see what Doc and Grandma wanted?"

"Okay, I'll do that." Lorelei headed out the doors, down the street and up the Wallers' steps. She smiled as she thought about the coming days. Eventually the predators would leave or get chased off, Jeff would have some free time, and they could go talk to Preacher Jo and see about getting married. She knocked on the door and waited. She'd speak to Jefferson as soon as she saw him that night – even if she was already in bed, she'd get up and they'd talk about it. She was so happy she wanted to cry.

The door opened … and Lorelei's smile disappeared, along with her hopes and dreams.

"Hello, lass," Dallan MacDonald declared, filling the Wallers' doorway. His green eyes seemed to glow like a Terminator's. "I'm glad ye're here. 'Tis past time for us to go."

CHAPTER TWENTY-FIVE

Lorelei didn't know whether to flee, faint, or punch him. Before she could decide, the Scotsman swept her into his arms, stepped into the house and kicked the door closed.

"What's going on?" Doc Waller called from the parlor.

Well, now she couldn't flee or faint, so … "Put me down!" Lorelei yelled as loud as she could, and slapped Dallan across the face. It hurt – she might as well have smacked a boulder.

Doc came into the front hall. "Dallan, what are you doing?"

Dallan glanced between a fuming Lorelei and a bewildered Doc and set her on her feet. "Just being gentlemanly. But the lass wants none of it."

She walked over to Doc – scant protection against a 6'5" Scotsman who was built like he should be on the Seahawks' roster, but it was the best option she had. "Go?" she replied. "What makes you think I'm going?!"

Dallan looked stunned. "What makes ye think ye're not?"

She was both terrified and angry at the same time and speaking from both. She'd been afraid much of her life, but also angry that her parents had died, that no one wanted her, that those that did take her in didn't care much either. And now that she found people who did, he was going to make her leave. "*I* think I'm not. Problem with that?" It was all bravado, she knew, but she was taking her stand.

"Now see here, Dallan," Doc said. "This young lady has a right to make up her own mind about things!"

Dallan looked at Doc, whose head barely reached the big man's shoulder. "Och, aye?"

"Aye! And if she doesn't want to go with you, then she doesn't have to!"

Dallan's eyebrows rose in amusement, as if to say *oh really?*

Lorelei fought down a wave of panic. The man could do whatever he wanted – he knew it, and she knew it. She looked around, wondering where his wife was.

"If ye're looking for Shona," Dallan said as if he'd just read her thoughts – and maybe he had, "she's out back with Grandma gathering eggs."

Lorelei groaned as anger rose past fear. She'd never make it to the door and wasn't sure where to go even if she did. She couldn't outrun him, and he was so much stronger than her he'd have her prisoner before she could blink. But she would not give in. This was the proverbial hill she would die on. She glared at him. "What are you doing here?"

"I just told ye. 'Tis time we were on our way."

"Where?"

He arched an eyebrow at her. "Dinna fash yerself, lass. Ye'll ken in time."

Her back went stiff, her anger drowning her terror. "Oh, no." She shook her finger at him. "We're not playing that game again. You kidnapped me once and dropped me somewhere with no warning, but I'll be darned if you do that to me twice!"

The big Scot's eyebrows shot up. "No?"

Lorelei set her jaw. "Did I stutter?"

His hands went to his hips as he cocked his head to one side. "D'ye mind telling me why ye're so set against leaving?" He leaned toward her. "I thought ye'd be overjoyed."

She mimicked his stance, and his accent. "Well, *d'ye* mind telling me why *ye* brought me here in the first place?"

Just then, the door burst open, someone ran in, whomped right into Dallan's back and fell behind him. Lorelei leaned slowly to the right to see around the Scot and … "Jeff!"

"*Jeff?*" Dallan and Doc said at once.

Jeff jumped to his feet, ran around Dallan before he could react, grabbed Lorelei and shoved her behind him and Doc. "Stay away from her!"

Dallan, now clearly confused, looked at Doc.

"You heard the boy," Doc said. "Leave Lorelei alone."

Colin entered the house, Belle right behind him. "Jefferson, what are you doing in town?" He saw Dallan and smiled. "Oh, hello. I had no idea you were back."

"Stay away from him!" Lorelei warned. "He's dangerous!"

Colin scratched his head. "Dangerous?"

The big Scot stood to his full height and narrowed his eyes. "I mean to be leaving soon."

"I'm not going with you!" Lorelei yelped and took hold of Jefferson. *How do we stop this guy?*

I'm thinking.

Dallan grinned wickedly. "Is that so?"

Lorelei gasped. He *could* hear them!

"Would someone kindly explain to me what's going on?" Colin asked.

"Why d'ye no ask yer son?" Dallan said, his eyes fixed on Jeff.

Colin and Belle turned to him. "Well, Jefferson? What's going on?"

Jeff took a deep breath. "I am *not* letting *him* take Lorelei."

Colin glanced at Belle and back. "Oh. Well, of course." He looked at Dallan. "You can't take Lorelei away from Jefferson. They're getting married."

"They're ..." Dallan looked at Lorelei and Jeff in befuddlement.

"Dallan, we've been friends a long time," Doc added. "But I'm warning you. Leave the younguns be."

"Dallan? What's going on?" Shona came into the room with Grandma. "What's all the ruckus?"

Dallan pointed at Jeff. "The lad here doesna want us to take Lorelei home."

"I see." She seemed less perturbed than her husband. In fact, she looked like she was doing her best not to smile.

"They're quite taken with each other," Colin said with a hint of nervousness.

The Scot's eyes narrowed on Jeff. "Oh? How taken?"

Jeff stood straight. "Like I'd die if she were taken away."

Lorelei gasped. *You too?*

Yeah – every time I have to go away, it's like my heart's being torn out.

Me too! I had no idea ... Then she noticed Shona looking back and forth between them. *Can she hear us?*

I don't know. Should I ask?

"How long have you been doing what I think you're doing?" Shona asked.

"Um ... we've been ... talking for a while now." Jeff replied, putting his arms around Lorelei.

Lorelei snuggled close. "Could you hear us?"

Shona looked at the confused faces around them. "Let's discuss that later." She poked her husband in the bicep. "Looks like we have a change of plans."

"Do we?"

Shona stared at him. Dallan's eyes widened, then narrowed. Shona nodded firmly.

Do you hear that? Lorelei asked Jeff.

That buzzing sound? It's like some bees snuck in ...

It's them. They're talking. Like we do! We can't understand what they're saying, but they're doing it. It's like they're ... No, the only analogy she could think of was radio wavelengths.

Well, how do you like that?

Dallan's eyes narrowed to slits. He walked over to the stairs, sat and put his head in his hands. "I hate changes of plans," he groaned.

Jeff put Lorelei behind him again. "I don't care what you hate. You'll take her over my dead body."

Dallan waved him off and looked at his wife. She smiled and shrugged. He shook his head. Lorelei and Jeff heard the buzzing again, like static. Finally, Dallan spoke. "Jefferson Cooke, d'ye love this woman?"

"Of course I do! What do you think this is all about?"

"He has you there," Shona commented dryly.

Dallan ignored her. "Ye love her enough to promise to take care of her for all her days? Protect and provide for her?" He looked Jefferson up and down. "Ye're a wee bit young ..."

"I'm eighteen, and yes, I plan to do those things! And you're not going to stop me."

Dallan stood up again and rubbed his chin. "Lorelei Carson, d'ye love this scraggly bairn?"

She stepped out from behind Jeff. "With all my heart."

"And ye're willing to stay in this place?" He waved at their surroundings. "Willing to leave all that ye know behind to be with him?"

"Yes, I am." She sighed. "It wasn't that great there."

Dallan trapped her with an intense stare. "Ye willingly give yerself to this man, then?"

Her eyes misted with tears. "Yes. I … I do."

Colin stepped forward. "Are you sure, Lorelei? You'll be giving up all those fancy machines …"

"And gaining a family, a community," she finished. "That's worth losing Netflix and smartphones." She paused, then added. "Don't worry about what those are. Doesn't matter."

"Right." Colin nodded. "Well, I know Jefferson is sure – I thought he might go to pieces on the fence line just from being away from you."

"Father!"

"You know it's true – and it's nothing to be embarrassed about." Colin turned to Dallan. "So what will it … what are you doing?!"

Dallan held up the pistol he'd just cocked. "I'm not one to leave loose ends."

"Good heavens, man!" Colin took a cautious step forward. "There's no need for that!"

"Dallan, I think it's pretty clear they're going to marry. You don't need to ensure they do with a shot gun-wedding," Shona warned. Then she squinted at him. *Bzzzz.*

He squinted back. *Bzzzzzzzzzz. Bzzzz.*

Bzzz bz bzzzzzz. Bzzzzzzz.

I wish they'd just talk out loud, Jeff groused.

As long as he's not shooting, I can live with this.

At last Dallan lowered the gun. "So how many of ye know where the lass is from?" he asked grudgingly.

"Everyone in this room," Grandma replied. "And Doc Drake. Not sure about Elsie."

"And Adele," Lorelei added.

"You told Adele?" Belle blurted.

"She's kept the secret," Lorelei pointed out.

Belle thought about it and nodded. "All right. Awful risk, though – she's such a chatterbox."

"We thought she was going to be chaperoning us for tea,

but then Father asked Grandma," Jeff clarified. "We told her, so we'd be able to talk freely."

Colin crossed his arms. "You really have become a wise young man."

"You did a good job with him, sir," Lorelei replied, and Colin beamed.

"They've all kept it to themselves," Shona told Dallan. "We both knew they were going to figure it out sooner or later. It was bound to happen."

"Aye, but if word gets out ..."

"... Nobody will believe us," Lorelei finished for him. "They'll just think those folks in Clear Creek are plumb loco, telling tall tales about their healing-hands doctor and their blind hotel manager who can still see and more gourmet cooks than San Francisco and their multicolored attack rooster and the African couple who appears and disappears out of nowhere. With all that, what's a time traveler or two?"

Five seconds of silence. Then Dallan and Shona burst out laughing, and soon everyone was howling at the absurdity of it all. It was a couple of minutes before they calmed down enough that Shona could say, "All right ... but let's not tell anyone else, okay. Just to be on the safe side."

"We promise," four people said at once, starting the laughter all over again.

A FEW MINUTES LATER, Lorelei and Jeff were walking through town toward the church. "I was so angry," she said.

"I still can't believe you slapped him." Jefferson squeezed her hand. "I wish I'd been there to see it."

"I wish I hadn't – it was like hitting a brick wall." She sighed and leaned toward him. "Coming here changed my life."

He looked at her and smiled. "Mine too." He glanced over his shoulder. His parents, the Wallers and the MacDonalds walked about ten yards behind them. "We still don't know why they brought you here."

She glanced at them and back. "No, we don't. But I suspect."

He almost tripped over his own feet. "You really think …?"

"Got any better ideas? I sure didn't belong anywhere in my time. Or with anyone there. But I belong here, with you."

Jeff grinned like the Cheshire cat. "I could kiss you right now."

"Not with all those watching eyes behind us. But soon we can. And more – oops, shouldn't have said that." She laughed, and he joined her.

"I want to hear all about your time," he said after a long silence.

She looked at him. "Really?"

"Really. What it's like. The things you can do. Everything."

She nodded. "I wish you could see it, even for a day or two. I told you I live over Dunnigan's."

"That's right. That's … what's your word? Awesome. Does it look the same?"

"Almost. It's in what we call Old Town." She squeezed his hand. "Most of the buildings from now are still standing, very well preserved. And as I mentioned, the Cookes are the richest family in the county, and the Turners aren't far behind."

"I'd love to see your Clear Creek."

"I'd love to show it to you."

He let go of her hand and wrapped her arm through his. "There's something special between us, Lorelei. I don't know what it is, only that it's there." He gazed at her as they walked. "It's as if you were made just for me. But look at everything that separated us. If it weren't for them ..." He tossed his head at the couple trailing behind them.

"I know, right?" She stopped them and waited for Dallan and Shona to catch up. As soon as they did, she held tight to Jeff. "Why did you *really* bring me here?"

Dallan smiled. "Is it not obvious, lass?"

She looked at Jeff and back. "Yeah, I guess it is. But I wanted to double-check."

"Aye."

"But why did you have to take her against her will?" Jeff asked.

"To save her," Dallan said calmly.

Lorelei's face screwed up in confusion. "What?"

Dallan glanced at Colin and the others, now walking ahead. "The two of ye are ... *compatible*. That's all ye need ken for now."

Lorelei's eyes narrowed. "Oh no, no, no. You're going to have to do better than that."

"Dallan," Shona said. "Let me explain it."

He glanced at her and smiled. "Verra well, Flower. Explain it as ye will."

Shona took a deep breath. "There's a lot I can't tell you – that I'm not allowed to explain. There are things at work here beyond your understanding."

"That sounds ... ominous," Lorelei commented.

"You have no idea," she said. "Suffice to say we're trying to clean up a very big mess."

"Of your own making?" Jeff asked, glaring at Dallan.

"No, someone else's. I *can* tell you that Lorelei cannot survive without you. It's why we brought her here. If we hadn't ... it would have been bad for her."

"I knew it!" Lorelei said in triumph. "But that still doesn't explain a lot of things."

"Like the ..." Jeff lowered his voice to a whisper. "... mind reading."

"It's not mind reading. It's something else entirely and has to do with your particular bond." She looked at Lorelei. "And it has to do with what you really are. But we'll talk about that another time. Just know that Dallan and I have that too. You're literally that close." She glanced at the ground and back. "And I'd also better tell you that it's not safe for you to stay here."

Jeff was slack-jawed. "What? You mean we have to leave Clear Creek?"

"Eventually, yes – for the same reason some others have left. Your Uncle Duncan has arranged everything."

Lorelei suddenly guessed something. "Was he Mr. Aerosol Cheese?"

Shona glanced at Dallan and smiled. "You figured that out, I see."

"Just now."

Jeff shook his head in confusion. "What does my uncle have to do with this?"

"He is a very powerful man in some circles," Shona said. "Circles that can't be talked about."

Lorelei thought it made him sound like James Bond but decided not to mention that right now. Things were confusing enough without having to explain fictional British spies.

"The upshot, Jefferson, is that your uncle wishes to groom you to take over the estate in England," Shona said. "Your father doesn't want to, nor does your uncle Harrison, and Duncan doesn't have any children. That makes you the next male heir."

Jeff thought a moment. "That's true. Father mentioned it once or twice. But I never thought anything would come of it."

"Yer father will be receiving a letter from your uncle soon," Dallan said. "Ye'll leave for England sometime in the coming year. Again, 'tis no something that hasna already been discussed."

"Is this true?" Lorelei asked.

Jeff nodded. "Yes. Nothing was decided because we never had a serious conversation on the matter. I always figured Duncan would have a son eventually, and that'd be that." He looked at Lorelei. "How would you feel about being a duchess?"

Lorelei now knew the full meaning of the word *gobsmacked*. "I … wow. It never … I don't know, but it sounds like a great adventure." She laughed nervously.

Dallan put his arm around Shona. "I ken it's hard to understand how ye two have bonded and all that comes with it, but a man brought me to Shona much like we brought Lorelei to you. If I hadna taken her as my wife, harm would have befallen her. I've never regretted my decision. Nor will you."

Lorelei gaped at them. "Wh … where are *you* from, then? I mean, when?"

Shona glanced at her husband and back. "I'm from the late 20th century. My birth certificate says I was born on June 6, 1976 in Portland."

Dallan shrugged. "Scotland, January 1672."

Lorelei took a breath. *1672?!* "And your friend Kitty?" she asked Shona.

Shona smiled. "We're the same age, from the same century, the same city. It doesn't matter where I am in time – she'll always be my 'bestie,' as you might say."

"Does she do what the two of you do?" Lorelei asked to clarify.

"Thank the saints, no," Dallan quipped.

Shona rolled her eyes and continued. "We know it's a lot

to take in and we wish we could tell you more, but you'd only be more confused."

Jefferson ran a hand through his hair. "I'm confused enough now."

Shona sighed. "Lorelei will understand this better than you and I'll let her explain more later." Shona turned to her. "Suffice to say, you carry a rare set of genes. To ensure they are passed on properly to your children, you must be with someone compatible or you and your children will die."

Lorelei could only stare. "Why didn't you just say so?"

"Would ye have believed us?" Dallan asked. "*And* come here to the past to meet the one man we found ye're compatible with?"

Lorelei felt like the village idiot. "Mm, no. I'd have said you were nuts."

"Aye." He shrugged.

"You cannot tell a soul what we've just told you," Shona added. "Not your friends, not the Wallers – not even your parents, Jefferson. You have to swear to us."

Jefferson stared at them a moment. "Is Lorelei in danger?"

"Not anymore," Dallan said. "Not so long as ye ..." He glanced at Shona and back. "... join. Marry."

Lorelei faced Jefferson. "I think I understand about the genes." She glanced at Dallan and Shona. "Marriage is just a way to make sure I don't have kids with the wrong guy?"

"Aye," Dallan said with a smile. "And let's face it, marriage is something taken much more seriously here than in yer own time, lass."

She couldn't argue with that. Still ... "There's a lot more, isn't there?"

"Of course," Dallan said. "But that's our problem, not yers." He stepped toward them. "Ye canna deny the bond between ye two, can ye?"

They looked at one another. It was true. They were tied together by something beyond their comprehension.

"That's what I mean by *compatible*. So marry, have children, live a wonderful life. That's all we ask."

"Sounds reasonable enough." Lorelei gave Dallan a hard stare. "But ... who *are* you?"

The Scot stood straight, then gave them a formal bow. "I am Dallan Keir MacDonald of the MacDonalds of Glencoe." He straightened again and looked them square in the eyes. "And I am a Time Master."

EPILOGUE

New Year's Day, 1880

"And do you, Lorelei Carson," said Preacher Jo, "take Jefferson Cooke to be your lawfully wedded husband?"

Lorelei shook with happiness and something else, she wasn't sure what. She couldn't get enough of Jeff. It was bizarre, and she was the first to admit it was too much to take in. No one would believe her or Jeff if they told them, and they couldn't begin to explain things. It's just as well that they were prohibited from talking about it with anyone but each other not to mention the fact they probably only knew half of what was really going on.

Most of the rest of Clear Creek still didn't know the truth about Dallan and Shona, but it was better that way. She knew there was more to them than just this whole time-travel business, but for now that was information she could live without. She wasn't sure she could comprehend it anyway.

But Jeff was all she needed, all she wanted. Her dreams of

having a loving family had finally come true, and she was marrying a man she could never have imagined being with before. Jeff was kind, loving, protective and accepting. She knew she was broken, but that wasn't what he saw when he looked at her. He wanted her, all of her, as-is, and she him. The trust between them was building, and marriage would help it along. After all, they were going to be together the rest of their lives.

Before she knew it, she was saying "I do" and facing a church full of cheering townspeople. *Her* people now. They'd pulled together to make her wedding possible. Her dress was borrowed from her new mother in-law – a little short, but that was minor. Some of the women from the town sewing circle took care of her veil and flowers. Cyrus Van Cleet and Paddy Mulligan put together her reception – what the town called a "wedding supper" – while Mrs. Dunnigan, with Sally and Rosie from the hotel, made all the food. She'd never seen anything like it.

"I love this place," she said as they started down the church aisle.

"It does kind of grow on you," Jeff agreed, then in a low voice, "I hate that we have to leave."

"But we can always visit."

He stopped them, turned and kissed her.

"That's the stuff!" Wilfred Dunnigan cried somewhere near them.

Jeff broke the kiss with a laugh. "Thank you, Uncle Wilfred." He smiled at the older man before gazing into her eyes. "Wilfred's kind of a hopeless romantic. A terrible gossip too."

"Well, we just won't tell him anything."

They continued down the aisle, out of the church and smiled at a wagon decorated with evergreen boughs and red ribbons. Colin was driving them to the hotel for the wedding supper. "If it were summer that wedding wagon would be covered with flowers," Jeff told her. "The only other winter weddings in Clear Creek that I know of were the Drakes' and my cousin Honoria's."

She smiled, nodded and breathed in a lungful of crisp winter air. She wasn't dreaming. She'd have to keep telling herself that.

She spied Dallan and Shona in the crowd pouring out of the church and smiled. "When will they leave?"

"Shona said sometime after the wedding supper. Speaking of which, let's get to the wagon. Everyone's waiting on us."

At the hotel, they received congratulations and well wishes from the townspeople. Lorelei was having the time of her life with the people, the food, the … ooh, music! A few folks were tuning fiddles at the other end of the hotel's dining room.

"Happy, lass?"

Lorelei and Jeff jumped, then spun to face Dallan and Shona. "Very. Are you leaving right now?"

"Not yet, but soon." Shona glanced at Dallan. "There's the small matter of your wedding present we need to discuss."

"Wedding present?" they said at once.

"Aye," Dallan said with a smile. "Something Shona said ye'd like. But we'll have to wait until everyone else has left."

Lorelei glanced at Jefferson, who could only shrug. "All right," she said. "But there'd better not be any sleepy drugs in it."

Dallan's face was a blank. "We'll come fetch ye from yer room. We've taken the liberty of providing ye each with a change of clothes."

Shona smiled. "Just be sure you're changed and ready by eight o'clock, okay?"

Lorelei nodded. "Fine."

The MacDonalds left to go speak to Doc and Grandma. "That was strange," Jeff commented.

Lorelei laughed. "What about this *hasn't* been? But it brought me to you – that's what matters."

He took her in his arms. "I love you, Lorelei Cooke."

She sighed in contentment. "Mmmm ... say that again."

"I love you, *Mrs.* Cooke."

"That's even better." She rested her head against his chest. "What do you think our wedding present is?"

"I can't imagine. But with those two, anything is possible."

She looked up at him. "You're right. I hope it's not some weird pet from outer space that looks like a Muppet."

"Like a what?"

"Ugh. So many cultural references, so little time. I'll explain later. Let's go take our place at the head table – Mrs. Dunnigan looks like she's ready to feed us." Lorelei pulled away, took his hand and led them to their seats to share their first meal together as husband and wife.

Dunnigan's Mercantile, present day ...

Lorelei took a deep breath, grabbed Jeff's hand, opened the door of the mercantile and stepped inside.

"Lorelei!" Mr. Jensen called. "There you are! And this must be that fine young man the MacDonalds told me about."

Lorelei smiled at Jeff as he gawked at his surroundings, then at Mr. Jensen. "Yes, he is." She held up her left hand and wiggled her ring finger, showing off her gold band. There was a slight commotion off to one side behind a display of Christmas decorations, but she ignored it. "Mr.

Jensen, I'd like to introduce you to my new husband, Jefferson Cooke."

"What?!" Cindy Crankshaw marched around the corner, took one look at them and Lorelei's ring and snorted in disgust. "You've got to be kidding me!"

Jefferson's eyebrows slowly rose. "What's the matter with her?"

Lorelei patted him on the chest. "That's what a jealous rage looks like, darling. But don't worry, I'm sure she'll get over it in a decade or so."

Heather and Melanie came up, stared at Cindy, then at Lorelei and Jeff. Heather took a few steps forward. "Wow, you got married?"

"Yes," Lorelei said with a smile.

Heather smiled back. "Congratulations."

"What?!" Cindy snapped. "Don't congratulate her!"

"Why not?" Heather fired back. "Geez, Cindy, don't you think it's kind of cool?"

"Yeah, none of us even knew you were dating." Melanie studied Jefferson. "Are you related to the Cookes from around here?"

"If you are referring to the Triple-C Cookes, yes, I'm related," Jeff confirmed. "Distantly."

"Are you going to live at the ranch?" Cindy squeaked.

"No, we're making our home in England," Jeff explained. "Now if you'll excuse us, my wife has things she needs to pick up."

Lorelei smiled at Mr. Jensen. "I'm sorry I'm leaving without notice."

"Oh, I understand. When Mr. MacDonald said you'd married a Cooke and that his work meant living elsewhere, well, who am I to get in the way of love?" He looked at Jeff. "You take good care of this girl. She's mighty special to us."

"To me too, sir," he said.

Heather elbowed Melanie in the ribs. "Is that an English accent?"

She shrugged, unable to take her eyes off them. Neither could Cindy, but she wasn't smiling like the others.

"We'll head upstairs now." Lorelei took Jefferson's hand again and went through the curtained doorway. Once behind it she looked at him and smiled.

Their "wedding present," as Dallan and Shona called it, was a weeklong honeymoon in her own time with her new husband. She didn't know how it all worked other than Shona said they could return them to the exact time they left so they'd never be missed.

The MacDonalds took them from the Van Cleet hotel the night of their wedding, loaded them into a wagon, drove to Amon Cotter's cabin and went to the same room she woke up in that fateful day. They refused to be drugged. Shona explained to Lorelei and Jeff that the … "transition into another time" would be bizarre, but they argued that so had the last few weeks, so what was the difference? The MacDonalds finally gave in but instructed them to look at the ceiling only. Period, nowhere else.

In the same commanding voice as before, Dallan said, "Shona, take us to Clear Creek." Only this time he said something else in a language she'd never heard. There was a bright light that suddenly appeared, spiraling fractal rainbows neither she nor Jefferson could take their eyes off of and a feeling of pins and needles all over. The room shook as if in an earthquake. And Shona sang … well, it sounded like her voice was an orchestra, only half the instruments were from other planets.

Then after a minute or two, they were in the cabin from her time and Jeff was rubbing his eyes to get the afterimages to stop.

Jeff's first taste of the 21st century was Kitty Morgan's

truck – they had to pull over halfway to town so he could get out and be furiously carsick. (Given Kitty's driving, Lorelei almost needed to join him.) They'd gone back to the Van Cleet hotel – ironically, to the same room as in the past – rested up a bit, then come to Dunnigan's so she could pack. Dallan promised to take them to the Triple-C later and introduce them to Titus Cooke, who also apparently knew Dallan was a Time Master. Lorelei wondered how he'd found out.

"Up there?" Jeff said as he looked at the stairwell.

"Follow me." She led him upstairs, unlocked the door, went inside and stuck the key in her purse. She wasn't surprised when Shona handed it to her before they left the truck. She headed for the back bedroom and went straight to the armoire.

"What are you looking for exactly?"

"You'll see." She opened it and did her best to open the bottom drawer. "It's stuck."

"It looks old."

"It was new when I put it in here."

"You were in the Dunnigans' living quarters?"

"Yes, the day I got my two new dresses."

He looked around. "To think that was what? A hundred and forty years ago?"

"That's right." She continued to tug. "But a week and a half ago for us."

"Here, honey, let me try." He gently waved her away, took hold of the handle and gave it a good pull, then another. It gave and he smiled in triumph.

"Showoff." She pulled the drawer out, peeked into the dark space below it and reached inside. "Got it!" She stood with a yellowed piece of paper. She smiled at him as she carefully unfolded it. Tears filled her eyes when she looked at her own handwriting. "Proof."

Jefferson peeked over her shoulder and read:

It wasn't a dream. You were really there. And yeah, he's super cute. I'm falling in love with him. Jefferson Cooke is da bomb!
Lorelei Ingrid Carson, 12/22/1879

He wrapped his arms around her from behind. *What is that supposed to mean?*

Lorelei looked at her signature and the date. *It means it's true. It happened. And I fell in love with the man of my dreams.*

But you called me a bomb. *You're going to have to teach me how people talk in this century. I'm afraid I'll be lost otherwise.*

You'll be fine. She grabbed a few things out of the armoire, put them into the suitcase she'd placed under the bed when she first moved in, then closed it. *I should show you the bookstore. I want to pick up a copy of* His Prairie Princess. *Then We should go see a movie.*

What's a movie?

You'll find out. Maybe we should just stream some instead. Preferably a Western – I don't think you could handle Star Wars or Godzilla.

Godzilla?

She hooked her hands behind his neck. *Imagine a hundred-foot lizard with Cindy's personality.*

I think I'd rather imagine kissing you.

Lorelei gazed into Jeff's eyes and smiled. *I think you can do better than imagine it.*

As a matter of fact, he could.

Meanwhile, across the street ...

"They've been in there too long. I should fetch them," Dallan said.

"Let them have a chance to visit with Lorelei's old boss. Don't worry, they'll be fine."

He sipped his mocha. "I'm not sure I like this drink, Flower. Too sweet."

She smiled at him. They were sitting in a small coffee place a few doors down from the museum. Or, in Jefferson's time, the Waller's house. She sipped her gingerbread spiced latte. "I like mine."

He smiled at her. "Weel, this wee assignment turned out better than I planned."

She gave him a flat look. "Oh, you mean the abduct the girl, abandon her near her future mate, then hope for the best plan?"

"It was better thought out than that." He smiled. "In fact, I think I'm getting the hang of this matchmaking business."

"You're not the one doing the matching, Dallan. You're the one doing the delivering, remember?"

"Oh, aye, still, I could tell they were compatible."

"Leave the matching to those assigned to do it. And you've only done it twice now, so don't get cocky. In fact, I'm not sure we should count our first assignment considering how it went."

"It was successful."

"Really? Shall I ask Duncan Cooke if he thinks so? Or how about Cozette?"

He rolled his eyes. "They've thanked us enough for seeing it done."

"Yes, for seeing they didn't get killed, which almost happened!"

"So there were a few wee mishaps ..." he said with a shrug.

"Dallan," she said in warning. "Those were more than little mishaps."

He gave her a grin. "Perhaps, but they did make things interesting."

"Oh, you!" She picked up her latte. "Did Melvale give you our next assignment?"

"Aye." He reached into the inside pocket of his jacket, pulled out a piece of paper and handed it to her.

She unfolded it and read, "Victoria Phelps, Stockton, California ... 2020 ...Human, and Sir Aldrich Barrow, 1877 ... also Human." She read further. "He's in Sussex, England." She looked at her husband. "That's convenient."

"Aye, and I can think of a certain duke and duchess we know that could help with this."

"So long as said duke doesn't slip Miss Phelps a cracker covered in drug-induced spray cheese, we'll be fine."

"Another wee mishap, but it did work," he countered.

"Well, I think things will go smoother next time without the spray cheese."

He smiled. "Aye, on that I'll have to agree. But dinna worry, we'll make sure she's none the wiser."

"When she discovers she's in the year 1877 in England?" Shona laughed. "I can't wait to see you pull that off."

"Have ye no confidence in me, woman?"

She arched an eyebrow, sighed and looked at Dunnigan's Mercantile across the street. "Maybe we should have told her."

"That she's part human and part yer kind, Flower?" He followed her gaze. "Nae, the lass couldna handle it. She was having a hard enough time with her heart bonding to Jefferson's. Let them be for now."

She nodded. "You're right. Besides, she's safe, surrounded

by the best people in the world and in one of our favorite places."

"Aye. She's found her home in Clear Creek and more importantly, her family in the Cookes. Ye ken family is what she feeds her heart with?"

"Yes, I guessed as much. I do hope she gets along all right."

"She'll be fine. Besides yer father has a ranger watching over the town. He'll keep an eye on her until they join Duncan in England."

She nodded. "Well then, what should we do while we're here for a week?"

He shrugged. "You tell me."

"I'm from the 90's, remember? There are things here I want to see."

"Like what?"

"I don't know, gadgets. We should go shopping. I could ask Kitty along since she's here with us. I'm sure she's just as curious."

"No! We'll never have any peace. Besides, isn't she working on another wee book of hers?"

"Yes, she is."

He leaned across the table. "Ye did tell her to stop writing about our work, did ye no?"

"Um … yes."

He leaned closer. "And?"

"She promised she wouldn't write any more about what we do."

"Including writing about the folks in Clear Creek and the town?"

She nodded.

He leaned back in his chair. "Good. I wouldna want her writing about this little adventure and turning it into a book."

Shona gave him a sheepish look.

"Lass? Ye didna already tell her how everything turned out, did ye?"

"Um, well ..."

Dallan ran a hand over his face a few times. "The lass is going to get us exposed one of these days or worse."

"She won't write a word. She knows better. Besides, how could she sugarcoat this story, what would she call it, Christmas with the Cookes or something?"

"I dinna care what she calls it. It's what she puts in it that worries me."

"Kitty will be fine. Stop worrying and finish your mocha. Then maybe we should go to a movie."

He picked up his drink. "Remind me what that is."

She smiled. "Maybe a Star Wars movie."

"What's Star Wars?"

Her smile turned mischievous. "You'll see. Just remember how much you love me when it's over."

He looked into her eyes. *I do love you, Flower. More than life itself.*

She smiled back. *I know.*

THE END

ABOUT THE AUTHOR

Kit Morgan, aka Geralyn Beauchamp, has been writing for fun all her life. When writing as Geralyn Beauchamp, her books are epic, adventurous, romantic fantasy at its best. When writing as Kit Morgan they are whimsical, fun, inspirational sweet and clean stories that depict a strong sense of family and community. Raised by a homicide detective one would think she'd write suspense, but no, Kit likes fun and romance. Kit has plenty of both in her books. Books often described as Green Acres meets Gun Smoke! Kit resides in the beautiful Pacific Northwest in a little log cabin on Clear Creek, for which the fictional town from her Prairie Brides and Prairie Grooms series is named.

And yes, Kitty Morgan (Kit) *has written* about Dallan and Shona's assignments. If you'd like to read Kit's other books you can check them out on Kit's amazon page in the Prairie Bride and Prairie Grooms series. And if you'd like to find out more about Dallan and Shona, you can check out the Time Master Series on Geralyn Beauchamp's amazon page.

Want to get in on the fun?

Find out about new releases, cover reveals, bonus content, fun times and more? Text Cooke to 22828